懶鬼子 英日語
Language
17buy.com.tw

懶鬼子 英日語 Language
17buy.com.tw

懶鬼子 英日語
Language
17buy.com.tw

懶鬼子 英日語 Language
17buy.com.tw

英美國語言學校都在教的

英語
會話課

使用說明

1 《超擬真情境對話》

每個情境都精心設計了一個超擬真對話，更能快速融入、身歷其境，輕鬆瞭解如何建構完整的情境對話。

Additional Vocabulary & Phrases｜補充單字 & 片語

● **book** v. 預定、預約
Jane has booked a flight from Thailand to Berlin.
珍妮已經預訂了一張從泰國飛往柏林的機票。

● **wake-up call service** n. 喚醒服務
This hotel offers wake-up call service for every customer.
這間飯店為每位顧客提供喚醒服務。

★隨機補充的單字和片語：亮黃底的補充單字和片語，配上生活化的例句，讓你一字不漏、學習更完整。

A Welcome to ABC Hotel. How can I help you?
歡迎光臨 ABC 飯店。我能為你服務嗎？

B I booked a double room online two days ago. I would like to check in now.
兩天前，我在網路上預約了一間雙人房。我現在要登記入房。

A No problem. Let me check your reservation on our website. May I know your name and your Identity Card number?
沒問題，讓我在我們的網路上查一下你的預約。可以告訴我你的名字和身份證號碼嗎？

A Welcome to ABC Hotel. How can I help you?
歡迎光臨 ABC 飯店。我能為你服務嗎？

B I booked a double room online two days ago. I would like to check in now.
兩天前，我在網路上預約了一間雙人房。我現在要登記入房。

2 《超高頻率使用句》

全書收錄超過 500 句的日常會話必備好用句，就是要讓你一分鐘學一句，快速學習，不怕不夠用！

Daily Sentences 超高頻率使用句｜一分鐘學一句不怕不夠用 02-02

● It's so hot today. I am melting. Let's go eat some ice cream to cool down.
今天好熱，我快融化了。我們去吃一點冰淇淋冷卻一下。

● Do you have any coupons?
你有任何優待券嗎？

● Can you recommend me some low-fat ice cream?
你能推薦一些低脂冰淇淋嗎？

● Janet, what is your favorite ice cream?
珍納特，妳最喜歡什麼口味的冰淇淋？

● Does this flavor come in popsicles?
這種口味有出冰棒嗎？

● I want a banana split with chocolate sauce and nuts.
我要一個加巧克力醬和核果的香蕉船。

● Can I have one scoop of vanilla*¹ ice cream in an ice cream cone?
我要一球香草冰淇淋用餅乾裝。

● Do you want some syrup on the top of your ice cream?
你想要在你的冰淇淋上淋上糖漿嗎？

● Could we take a look at the menu?
我們能看一下菜單嗎？

● This smells delicious.
這聞起來好美味。

3 《換個單字說說看》

Amy 老師精心設計舉一反三的完美心機學習方塊，用單字累積句子的豐富度，讓你的句子更漂亮，再多的突發狀況也不怕！

★可依照文內藍色字旁的星星編號，依照號碼對照練習！

★ 換個單字說說看｜用單字累積句子的豐富度，讓句子更漂亮！

vanilla*¹ 可替換：

marshmallow 棉花糖	wild berry 野莓	caramel 焦糖

Can I have one scoop of _____ ice cream?
我想要一球_____（口味）冰淇淋。

of ____ ice
____（口味）冰淇淋。

oupons?

Daily Vocabulary 語言學校都會教的超實用日常單字 🎧 MP3 02-06

① cake 蛋糕

blueberry cheesecake ph	藍莓起司蛋糕
marble cheesecake ph	大理石起司蛋糕
carrot cake ph	胡蘿蔔蛋糕
blueberry mousse ph	藍莓幕斯
chocolate cake ph	巧克力蛋糕
mango mousse ph	芒果慕斯

② bread 麵包

toast [tost] n	吐司,烤麵包片
butterbread [`bʌtɚ] n	奶油麵包
biscuit [`bɪskɪt] n	小麵包
croissant [krwɑˋsɑn] n	可頌

4 《語言學校都會教的超實用日常單字》

Amy 老師在每個情境裡,都詳細列出國外語言學校都會教的實用日常單字,搭配照片圖解,用圖片記單字,印象更深刻,不用再怕背的單字用不到,100% 符合情境、100% 超實用!

詞性符號說明
- n 名詞
- v 動詞
- a 形容詞
- ad 副詞
- ph 片語

Daily Q&A

〔會話一〕	〔會話二〕	〔會話三〕
Q▶ Do you microwave to cook food?	Q▶ How many bedrooms do you have?	Q▶ Where do you put your earrings?
你會用微波爐煮東西嗎?	你有幾間房間啊?	你把耳環放在哪裡?
A▶ Yes, I usually use it to heat some food.	A▶ There are three bedrooms.	A▶ I think I put them on the dressing table.
會啊,我通常用它來熱食物。	總共三間。	我想我把它們放在化妝台上。

5 《Daily Q&A》

Amy 老師貼心設計生活中常見的簡易 Q&A,讓你學完單字馬上能應用在日常的簡單對話當中,不再只是死記單字而已!

Proverbs & Idioms 道地諺語與慣用語 | 讓句子更錦上添花

be home and dry 成功的完成某事
I've just got one more report to finish and I will be home and dry.
我還有一個報告要完成。我會成功的完成它。

make oneself at home 把自己當作像在家一般
Welcome to my home. Please make yourself at home.
歡迎來到我家,當成自己家一樣吧。

hit a home run 在某方面成功
Our performance last night was the best we ever gave. We felt our group hit a home run.

6 《道地諺語與慣用語》

連學校老師都驚豔的超道地諺語與慣用語!課本一定沒有教,Amy 老師通通傳授給你!有趣又道地的用法,一看就懂,一學就會,讓你出其不意的用在日常對話中,絕對讓你的口語更錦上添花!

7天學習進度表
每個時段讀 1～2 個單元,輕鬆學習毫無負擔!只要 7 天,英文口說就能呱呱叫!

★每完成一個 Unit 請在框框裡打勾!

Time Day	早上 Morning	下午 Afternoon	晚上 Evening
Day 1	Unit 1 Unit 2	Unit 3 Unit 4	Unit 5 Unit 6
Day 2	Unit 7 Unit 8	Unit 9 Unit 10	Unit 11 Unit 12
Day 3	Unit 13 Unit 14	Unit 15 Unit 16	Unit 17 Unit 18
Day 4	Unit 19 Unit 20	Unit 21 Unit 22	Unit 23 Unit 24
Day 5	Unit 25 Unit 26	Unit 27 Unit 28	Unit 29 Unit 30
Day 6	Unit 31 Unit 32	Unit 33 Unit 34	Unit 35

7 《7天學習進度表》

Amy 老師特別將語言學校課程設計成「1分鐘學 1 句」,一個時段只要輕鬆讀 1-2 個單元,只要 7 天就能用英文行遍全世界!隨書附上學習進度檢視表,按表操課,愈讀愈有成就感!

MP3 01-04

8 《外籍老師親錄 MP3》

全書英文單字、會話完整收錄 MP3,同時跟讀、矯正發音。就是要讓你不用花大筆銀子出國,也能說一口道地流利的英語!
★本書附贈CD片內容音檔為MP3格式★

作者序

　　説英語是不是讓你有點膽怯？明明就是學了好幾年的英語，也背了好多單字，但當要開口的時候，卻腦袋一片空白不知道如何開口？在台灣教授英語近 10 年，發現台灣學生最普遍的問題就是不知道如何將學校所學的英文融入日常生活之中，導致遇到外國人卻不知如何開口，出國旅行還是比手畫腳無法暢所欲言。台灣填鴨式的英語教育，讓許多想要開口説英語的學生們堆上一層又一層的阻礙。

　　為了能和更多朋友分享有效率並輕鬆有趣的英語學習理念，本書將海外生活或旅行時會遇到的情境與需要使用到的英語會話以清楚有趣的編排方式讓讀者對説流利的英文這件事情不再是遙不可及的夢想。運用日常生活情境式的方式來學英語會話將是最紮實，最實用，最有趣，也最輕鬆快速的方法。運用本書所學的內容，進而運用到生活之中，用英文和他人聊天 just a piece of cake（輕而易舉）。

　　透過每個單元的五大元素，包含：擬真對話、常用句型、日常單字、道地諺語以及外籍老師 MP3 的跟讀，同時也搭配照片，由圖像的方式去記憶，一個一個完整紮實地建構你的英語會話能力，拋開過時的死背死記，讓英語會話像喝咖啡、看電影一樣自然的圍繞在你的生活當中。

　　祝福每一位學子在學習英語的道路上，都能滿載而歸！

Amy 黃文俞 2015. 07

Chapter 4 Exercising
運動身體好

Chapter 5 Shopping
逛街好心情

Chapter 6 Transportation
交通工具暢行無阻

Chapter 7 Close to Nature
享受大自然

目 錄

Unit 30
Unit 31
Unit 32
Unit 33
Unit 34
Unit 35
Unit 36
Unit 37
Unit 38

學習進度表

7天學習進度表

每個時段讀 1～2 個單元，輕鬆學習沒有負擔！
只要 7 天，英文口說就能不一樣！

★每完成一個 Unit 請在框框裡打勾！

Time Day	早上 Morning	下午 Afternoon	晚上 Evening
Day 1	Unit 1 Unit 2	Unit 3 Unit 4	Unit 5 Unit 6
Day 2	Unit 7 Unit 8	Unit 9 Unit 10	Unit 11 Unit 12
Day 3	Unit 13 Unit 14	Unit 15 Unit 16	Unit 17 Unit 18
Day 4	Unit 19 Unit 20	Unit 21 Unit 22	Unit 23 Unit 24
Day 5	Unit 25 Unit 26	Unit 27 Unit 28	Unit 29 Unit 30
Day 6	Unit 31 Unit 32	Unit 33 Unit 34	Unit 35
Day 7	Unit 36	Unit 37	Unit 38 CONGRATULATIONS!

Chapter 1

Accommodation& Housing
一天的起點和終點

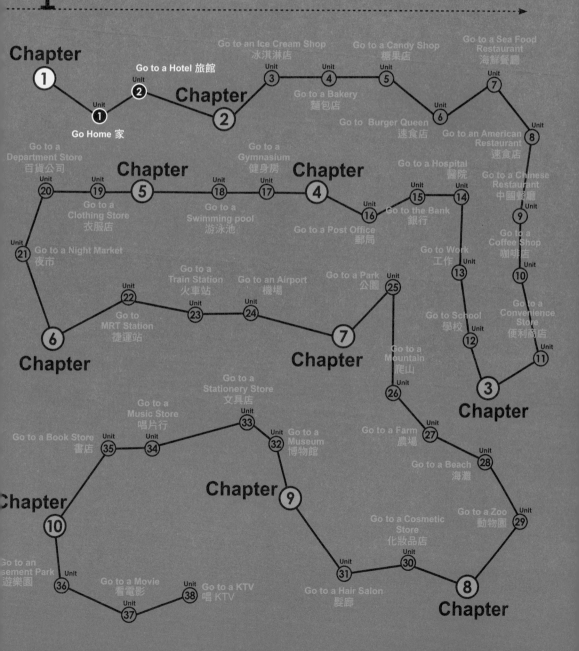

Chapter
1

Go to a Hotel 旅館
Unit **2**

Unit **1**
Go Home 家

Chapter
2

Go to an Ice Cream Shop
冰淇淋店
Unit **3**

Unit **4**

Go to a Candy Shop
糖果店
Unit **5**

Go to a Sea Food Restaurant
海鮮餐廳
Unit **7**

Go to a Bakery
麵包店

Go to Burger Queen
速食店
Unit **6**

Go to an American Restaurant
速食店
Unit **8**

Go to a Department Store
百貨公司
Unit **20**

Chapter
5

Unit **19**

Go to a Clothing Store
衣服店

Go to a Gymnasium
健身房
Unit **18**

Go to a Swimming pool
游泳池
Unit **17**

Chapter
4

Go to a Hospital
醫院

Unit **15**

Go to the Bank
銀行
Unit **14**

Go to a Chinese Restaurant
中國餐廳
Unit **9**

Go to a Post Office
郵局
Unit **16**

Go to Work
工作

Go to a Coffee Shop
咖啡店

Unit **21**
Go to a Night Market
夜市

Go to a Train Station
火車站
Unit **22**

Go to an Airport
機場

Go to a Park
公園
Unit **25**

Unit **13**

Go to a Convenience Store
便利商店
Unit **10**

Unit **23**

Unit **24**

Go to School
學校

Unit **12**

Unit **11**

Go to MRT Station
捷運站

Chapter
6

Chapter
7

Go to a Mountain
爬山
Unit **26**

Chapter
3

Go to a Stationery Store
文具店
Unit **33**

Go to a Music Store
唱片行

Unit **32**
Go to a Museum
博物館

Go to a Farm
農場
Unit **27**

Go to a Beach
海灘
Unit **28**

Go to a Book Store
書店
Unit **35**

Unit **34**

Chapter
9
Unit **9**

Chapter
10
Unit **10**

Go to a Cosmetic Store
化妝品店

Go to a Zoo
動物園
Unit **29**

Go to an Amusement Park
遊樂園
Unit **36**

Go to a Movie
看電影

Unit **38**
Go to a KTV
唱 KTV

Unit **31**

Unit **30**

Go to a Hair Salon
髮廊

Chapter
8

Unit **37**

A Welcome to my home. I just moved into this apartment a month ago.
歡迎來我家。我一個月前才剛搬進這間公寓。

B Wow. Congratulations. No wonder everything looks brand new in your house.
哇，恭喜！難怪你的房子裡，所有的東西看起來都超新的。

A Yes. I spent a lot of time thinking how to make it the coziest place in the world.
是啊，我花了好多的時間想要如何讓它變成世界上最溫馨的地方。

B It does look like you have what you want.
看起來你真的擁有你想要的。

A Are you hungry? I prepared some cookies in the oven. Would you like to have some?
你餓了嗎？我有準備一些餅乾在烤箱裡。你想吃一些嗎？

B Sure. Can I also have a cup of hot coffee? Coffee and cookies are the perfect match.
當然，我可以來一杯熱咖啡嗎？咖啡和餅乾是完美的組合。

A No problem. Hold on a second.
沒問題，等一下。

Additional Vocabulary & Phrases | 補充單字 & 片語

- **no wonder** ph 難怪
  Carrie had a terrible cold last week. No wonder she didn't come to our party.
  上星期卡麗得了重感冒，難怪她沒有來我們的派對。

- **brand new** ph 全新、嶄新的
  My parents moved into a brand new house last week.
  我的父母上星期搬進了一間全新的房子。

- **cozy** a 舒適的、愜意的、舒服的 (cozy-cozier-coziest)
  The blanket is warm and cozy.
  毯子蓋起來又溫暖又舒服。

- **perfect match** ph 完美組合
  Do you think John and Lily are perfect match?
  你覺得約翰和莉莉是完美組合嗎？

Daily Sentences 超高頻率使用句 | 一分鐘學一句不怕不夠用 🎧 MP3 01-02

- I still need to buy a new **washing machine** ★¹.
  我還需要買一台新的洗衣機。

- I love big living rooms. I think a living room is a place where you can enjoy your time with friends and family.
  我喜歡大客廳。我認為客廳是你可以和朋友、家人一起享受時光的地方。

- Lying casually on the sofa and watching TV with friends and family are the most enjoyable things after finishing a tiring day.
  輕鬆的倒在沙發上和朋友、家人一起看電視，是累人的一天結束後最享受的事情。

- I love watching some DVDs on my bed. 我喜歡在床上看一些 DVD。

- LCD TVs are much cheaper than Plasma TVs.
  液晶電視比電漿電視便宜很多。

- We ran out of **light bulbs** ★². Can you run errands to buy them?
  我們用完燈泡了，你可以替我跑腿買新的嗎？

- Don't be like a couch potato sitting on the sofa and doing nothing but eating and watching TV. 不要像一個沙發馬鈴薯坐在沙發上什麼都不做，只有吃和看電視

- The refrigerator is empty. Let's go to the supermarket to do some grocery shopping. 冰箱空了，我們去超市買一些吃的食物吧。

- You can wash your dishes in a dishwasher. What you need to do is turn on the machine, put some detergent in and press the start button.
  你可以用洗碗機洗碗，你需要做的就是打開機器，放一些洗碗精和按下開始鍵就可以了。

★ 換個單字說說看 | 用單字累積句子的豐富度，讓句子更漂亮！

washing machine★¹ 可以替換：

| dryer 烘乾機 | air conditioner 冷氣機 | dish washer 洗碗機 |

I still need to buy a new _____.
我還需要買一台新的 _____。

light bulbs★² 可以替換：

| toilet paper 衛生紙 | shampoo 洗髮精 | garbage bag 垃圾袋 |

We are out of _____.
我們 _____ 用完了。

Additional Vocabulary & Phrases | 補充單字 & 片語

- **casually** ad 輕鬆地、偶然地
  Mom and dad walked casually along the beach.
  爸媽輕鬆地沿著海岸散步。

- **run errands** ph 跑腿、為某人辦事
  Cindy ran errands for the boss.
  辛蒂替老闆跑腿去了。

- **detergent** n 洗潔劑
  I need to buy some detergent.
  我得買些洗潔劑。

- **press** v 按、壓
  You need to press this button to start the computer.
  要將電腦開機你得按這顆按鈕。

❶ living room 客廳

television [ˋtɛləˌvɪʒən] n	······	電視
sofa [ˋsofə] n	······	沙發
chair [tʃɛr] n	······	椅子
table [ˋtebḷ] n	······	桌子
window [ˋwɪndo] n	······	窗戶
light [laɪt] n	······	日光燈

❷ bedroom 臥室；寢室

single bed ph	······	單人床
double bed ph	······	雙人床
blanket [ˋblæŋkɪt] n	······	毯子
pillow [ˋpɪlo] n	······	枕頭
sheet [ʃit] n	······	床單
dressing table ph	······	梳妝台
bedside lamp ph	······	床頭燈

❸ bathroom 浴室

toilet [ˋtɔɪlɪt] n / **restroom** n （有沖
洗式馬桶的）廁所；洗手間；盥洗室

bathtub [ˋbæθˌtʌb] n ······ 浴缸

shower nozzle ph ······ 蓮蓬頭

mirror [ˋmɪrɚ] n ······ 鏡子

toilet [ˋtɔɪlɪt] n ······ 馬桶

faucet [ˋfɔsɪt] n ······ 水龍頭

sink [sɪŋk] n ······ 洗手台

❹ kitchen 廚房

stove [stov] ⓝ	瓦斯爐	
refrigerator [rɪˋfrɪdʒəˌretə] ⓝ	冰箱	
oven [ˋʌvən] ⓝ	烤箱	
cooker [ˋkukə] ⓝ	炊具；烹調器具	
turner [ˋtɝnə] ⓝ	鍋鏟	
pan [pæn] ⓝ	平底鍋	

pot [pɑt] ⓝ	鍋；罐；壺
chopping board ⓟⓗ	砧板
hot water dispenser ⓟⓗ	熱水機
toaster [ˋtostə] ⓝ	烤麵包機
microwave [ˋmaɪkroˌwev] ⓝ	微波爐

❺ housewares 家庭用品

bowl [bol] ⓝ	碗
chopsticks [ˋtʃɑpˌstɪks] ⓝ	筷子
spoon [spun] ⓝ	湯匙
cup [kʌp] ⓝ	杯子
dish [dɪʃ] ⓝ / **plate** [plet] ⓝ	盤子
kettle [ˋkɛtl̩] ⓝ	水壺

❻ storage 儲藏室

broom [brum] ⓝ	掃把
dustpan [ˋdʌstˌpæn] ⓝ	畚斗
lawnmower [ˋlɔnˌmoə] ⓝ	割草機
mop [mɑp] ⓝ	拖把
trash can ⓟⓗ	垃圾桶
vacuum cleaner ⓟⓗ	吸塵器

7 yard 院子

barbecue [ˋbɑrbɪkˌju] n ……………… 烤肉架
doghouse [ˋdɔɡˌhaʊs] n ……………… 狗屋
fence [fɛns] n ……………… 圍籬
garden [ˋɡɑrdn̩] n ……………… 花園
greenhouse [ˋɡrinˌhaʊs] n ……………… 溫室
patio [ˋpɑtɪˌo] n ……………… 露臺

8 library 圖書室

lamp [læmp] n ……………… 檯燈
carpet [ˋkɑrpɪt] n ……………… 地毯
fireplace [ˋfaɪrˌples] n ……………… 壁爐
bookshelf [ˋbʊkˌʃɛlf] n ……………… 書櫃
blinds [blaɪndz] n ……………… 百葉窗

ceiling [ˋsilɪŋ] n ……………… 天花板
doorknob [ˋdorˌnɑb] n ……………… 門把
recreation room ph ……………… 遊戲室
light switch ph ……………… 電燈開關
floor mat ph ……………… 地墊

Daily Q&A

〔會話一〕

Q▸ Do you use microwave to cook food?
你會用微波爐煮菜嗎？

A▸ Yes, I usually use it to heat some food.
會啊，我通常用它來熱食物。

〔會話二〕

Q▸ How many bedrooms do you have?
你有幾間房間啊？

A▸ There are three bedrooms.
總共三間。

〔會話三〕

Q▸ Where do you put your earrings?
你把耳環放在哪裡？

A▸ I think I put them on the dressing table.
我想我把它們放在化妝台上。

Proverbs & Idioms 道地諺語與慣用語｜讓句子更錦上添花

be home and dry 〉 成功的完成某事

I've just got one more report to finish and I will be home and dry.
我還有一個報告要完成。我會成功的完成它。

make oneself at home 〉 把自己當作像在家一般

Welcome to my home. Please make yourself at home.
歡迎來到我家，當成自己家一樣吧。

hit a home run 〉 在某方面成功

Our performance last night was the best we had ever given. We felt our group hit a home run.
昨晚的表演是我們目前為止最好的表演。我覺得我們團在這方面是成功的。

until the cows come home 〉 花很長的時間

We can talk about the problem until the cows come home but it still wouldn't solve anything.
我們可以花很長的時間討論那個問題，但是那沒有幫助。

home is where the heart is 〉 心在哪裡家就在哪裡

I don't mind traveling around all the time because home is where the heart is.
我不介意到處旅行，因為心在哪裡，家就在哪裡。

the longest way round is the shortest way home 〉 欲速則不達

You had better read the instructions before trying to use your new cellphone. It may take some time, but the longest way round is the nearest way home.
你最好在你使用新手機前先閱讀說明書。這可能會花你一些時間但是欲速則不達。

Charity begins at home. 〉 行善始於近親

If you really want to make the world a better place, you can start by being kind to your family and friends. Charity begins at home.
如果你真的想要讓世界變成更好的地方，那麼你可以先從善待你的家人和朋友開始。行善始於近親。

East or west, home is best. 〉 天崖海角，自家最好。

You may think that traveling all the time is fun, but eventually you'll discover that east or west, home is best.
你可能覺得旅行很有趣，但是最終你會發現天崖海角，自家最好。

Go to a Hotel 旅館

01-04

A Welcome to ABC Hotel. How can I help you?
歡迎光臨 ABC 飯店。我能為你服務嗎？

B I booked a double room online two days ago. I would like to check in now.
兩天前，我在網路上預約了一間雙人房。我現在要登記入房。

A No problem. Let me check your reservation on our website. May I know your name and your Identity Card number?
沒問題，讓我在我們的網路上查一下你的預約。可以告訴我你的名字和身份證號碼嗎？

B Sure. It's Jeremy Pitt, F983412324.
當然，我的名字是皮特 · 傑若米，F983412324.

A Yes. I saw your reservation. Here is your room key and your room is 709. It's on the 7th floor next to the stairs.
是的，我看到你的預約了。這是你的鑰匙，你的房間在 709，在七樓的樓梯旁。

B By the way, I would like to have the wake-up call service. I will have to get up early in the morning to attend a very important meeting tomorrow.
順帶一提，我想請你們提供晨醒服務，我明天需要一早起床參加一個非常重要的會議。

A No problem. What time do you want to wake up tomorrow?
沒問題。你明天要幾點起床？

B 6 o'clock. Thank you very much! 六點。非常謝謝你！

Additional Vocabulary & Phrases | 補充單字 & 片語

- **book** v 預定、預約
  Jane has booked a flight from Thailand to Berlin.
  珍已經預訂了一張從泰國飛往柏林的機票。

- **wake-up call service** ph 晨醒服務
  This hotel offers wake-up call service for every customer.
  這間飯店提供每位房客晨醒服務。

Daily Sentences 超高頻率使用句 | 一分鐘學一句不怕不夠用 🎧MP3 01-05

- You can go to our hotel website and make room reservations on the Internet.
  你可以上我們旅館的網站訂房間。

- Is there any vending machine on this floor?
  這一樓有販賣機嗎？

- Can we have a floor map of this hotel?
  可以給我一張這間飯店的平面圖嗎？

- Can you hire a taxi for me? I need to go to the airport by 4 o'clock in the morning.
  可以請你幫我叫計程車嗎？早上四點前我要到機場。

- What time do I need to check out of the hotel?
  我幾點必須退房？

- Would you like to ask a porter to carry your luggage to your room?
  你想請行李員把你的行李拿到房間嗎？

- Excuse me. There is something wrong with my room. The **hairdryer**[1] keeps making funny noises.
  不好意思，我的房間有些問題。吹風機一直發出怪聲音。

- The sink in the bathroom is clogged.
  淋浴間的洗手台塞住了。

- We should put some tips on the table in the morning if we need to stay here for two nights.
  早上我們要放一些小費在桌上，如果我們要在這裡待上兩夜的話。

- This hotel offers some free maps with some discount vouchers.
  這間飯店提供一些免費的、含有折扣券的地圖。

★ 換個單字說說看 | 用單字累積句子的豐富度，讓句子更漂亮！

hairdryer[1] 可替換：

television 電視	**air conditioner** 冷氣	**toilet** 馬桶

The _____ keeps making funny noise.
_____ 一直發出怪聲音。

Additional Vocabulary & Phrases | 補充單字 & 片語

- **porter** n 行李員
  You can give your luggage to the porter.
  你可以把你的行李拿給行李員。

- **sink** n 洗手台
  Can you clean the sink, please?
  可以麻煩你清理一下洗手台嗎？

- **clog** v 堵塞、塞滿
  The tourists clogged the road into the amusement park.
  要往遊樂園的路被遊客塞滿了。

- **discount voucher** ph 折價券
  You can pay this item with the discount voucher.
  你可以用折價券買這樣商品。

❶ lobby 大廳

enquire [ɪnˋkwaɪr] v	諮詢
introduce [͵ɪntrəˋdjus] v	介紹
baggage [ˋbægɪdʒ] n	行李
wait [wet] v	等待
arrange [əˋrendʒ] v	安排
guard [gɑrd] n	守衛
check in ph	到達並登記；報到
check out ph	結帳離開；退房

❷ supply 供給

toothbrush [ˋtuθ͵brʌʃ] n	牙刷
toothpaste [ˋtuθ͵pest] n	牙膏
towel [ˋtauəl] n	毛巾
bathing kit ph	沐浴組
bath robe ph	浴袍

❸ features 特色

furniture [ˋfɜnɪtʃɚ] n	傢俱	bathroom [ˋbæθ͵rum] n	淋浴間
safe [sef] n	保險箱	minibar [ˋmɪnɪbɑr] n	冰箱酒櫃
air conditioner ph	空調		

4 facility 設施

banquet hall [ph]	⋯⋯⋯ 宴會廳	**parking lot** [ph]	⋯⋯⋯ 停車場
conference room [ph]	⋯⋯⋯ 會議室	**restaurant** [ˋrɛstərənt] [n]	⋯⋯⋯ 餐廳
gymnasium [dʒɪmˋnezɪəm]	健身房	**pub** [pʌb] [n]	⋯⋯⋯ 酒吧

5 room service 客房服務

tip [tɪp] [n] ⋯⋯⋯⋯⋯⋯⋯⋯⋯⋯ 小費
laundry service [ph] ⋯⋯⋯⋯⋯ 洗衣服務
housekeeper [ˋhausˌkipɚ] [n] 房務人員
doorman [ˋdorˌmæn] [n] ⋯⋯ 飯店門房
bellboy [ˋbɛlˌbɔɪ] [n] ⋯⋯⋯⋯ 行李員

6 accommodation 住宿

hotel [hoˋtɛl] [n] ⋯⋯⋯⋯⋯⋯ 飯店
B&B (bed & breakfast) [ph] 民宿
guesthouse [ˋgɛstˌhaus] [n] ⋯ 小型家庭旅館
hostel [ˋhɑstl̩] [n] ⋯⋯⋯⋯⋯⋯ 青年旅社
campsite [ˋkæmpˌsaɪt] [n] ⋯⋯ 露營地

7 guest room 客房

single room [ph] .... 單人房
double room [ph] .... 單床雙人房
twin room [ph] .... 雙床雙人房
triple room [ph] .... 三人房
suite [swit] [n] .... 套房

8 gift shop 禮品店

souvenir [ˋsuvəˌnɪr] [n] .... 紀念品
money exchange [ph] .... 兌幣處
newsstand [ˋnjuzˌstænd] [n] ... 報刊販賣攤

vending machine [ph] .... 販賣機
information desk [ph] .... 詢問處
brochure [broˋʃur] [n] .... 資訊小冊子

Daily Q&A

〔會話一〕

Q▸ **What kinds of rooms does this hotel have?**
這間旅館有什麼樣的房間？

A▸ **We have single rooms, double rooms and suits.**
有單人房、雙人房和套房。

〔會話二〕

Q▸ **Where is the elevator?**
電梯在哪裡？

A▸ **It is in the middle of the lobby.**
在大廳的中間。

〔會話三〕

Q▸ **Excuse me. The TV is broken. It just won't turn on.**
不好意思，電視壞了，它沒有辦法打開。

A▸ **OK. I will ask someone to check the problem.**
好，我會請人去查看問題。

7天就能用英文
行遍全世界！ **1** ─○─○─○─○

Chapter **1**
Chapter **2**
Chapter **3**
Chapter **4**
Chapter **5**
Chapter **6**
Chapter **7**
Chapter **8**
Chapter **9**
Chapter **10**

Proverbs & Idioms 道地諺語與慣用語 | 讓句子更錦上添花

be part of the furniture 如同傢俱一般，固定班底

I have been working for this company for so long, and now I am part of the furniture now.
我在這間公司已經工作很久了，我已經是固定班底了。

a rubber check 空頭支票，芭樂票

The woman was accused of writing more than 10,000 dollars in rubber checks to pay for expensive jewelry.
那個女人被控告開了一萬元的空頭支票，購買昂貴的珠寶。

some elbow room 再多一些空間

The room is so crowded. We all need some elbow room.
這間房間很擠，我們需要再多一點空間。

don't let it out of this room 不能將事情說出去

This is a top secret. Don't let it out of this room.
這是終極機密，千萬不要說出去。

not enough room to swing a cat 僅容旋馬的狹窄的空間

Their living room is very small. There is not enough room to swing a cat.
他們的客廳很小，僅容旋馬。

lobby for something 遊說通過議案

The manufacturers lobbied for tax relief.
製造商們遊說通過減稅的議案。

lobby against something 遊說反對議案通過

They lobbied against the tax increase.
他們遊說反對增加稅收的議案。

make a reservation 預約；預訂

I made a reservation for a flight at twelve .
我預訂中午十二點的飛機。

travel broadens the mind 旅行使視野變得更廣。

It's rather true that travel broadens the mind. You will learn to see things from different perspectives.
旅行使視野變得更廣這個說法蠻對的。你會學習用不同的角度看事情。

- Can I make my reservation on the Internet?

  我可以在網際網路上訂房嗎？

- There is something fragile in my hand carry. Can you ask the porter to be more careful?

  我的手提行李中有易碎物品。你可以請行李員小心一點嗎？

- Just go to our hotel website. Find the icon for hotel reservation and complete the form.

  只要到我們旅館的網站，找到旅館訂房的標示，然後填完表格就可以了。

- Is there still anything I can help you?

  還有什麼事我可以服務嗎？

- After I put all my luggage in my room, I would like to walk around here. Do you offer any free map?

  我把我的行李放在房間後，我想要在附近走走。你們有提供免費的地圖嗎？

- Can you recommend me a good restaurant near here?

  你可以建議我一間附近不錯的餐廳嗎？

- You can try our Japanese sushi bar in our gourmet street in the basement. A lot of our customers like it.

  你可以試試地下室美食街的日本壽司吧，很多客人都喜歡。

- Our bartender can make all kinds of cocktails. They all taste great.

  我們的酒保可以調出各種雞尾酒，它們嘗起來都很棒。

- We're out of coffee. How about some milk instead?

  我們沒咖啡了，改喝牛奶好嗎？

- Taking a shower will help me wake up.

  沖個澡可以讓我清醒一點。

MEMO

From AM-PM 從早到晚都用得到的必備好用句

- I'll call a taxi to pick us up.
  我叫計程車來載我們。

- Could you drive a bit faster? I'm in a rush.
  能請你開快一點嗎？我在趕時間。

- How fresh are these fish?
  這些魚有多新鮮？

- I ride the bus to work every morning.
  我每天搭公車上班。

- I need to catch the bus.
  我得趕公車。

- Where can I take Bus 287?
  我在哪可以搭到 287 公車？

- I ride my bicycle to school every day.
  我每天騎腳踏車上學。

- This is my stop.
  我的站到了。

- Where's the nearest subway station?
  最近的地鐵站在哪？

- Where can I buy a subway token?
  我要在哪買地鐵搭乘幣？

- What do you recommend?
  你有什麼建議呢？

MEMO

- What is today's special?
  今日特餐是什麼？

- What is the soup of the day?
  今天濃湯是什麼？

- Which subway line should we take?
  我們要搭哪一線地鐵啊？

- This smells delicious.
  這聞起來好美味。

- No sugar, please.
  不要糖，謝謝。

- I don't drink coffee. What other drinks do you have?
  我不喝咖啡。你們有其他飲料嗎？

- Do you serve any dessert here?
  妳們這有甜點嗎？

- Do you have wireless Internet in this coffee shop?
  這家咖啡店有無線上網嗎？

- I'm going to the coffee shop to read and drink coffee.
  我要去咖啡店看書喝咖啡。

- This coffee is too bitter. Could I have more sugar, please?
  這咖啡好苦。可以再幫我加一些糖嗎？

- I want some whipped cream on top of my cappuccino.
  我的卡布奇諾要加鮮奶油。

MEMO

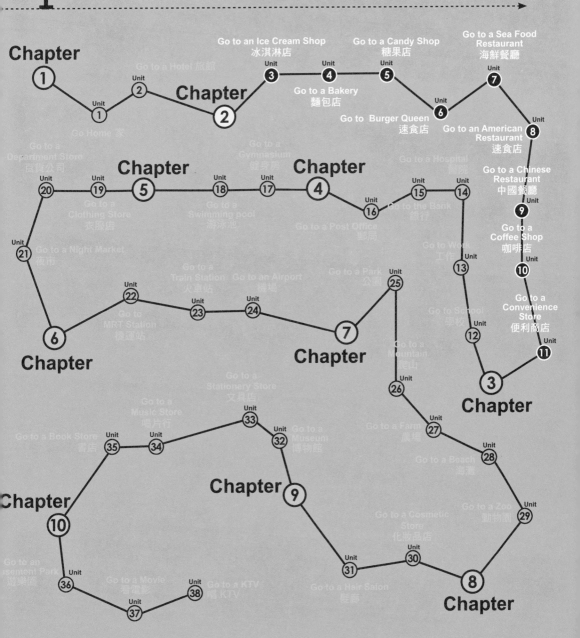

Chapter 2

Food
祭祭五臟廟

Go to an Ice Cream Shop 冰淇淋店

A Look at the ice cream counter. Isn't the ice cream lovely?
你看那冰淇淋櫃，那些冰淇淋好令人垂涎欲滴，不是嗎？

B It is. I can't wait to have it.
是呀，我等不及吃它了。

A I feel like eating Swiss chocolate and rum and raisin. They are my favorite flavors.
我想吃瑞士巧克力和蘭姆葡萄，它們是我最愛的口味。

B I would like to have vanilla and mango with some nuts on the top. I would like to have it in a cup.
我想要香草和芒果口味的，要加核果配料。我要用杯子裝。

A Do you want to order another blueberry sorbet with me? We can share.
你想要和我再點一杯藍莓冰沙嗎？我們可以一起喝。

B Sure!
好啊！

Additional Vocabulary & Phrases | 補充單字 & 片語

● **counter** n 長櫃、櫃台
You can pay your items at the counter over there.
你可以在那邊的櫃台結帳。

● **order** v 訂購、點（餐、菜、飲料等）
I would like to order two hamburgers, please.
我想要點兩份漢堡。

7天就能用英文
行遍全世界！ ① ─○─○─○─○─○

Chapter 1
Chapter 2
Chapter 3
Chapter 4
Chapter 5
Chapter 6
Chapter 7
Chapter 8
Chapter 9
Chapter 10

Daily Sentences 超高頻率使用句 | 一分鐘學一句不怕不夠用

🎧 MP3 02-02

- It's so hot today. I am melting. Let's go eat some ice cream to cool down.
  今天好熱，我快融化了。我們去吃一點冰淇淋冷卻一下。

- Do you have any coupons?
  你有任何優待券嗎？

- Can you recommend me some low-fat ice cream?
  你能推薦一些低脂冰淇淋嗎？

- Janet, what is your favorite ice cream?
  珍納特，妳最喜歡什麼口味的冰淇淋？

- Does this flavor come in popsicles?
  這種口味有出冰棒嗎？

- I want a banana split with chocolate sauce and nuts.
  我要一個加巧克力醬和核果的香蕉船。

- Can I have one scoop of **vanilla**[1] ice cream in an ice cream cone?
  我可以點一球香草冰淇淋用餅乾裝嗎？

- Do you want some syrup on the top of your ice cream?
  你想要在你的冰淇淋上淋上糖漿嗎？

- Could we take a look at the menu?
  我們能看一下菜單嗎？

- This smells delicious.
  這聞起來好美味。

★ 換個單字說說看 | 用單字累積句子的豐富度，讓句子更漂亮！

vanilla[1] 可替換：

marshmallow 棉花糖	wild berry 野莓	caramel 焦糖

Can I have one scoop of ＿＿＿＿＿＿＿＿ ice cream?
我想要一球＿＿＿＿＿＿＿＿（口味）冰淇淋。

Additional Vocabulary & Phrases | 補充單字 & 片語

- **melt** [v] 融化
  The ice cube is melting quickly.
  冰塊正快速地融化中。

- **coupon** [n] 折價券
  Do you have any coupons?
  你有折價券嗎？

① fruity 水果味的

strawberry [`strɔbɛrɪ] n	草莓
cherry [`tʃɛrɪ] n	櫻桃
melon [`mɛlən] n	香瓜
mango [`mæŋgo] n	芒果
banana [bə`nænə] n	香蕉
cranberry [`kræn͵bɛrɪ] n	蔓越莓

② flavor 口味，味道

coffee [`kɔfɪ] n	咖啡
brownie [`braʊnɪ] n	布朗尼
vanilla [və`nɪlə] n	香草
mint chocolate ph	薄荷巧克力
Swiss chocolate ph	瑞士巧克力
green tea ph	抹茶
rum and raisin ph	蘭姆葡萄
Macadamia nut ph	夏威夷豆

③ toppings 填料；調料

syrup [`sɪrəp] n	糖漿	cinnamon [`sɪnəmən] n	肉桂
fudge [fʌdʒ] n	巧克力乳脂糖	caramel [`kærəml̩] n	焦糖
toffee sauce ph	太妃糖漿	whipped cream ph	鮮奶油

④ ice cream sandwich 冰淇淋三明治

popsicle [ˋpɑpsəkəl] ·············· 冰棒

ice cream cone ph ·········· 冰淇淋蛋捲筒

soft-serve ice cream ph ········· 霜淇淋

⑤ sundae 聖代冰淇淋

sorbet [ˋsɔrbɪt] n ·························· 雪酪；雪寶
（鮮果製成的冰沙甜品）

strawberry sundae ph ············ 草莓聖代

banana milkshake ph ··········· 香蕉奶昔

gelato n ························· 義式冰淇淋

frozen yogurt ph ················ 優格冰

scoop [skup] n ················· 冰淇淋勺

one scoop of ice cream ph 一球冰淇淋

Chapter 1
Chapter 2
Chapter 3
Chapter 4
Chapter 5
Chapter 6
Chapter 7
Chapter 8
Chapter 9
Chapter 10

6 nuts 堅果

pecan [pɪˋkæn] 🄝 ········· 美國薄殼胡桃	**hazelnut** [ˋhezḷˏnʌt] 🄝 ········· 榛果
almond [ˋɑmənd] 🄝 ········· 杏仁	**peanut** [ˋpiˏnʌt] 🄝 ········· 花生
cashew [ˋkæʃu] 🄝 ········· 腰果	**pine nut** 🄟 ········· 松子

7 ice cream topping 冰淇淋的配料

cereal [ˋsɪrɪəl] 🄝 ········· 玉米片

waffle [ˋwɑfḷ] 🄝 ········· 格子餅

coconut [ˋkokəˏnət] 🄝 ········· 椰子

chocolate sprinkles 🄟 ····· 巧克力米

gummy bear 🄟 ········· 小熊軟糖

Daily Q&A

〔會話一〕

Q▸ What flavors of ice cream do you have?
你們有哪些冰淇淋口味？

A▸ We have at least 20 different flavors.
我們有超過二十種不同的口味。

〔會話二〕

Q▸ Can I taste some blackberry sorbet?
我可以試吃一些黑櫻桃冰沙嗎？

A▸ No problem.
沒問題。

〔會話三〕

Q▸ How much is a scoop of ice cream?
一球冰淇淋多少錢？

A▸ It's 90 dollars in a cone and 70 dollars in a cup.
用餅乾裝的是九十元，杯裝的是七十元。

Proverbs & Idioms 道地諺語與慣用語 | 讓句子更錦上添花

---

break the ice 〉 打破僵局，打破沉默

When I go to a party, it is hard for me to break the ice. I really don't know how to start the conversation with a stranger.

當我去派對時，打破沉默對我而言很難。我真的不知該如何和陌生人開始先説話。

ice something down 〉 用冰降溫

They are icing the coke down now.

他們正用冰塊將可樂降溫。

ice something over 〉 覆蓋上一層薄冰

In winter, the river will ice over, so people can skate on the river.

冬天時，河上面會結一層薄冰，所以人們可以在河面上溜冰。

on thin ice 〉 處於危險狀態中

It's a very dangerous case. Don't do it, or you will find yourself on thin ice.

這是很危險的事，不要做，不然你會很危險。

cut no ice with someone 〉 對某人無影響

I don't care how people see me. They cut no ice with me.

我不管人們怎麼看我，他們對我沒影響。

cream of the crop 〉 最棒的

Fiona is very smart and hardworking. She is cream of the crop at her school. She always gets the best scores on every test.

費歐娜非常聰明和努力。她是全校最棒的。她每次考試總是得最高分。

ice queen 〉 冰山美人

Tiffany is known for her poker face. She is an ice queen.

蒂芬妮以她的撲克臉聞名。她是個冰山美人。

tip of the iceberg 〉 冰山一嶼

The problem that many people see is just the tip of the iceberg. There are many other hidden ones waiting to be found.

這個問題只是冰山一嶼。還有很多待發現的問題在那裡。

ice palace 〉 珠寶店

What can you afford to buy in that ice palace?

在珠寶店裡有什麼你可以買得起的東西？

Go to a Bakery 麵包店

Daily Conversation 日常對話 | 快速融入超擬真的日常對話

A Their cookies are just freshly made from the oven. They are 6 for 20 dollars.
他們的餅乾才剛出爐，六個售價二十元。

B Sounds like a good bargain. I want 12.
聽起來很划算，我要十二個。

A Look at the Swiss roll over there. They look delicious, too. I am thinking about buying one.
看看那邊的瑞士捲，看起來很好吃，我在想要不要買一個。

B You can taste it before you buy it. They have food tasting at the counter.
你可以先試吃再買，櫃檯那邊有提供試吃。

A I am starting to love this bakery.
我開始漸漸喜歡這間麵包店了。

B It's one of my favorite bakeries.
這是我最愛的麵包店中其中一家。

A You should have told me earlier. I am a cookie lover.
你應該早一點告訴我，我是一個餅乾愛好者。

Additional Vocabulary & Phrases | 補充單字 & 片語

- **bargain** n 特價商品、便宜貨
  These clothes are a real bargain.
  這些衣服真的很划算。

- **food tasting** ph 試吃
  This supermarket usually offers many food tastings on the weekend.
  這間超市在週末的時候都有很多試吃。

Daily Sentences 超高頻率使用句｜一分鐘學一句不怕不夠用
MP3 02-05

- Can I have the **pineapple roll** ★1 next to the cake?
  我可以買蛋糕旁的鳳梨捲嗎？

- How many flavors do the cookies come in?
  餅乾有多少種口味？

- What is the most popular bread at this bakery?
  這家麵包店最受歡迎的麵包是哪一種？

- Do you sell **gingerbread** ★2 ?
  你們有賣薑餅嗎？

- I can't resist the temptation of bread and cookies.
  我無法抗拒麵包和餅乾的誘惑。

- The cookies and bread are freshly made in the oven every two hours.
  餅乾和麵包每二小時新鮮出爐。

- The cookies of the bakery are very popular in town.
  這間麵包店的餅乾在鎮上很受歡迎。

- The bakery invites a famous baker from the USA. He is good at making cookies.
  那間麵包店邀請了一位來自美國的有名麵包師傅，他很擅長做餅乾。

- Let's go get some cookies. I am hungry now.
  我們去買些餅乾吧，我現在好餓喔！

★ **換個單字說說看**｜用單字累積句子的豐富度，讓句子更漂亮！

pineapple roll★1 可以替換：			gingerbread★2 可以替換：		
baguette 法式長棍	**quiche** 鹹派	**cream puff** 泡芙	**macaroon** 馬卡龍	**cinnamon roll** 肉桂捲	**tiramisu** 提拉米蘇

Can I have the _____ **next to the cake?**
我可以買蛋糕旁的_____嗎？

Do you sell _____?
你們有賣_____嗎？

Additional Vocabulary & Phrases｜補充單字 & 片語

- **temptation** n 誘惑
  He has been able to resist the temaptation.
  他一直以來都能夠拒絕誘惑。

- **freshly made** ph 新鮮現做
  They have various kinds of pie freshly made every day.
  他們每天都有很多種新鮮現做的派。

- **good at...** ph 擅長於…
  She is good at playing the piano.
  她很擅長於彈琴。

033

語言學校都會教的超實用日常單字
02-06

1 cake 蛋糕

blueberry cheesecake ph	藍莓起司蛋糕
marble cheesecake ph	大理石起司蛋糕
carrot cake ph	胡蘿蔔蛋糕
blueberry mousse ph	藍莓幕斯
chocolate cake ph	巧克力蛋糕
mango mousse ph	芒果慕斯

2 bread 麵包

toast [tost] n	吐司，烤麵包片	
butterbread [`bʌtɚ] n	奶油麵包	
biscuit [`bɪskɪt] n	小麵包	
croissant [krwɑ`sɑn] n	可頌	

3 pastry 酥皮點心

pie [paɪ] n	有內餡的派	**egg roll** ph	蛋捲
almond flakes ph	杏仁酥片	**red bean green tea roll** ph	
strawberry tart ph	草莓塔		紅豆綠茶蛋糕捲
pineapple roll ph	鳳梨捲		

7天就能用英文
行過全世界！ ①－○－○－○－○－○

Chapter 1
Chapter 2
Chapter 3
Chapter 4
Chapter 5
Chapter 6
Chapter 7
Chapter 8
Chapter 9
Chapter 10

④ **utensil** 器具

baking paper ph	烘焙紙	**scale** [skel] n	磅秤
foil [fɔɪl] n	鋁箔紙	**measuring spoon** ph	量匙
mixing bowl ph	攪拌容器	**rolling pin** ph	麵棍

⑤ **ingredient** 原料

cream cheese ph 奶油起司
whipping cream ph 淡的鮮奶油
unsalted butter ph 淡牛油
baking soda ph 蘇打粉
gelatin [ˋdʒɛlətn] n 吉利丁（用於果凍凝膠類）
baking powder ph 泡打粉
cocoa powder ph 可可粉

⑥ **cookie** 甜餅乾

butter shortbread ph 牛油酥餅
gingerbread [ˋdʒɪndʒɚˏbrɛd] n 薑餅
coconut cookies ph 椰絲酥餅
oatmeal cookies ph 燕麥酥餅
mixed sesame cookies ph
黑白芝麻酥餅

❼ cupcake 杯子蛋糕

scone [skon] n .... 司康
cheese stick ph .... 起司條
waffle [ˋwɑfl] .... 鬆餅
upside down cake ph .... 反轉蛋糕
doughnut [ˋdoˏnʌt] n .... 甜甜圈

❽ baker 麵包（糕點）師傅

bake [bek] v .... 烘、烤
heat up ph .... 加熱
cook [kʊk] v .... 烹煮
mix [mɪks] v .... 混合

freeze [friz] v .... 冷凍
melt [mɛlt] v .... 融化
pour [por] v .... 倒入
coat [kot] v .... 塗在上面
preheat [priˋhit] v .... 預熱

Daily Q&A

〔會話一〕

Q▸ How do you like the cake?
你覺得蛋糕怎麼樣？

A▸ It is very delicious.
很可口。

〔會話二〕

Q▸ How much are the cookies?
餅乾多少錢？

A▸ They are 6 for 20 dollars.
六個二十元。

〔會話三〕

Q▸ Do you have any food tasting?
你們有試吃嗎？

A▸ Sure. It's right over the corner.
當然有，在角落那裡。

Proverbs & Idioms 道地諺語與慣用語｜讓句子更錦上添花

someone's bread and butter ＞ 基本收入

Working as a bartender is his bread and butter.
當一個調酒師是他基本的收入來源。

bread always falls on the buttered side ＞ 禍不單行

Not only did my motorcycle break down on the road, but my cell phone was out of batteries. I think bread always falls on the buttered side.
我不只在半路上機車壞了，連手機也沒電了。我想真的是禍不單行。

bread-and-butter letter ＞ 追蹤信

When I got back home from the international meeting, it took me two days to finish with some bread-and-butter letters.
在我結束國際會議回家後，我花了將近兩天的時間寫完我的追蹤信。

cast one's bread upon the waters ＞ 無怨無悔的付出

Tina is casting her bread upon the waters, supporting her husband while he works on every of his projects.
每當蒂娜的老公在做每個計畫時，蒂娜都無怨無悔的付出。

know which side one's bread is buttered on ＞ 知道經濟來源來自何處

I know which side our bread is buttered on.
我知道經濟來源來自何處。

have your cake and eat it too ＞ 又要馬兒好，又要馬兒不吃草。

You can't have your cake and eat it too. If you want to have a better service, you need to pay more money.
你又要馬兒好，又要馬兒不吃草。如果你想要更好的服務，你就需要付更多的錢。

icing on the cake ＞ 令人更興奮的事

Fiona is my best friend and her visiting is definitely icing on the cake.
費歐娜是我最好的朋友，她的來訪當然是令人非常興奮的事。

sell like hotcakes ＞ （產品）熱賣；暢銷

i-Phone 6 is so popular. It sold like hotcakes.
i-Phone 6 很受歡迎。它很熱賣。

Go to a Candy Shop 糖果店

MP3
02-07

A A new candy shop just opened around the corner last week. They have a variety of candies and it is always full of people.
上星期，有一間糖果店才剛剛在附近開幕，他們有各式各樣的糖果，而且總是充滿了人潮。

B That sounds really attractive. Let's go to that candy shop now.
聽起來很吸引人，我們現在去糖果店吧。

(At the candy shop)
（在糖果店裡）

A Look at the candy bar over there. It is so colorful and tasty.
看那裡的糖果櫃，它們有好多顏色，而且好好吃的樣子。

B They have lollypops, chocolate drops, fruit candy, mints, peanut brittle and toffee. They are in different colors and flavors.
他們有棒棒糖、粒狀巧克力、水果糖、薄荷糖、花生薄片和太妃糖。他們有不同的顏色和口味。

A I want to get a big bag and buy a little of everything.
我想要拿一個大袋子，然後各種口味買一些。

B Me too!
我也要！

Additional Vocabulary & Phrases | 補充單字 & 片語

- **full of** ph 充滿
  The room is full of kids.
  整間房間都是小孩。

- **attractive** a 吸引人的、有吸引力的
  That beautiful woman is very attractive.
  那個漂亮的女人非常有吸引力。

- **colorful** a 鮮豔的、多采多姿的
  This story book is very colorful.
  這本故事書的顏色很鮮豔。

- **tasty** a 可口的、美味的
  This cheesecake is very tasty.
  這塊起司蛋糕真的非常美味。

- I really can't live without **candy** [1].
  我真的沒不能沒有糖果。

- I have a cavity. It's killing me. I think I must have eaten too much candy.
  我有蛀牙，痛死了。我覺得一定是吃太多糖。

- You can still eat candy. What you need to do is watch the calories. Don't eat too much.
  你還是可以吃糖果的。你要做的只是要小心卡路里。不要吃太多。

- Christmas is coming. Let's go buy some candy canes to decorate our Christmas tree.
  聖誕節快到了。我們買些糖果拐杖來裝飾我們的聖誕樹。

- I know a famous candy shop on the first floor in the department store.
  我知道有一間有名的糖果店在百貨公司的一樓。

- You put an apple on a stick and cover it with a lot of toffee. It's tasty.
  你把蘋果放在一根棍子上，然後加上太妃糖。很好吃的。

- You can put some marshmallows in hot chocolate. It's tasty.
  你可以放一些棉花糖在你的熱巧克力裡，很好吃。

- Eat some candy can boost your energy.
  吃糖果可以提振你的活力。

- Some candy is made of fresh fruit juice and is very natural.
  有些糖果是用新鮮果汁做成的，非常天然。

★ 換個單字說說看｜用單字累積句子的豐富度，讓句子更漂亮！

candy [1] 可以替換：

chocolate 巧克力	peanut butter cup 巧克力花生杯	gummy candy 軟糖

I really can't live without _____.
我真的不能沒有_____。

Additional Vocabulary & Phrases｜補充單字 & 片語

- **cavity** n 蛀洞、蛀牙
  Brushing your teeth every day can prevent a cavity.
  每天刷牙能預防蛀牙。

- **calorie** n 卡路里
  Cathy is instructed to start a low calorie and low fat diet.
  凱希被指示要開始執行低卡低脂的飲食習慣。

- **decorate** v 裝飾
  My mom decorated the living room with flowers.
  媽媽用鮮花裝飾客廳。

- **boost** v 推動、促進
  An energy drink can boost you through the day.
  能量飲料可以促進你一整天的動力。

1 snack 零食

candied fruit ph	蜜餞
cookie [ˋkʊkɪ] n	（甜的）餅乾
cracker [ˋkrækɚ] n	（淡或鹹的）餅乾
jelly [ˋdʒɛlɪ] n	果凍
pretzel [ˋprɛtsl̩] n	蝴蝶餅乾（椒鹽脆餅）

2 chocolate 巧克力

brownie [ˋbraʊnɪ] n	布朗尼
white chocolate ph	白巧克力
milk chocolate ph	牛奶巧克力
dark chocolate ph	巧克力
fudge [fʌdʒ] n	巧克力乳脂軟糖

3 candy 糖果

candy bar ph	單獨包裝的塊狀糖	**bubble gum** ph	泡泡糖
mint [mɪnt] n	薄荷糖	**cotton candy** ph	棉絮狀的棉花糖
chewing gum ph	口香糖		

4 **marshmallow 棉花糖**

caramel [ˋkærəml̩] n ──────────── 焦糖
toffee [ˋtɔfɪ] n ───────── 太妃糖；乳脂糖
peanut brittle ph ───────── 花生糖
nougat [ˋnugɑ] n 奶油杏仁花生糖；牛軋糖

5 **nut　堅果**

pumpkin seeds ph ──────── 南瓜子
sunflower seeds ph ─────── 葵花子
pistachio nuts ph ─────── 開心果
popcorn [ˋpɑpˏkɔrn] n ────── 爆米花

6 **jelly beans 雷根糖**

gummy bear ph ─────── 小熊軟糖
candy cane ph ─────── 拐杖糖
icing cookies ph ─────── 糖霜餅乾
lollipop [ˋlɑlɪˏpɑp] n ─────── 棒棒糖
cranberry truffles ph ───── 蔓越莓松露

❼ flavors 味道

taste [test] ⓥ ⸺⸺⸺⸺⸺ 嚐、辨（味）
sweet [swit] ⓐ ⸺⸺⸺⸺⸺ 甜的
sour [`saʊr] ⓐ ⸺⸺⸺⸺⸺ 酸的
bitter [`bɪtɚ] ⓐ ⸺⸺⸺⸺ 有苦味的
spicy [`spaɪsɪ] ⓐ ⸺ 加有香料的；辛辣的
hot [hɑt] ⓐ ⸺⸺⸺⸺⸺ 辣的
salty [`sɔltɪ] ⓐ ⸺⸺⸺⸺ 鹹味濃的

❽ unit 單位

bar [bɑr] ⓝ ⸺⸺⸺⸺⸺ 條、棒
bowl [bol] ⓝ ⸺⸺⸺⸺⸺ 碗
piece [pis] ⓝ ⸺⸺⸺ 片、塊、張、個
slice [slaɪs] ⓝ ⸺⸺⸺⸺ 片、份
box [bɑks] ⓝ ⸺⸺⸺⸺⸺ 盒
bag [bæg] ⓝ ⸺⸺⸺⸺⸺ 袋
gram [græm] ⓝ ⸺⸺⸺⸺ 公克
pound [paʊnd] ⓝ ⸺⸺⸺⸺ 磅
kilogram [`kɪləˌgræm] ⓝ ⸺⸺ 公斤
dozen [`dʌzn̩] ⓝ ⸺⸺⸺⸺⸺ 打
package [`pækɪdʒ] ⓝ ⸺⸺⸺⸺ 包
liter [`litɚ] ⓝ ⸺⸺⸺⸺⸺ 公升

Daily Q&A

〔會話一〕

Q▸ What flavor does the candy come in?
這些糖果有哪些口味？

A▸ It comes in strawberry and honey melon.
有草莓和哈密瓜口味。

〔會話二〕

Q▸ Have you tried toffee apple before?
你有沒有吃過太妃糖蘋果？

A▸ Nope. What is that?
沒有耶，那是什麼？

〔會話三〕

Q▸ What is your favorite candy?
你最喜歡的糖果是什麼？

A▸ Gummy bears are my favorite.
我最喜歡小熊軟糖。

Proverbs & Idioms 道地諺語與慣用語 ｜讓句子更錦上添花

be like taking candy from a baby ⟩ 像從嬰兒身邊拿走糖一般容易
Making a cup of good coffee is really easy. It is like taking candy from a baby to him.
泡一杯咖啡真的很簡單，就好像從嬰兒身邊拿走糖一樣容易。

be like a kid in a candy store ⟩ 像小孩到糖果店一樣快樂無法控制
He is like a kid in a candy store. He cannot help trying everything he sees in this room.
他真的像小孩子到糖果店一樣，沒辦法控制自己的興奮。他忍不住試試每一樣他在房間裡看到的東西。

be eye candy ⟩ 漂亮吸引目光的人事物
Some people think Fiona is just eye candy. She cannot really be a good actress.
有些人覺得菲歐娜只是個漂亮的花瓶，她沒辦法真的成為一個好的女演員。

chocolate box ⟩ 非常漂亮的事物
We drove through a series of chocolate box wooden houses on our way to the beach.
我們在去海灘的路上，開車經過一整排漂亮的木造房屋。

toffee-nosed ⟩ 高傲的
She is so toffee-nosed. She always thinks she is much better than other people.
她很高傲，她總是覺得她比別人都好。

sweet as honey ⟩ 甜心，迷人的
Tina is sweet as honey. No wonder everyone loves her.
緹娜很甜心又迷人。難怪每個人都愛她。

sugar and spice ⟩ 友善溫柔
Sara can be all sugar and spice when she wants to be. But, she can also be pretty evil.
當莎拉想變得友善溫柔時，她可以完全的友善溫柔。但是，她也可以變得相當邪惡。

A Let's go to Burger Queen for lunch. They have good cheese burgers.

我們去「漢堡皇后」吃午餐,他們有好吃的吉士漢堡。

B OK. I am hungry, too. I like their milkshake. They're very creamy and tasty.

好啊,我也餓了。我喜歡他們的奶昔,非常的香醇、濃郁。

(At Burger Queen) (在「漢堡皇后」)

A Look at the long line. There are always a lot of people waiting in line just for the cheese burgers. They must be very delicious.

看那一排長隊伍,總是有很多人在那裡排隊要買吉士漢堡,一定很好吃。

B Yup. But, this also means we have to wait to order our food.

是啊,但是這也是說,我們必須等候才能點餐。

A Come on. It is worth waiting. Their cheese burgers are really popular. Once you have it, you will love it.

拜託,這是值得等的,他們的吉士漢堡真的很受歡迎,一旦你吃過,你就會愛上。

B Well, sounds very attractive. I tried their vanilla milkshake last time, and it was really delicious.

嗯,聽起來很吸引人。我上次只有喝過他們的香草奶昔,真的很好喝。

Additional Vocabulary & Phrases | 補充單字 & 片語

- **creamy** [a] 奶香濃郁的、多乳脂的
  This pumpkin soup is very creamy.
  這個南瓜濃湯非常的濃郁。

- **attractive** [a] 有吸引力的、引人注目的
  That beautiful woman is very attractive.
  那位美麗的女人真的很有吸引力。

- **worth** [a] 值得;有價值的
  That terrible movie is not worth watching.
  那部糟糕的電影不值得一看。

- **vanilla** [n] 香草
  Mandy loves vanilla ice cream.
  曼蒂非常喜歡香草冰淇淋。

Daily Sentences 超高頻率使用句 | 一分鐘學一句不怕不夠用 🎧MP3 02-11

● How many set meals do you have? What are they?

你們有幾種套餐？什麼套餐？

● What drinks can I choose from for my set meal?

我的套餐可以點什麼飲料？

● We have 5 set meals. They are Big Cheeseburger, Giant Fish Burger, Big Chicken Burger, Chicken Nuggets, and Fried Chicken.

我們有五種套餐，它們是大吉士漢堡套餐、巨無霸魚堡套餐、大雞堡套餐、雞塊套餐和炸雞套餐。

● You can choose the drinks under 30 dollars.

你可以點一個低於三十元的飲料。

● Can I upgrade my drink and my fries?

我可以升級我的飲料和薯條嗎？

● What's on the **cheese burger**[1]?

吉士漢堡裡有什麼？

● You can only upgrade one thing for every set meal.

每一種套餐只能升級一樣東西。

● I would like to have a **large Coke**[2].

我想要一杯大杯可樂。

● Can I have the fried chicken with a chicken thigh only?

我可以只要雞大腿的炸雞嗎？

★ 換個單字說說看 | 用單字累積句子的豐富度，讓句子更漂亮！

cheese burger[1] 可以替換：			**large Coke**[2] 可以替換：		
burrito 墨西哥捲餅	**chicken wrap** 雞肉捲	**ceasar salad** 凱薩沙拉	**diet coke** 低卡可樂	**small iced tea** 小杯冰茶	**medium orange juice** 中杯柳橙汁

What on the _____?
_____ 裡有什麼？

I would like to have a _____.
我想要一杯_____。

Additional Vocabulary & Phrases | 補充單字 & 片語

● **set meal** ph 套餐
I would like to have the rice burger set meal.
我想要米漢堡套餐。

● **upgrade** v 升級
I got a flight upgrade last time when I went to Rome.
上次我去羅馬的時候我的機位被升等。

● **thigh** n 大腿
I exercise every day in order to make my thigh slimmer.
我為了瘦大腿所以每天運動。

1 fast food 速食

fast [fæst] a ⸺⸺⸺⸺⸺⸺ 快速的

convenience [kən`vinjəns] n ⸺ 便利

chain-store restaurant ph 連鎖餐廳

combo [`kɑmbo] n ⸺⸺⸺⸺ 套餐

meal [mil] n ⸺⸺⸺⸺⸺ 一餐；膳食

2 hamburger 漢堡

cheeseburger [`tʃiz͵bɝgɚ] n ⸺ 起司堡

rice burger ph ⸺⸺⸺⸺ 米香堡

chicken sandwich ph ⸺⸺ 香雞堡

fish burger ph ⸺⸺⸺⸺ 香魚堡

veggie burger ph ⸺⸺⸺ 蔬菜堡

3 fried chicken 炸雞

chicken nugget ph ⸺⸺⸺ 雞塊

french fries ph ⸺⸺⸺⸺ 薯條

onion rings ph ⸺⸺⸺⸺ 洋蔥圈

hash brown ph ⸺⸺⸺⸺ 馬鈴薯餅

cheese sticks ph ⸺⸺⸺⸺ 起司條

4 snack and side 副餐點心

ice cream ph ·················· 冰淇淋
apple pie ph ·················· 蘋果派
salad [ˋsæləd] n ·················· 沙拉

corn soup ph ·················· 玉米濃湯
yogurt [ˋjogɚt] n ·················· 優格

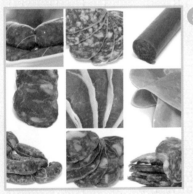

5 bacon 培根

ham [ˋhæm] n ·················· 火腿
sausage [ˋsɔsɪdʒ] n ·················· 臘腸
pepperoni [͵pɛpɚˋronɪ] n ·········· 義式辣味臘腸
salami [səˋlɑmɪ] n 莎樂美腸（義式蒜味香腸）
lunch meat ph ·················· 冷肉（午餐肉）

6 drinks 飲料

Coke [kok] n ·················· 可樂
iced tea ph ·················· 冰紅茶
coffee [ˋkɔfɪ] n ·················· 咖啡
milkshake [͵mɪlkˋʃek] n ·················· 奶昔
cocoa [ˋkoko] n ·················· 可可
juice [dʒus] n ·················· 果汁
milk [mɪlk] n ·················· 牛奶

7 ask 詢問

straw [strɔ] n ·· 吸管

napkin [ˋnæpkɪn] n ··························· 紙巾

free-refill ph ··································· 免費續杯

hot [hɑt] a ···································· 熱的

cold [kold] a ·································· 冰的

8 sauce 調味醬

ketchup [ˋkɛtʃəp] n ·········· 蕃茄醬

mustard [ˋmʌstɚd] n ·········· 芥末

barbecue [ˋbɑrbɪkju] n ······ 烤肉醬

mayonnaise [ˌmeəˋnez] n ···· 美乃滋

sweet and sour sauce ph ···· 糖醋醬

pepper [ˋpɛpɚ] n ················· 胡椒

salt [sɔlt] n ··························· 鹽

sugar [ˋʃʊgɚ] n ·················· 糖

chili sauce ph ···················· 辣醬

pickled relish ph ················ 酸黃瓜

Daily Q&A

〔會話一〕

Q▸ What would you like to order?
你想要點什麼？

A▸ I would like to have a cheese burger.
我想要一個吉士漢堡。

〔會話二〕

Q▸ For here or to go?
你想要在這邊吃，還是帶走？

A▸ To go, please.
帶走。

〔會話三〕

Q▸ Can I have some straws and mayonnaise?
可以給我一些吸管和美乃滋嗎？

A▸ Sure. There you go.
沒問題，在這裡。

Proverbs & Idioms 道地諺語與慣用語｜讓句子更錦上添花

make hamburger out of someone 〉 揍某人
If you don't behave well I will make hamburger out of you!
如果你不好好守規矩，我會揍你喔！

toss a salad 〉 拌沙拉
The host tossed the salad in front of all the guests and served every one of them a plate of fresh salad.
那個主人在所有客人面前拌沙拉，然後在每個人的盤子上放一份新鮮的沙拉。

in one's salad days 〉 在某人年輕時
Irene always recalls the joy she experienced on her school vacation in her salad days.
艾琳總是回想在她年輕時學校放假時所經歷過的愉快時光。

have one's finger in too many pies 〉 參與太多事
You make yourself too busy by having your finger in too many pies.
你參與太多事了，所以太忙了。

pie in the sky 〉 不切實際的想法計劃
Be realistic! Don't just make your plans like pie in the sky.
實際一點！不要只是在空中畫大餅，做些不實際的計畫。

bring home the bacon 〉 工作賺錢養家
Jason is a father. He works very hard to bring home the bacon.
傑森是個父親。她非常努力工作賺錢養家。

no spring chicken 〉 不再是年輕小夥子
He is 58 years old now. He is no spring chicken.
他現在五十八歲了。他不再是一個年輕小夥子。

butter (someone) up 〉 阿諛奉承
Jerry often butters up his boss in order to get the latest news about the policy of his company.
傑瑞常常阿諛奉承他的老闆來取得公司政策最新的消息。

Unit 7 Go to a Sea Food Restaurant 海鮮餐廳

MP3 02-13

A Let's go to the seafood restaurant in our neighborhood.
我們去我們家附近的那間海鮮餐廳。

B Sounds great. Let's go! 聽起來不錯，我們走吧！

(At the seafood restaurant) （在海鮮餐廳）

A Look at the crystal clear fridge. You can see a variety of seafood in it. They all look very fresh and delicious.
看那清澈透明的冰箱，你可以在那裡看到各式各樣的海鮮，它們都看起來很新鮮、很可口。

B True. I would like to have some salmon sashimi and a roast salmon head.
真的耶！我想要吃一些鮭魚生魚片和烤鮭魚頭。

A You sound like a seafood expert. I would like to have some stir-fried squids and steamed shrimps.
你聽來是個海鮮專家。我想要一些炒花枝和清蒸蝦子。

B You are not too bad as well. I also want to have a steamed lobster. It really tastes like its from the heaven.
你聽起來也不賴嘛！我還想叫一隻清蒸龍蝦，它們吃起來像來自天堂的味道。

Additional Vocabulary & Phrases | 補充單字 & 片語

- **neighborhood** n 鄰近地區
  She lives around our neighborhood.
  她住離我們家很近。

- **crystal** a 水晶的
  Dad uses his crystal glass to drink wine.
  爸爸用他的水晶杯喝紅酒。

- **expert** n 專家
  She's an expert in baking.
  她在烘焙方面是個專家。

- **steam** v 蒸
  I want to steam some bun for breakfast.
  我想要蒸些饅頭當早餐。

Daily Sentences 超高頻率使用句｜一分鐘學一句不怕不夠用 02-14

- Do you think we should try some deep fried oysters?
  你覺得我們要試試看炸蚵仔嗎？

- Oysters are tasty and contain a lot of nutrition.
  牡蠣很好吃，而且具有很多營養。

- I am allergic to seafood, and I dislike the smell. Whenever I have seafood, I will have diarrhea.
  我對海鮮過敏，而且我也不喜歡那個味道。每次我吃海鮮就會拉肚子。

- I would like my **salmon**[1] in a soup.
  我想要把鮭魚煮湯。

- Eating oysters is good for your skin. They are nicknamed sea milk.
  吃蚵仔對你的皮膚很好。牠們有一個綽號叫做「海中牛奶」。

- You can tell the seafood from the color. If the color looks transparent, it is fresh.
  你可以從顏色判斷海鮮。如果顏色看起來是透明的，就是新鮮。

- Have you eaten **sea urchin**[2] before?
  你吃過海膽嗎？

- I would like to have some clam chowder. It goes well with crackers.
  我想要喝一些蛤蜊濃湯，它們配蘇打餅乾很好吃。

- I would like to stir-fry some shellfish like clams, scallop, and mussels.
  我想要吃一些帶殼海鮮，像是蛤蜊、干貝，還有淡菜。

★ **換個單字說說看**｜用單字累積句子的豐富度，讓句子更漂亮！

salmon[1] 可以替換：			**sea urchin**[2] 可以替換：		
arctic char 北極鮭魚	**mackerel** 鯖魚	**sea bass** 鱸魚	**king crab** 帝王蟹	**bluefin tuna** 黑鮪魚	**jellyfish salad** 涼拌海蜇皮

I would like my ＿＿＿＿＿＿＿＿＿ in a soup.　　Have you eaten ＿＿＿＿＿＿＿＿ before?
我想要把＿＿＿＿＿＿煮湯。　　　　　　　　你吃過＿＿＿＿＿＿嗎？

Additional Vocabulary & Phrases ｜補充單字 & 片語

- **nutrition** n 營養、滋養
  Fish contains a lot of nutrition.
  魚含有很多營養。

- **allergic** a 過敏的
  I am allergic to nuts.
  我對堅果類過敏。

- **diarrhea** n 腹瀉
  He suffered from diarrhea due to the milk.
  他因為喝了牛奶而腹瀉。

- **nickname** n 暱稱、綽號
  What's her nickname?
  她的綽號是什麼？

1 **marine organism** 海洋生物

octopus [ˋɑktəpəs] n	⋯⋯⋯⋯	章魚
squid [skwɪd] n	⋯⋯⋯⋯	烏賊
cuttlefish [ˋkʌtḷ͵fɪʃ] n	⋯⋯	花枝
urchin [ˋɝtʃɪn] n	⋯⋯⋯⋯	海膽
jelly fish ph	⋯⋯⋯⋯	水母

2 **fish** 魚

anchovy [ˋæntʃəvɪ] n	⋯⋯	鯷魚
salmon [ˋsæmən] n	⋯⋯⋯	鮭魚
bass [ˋbæs] n	⋯⋯⋯⋯	鱸魚
cod [kɑd] n	⋯⋯⋯⋯⋯	鱈魚
tuna [ˋtunə] n	⋯⋯⋯⋯	鮪魚

3 **shellfish** 貝；有殼的水生動物

oyster [ˋɔɪstɚ] n	牡蠣	**lobster** [ˋlɑbstɚ] n	龍蝦
crab [kræb] n	螃蟹	**clam** [klæm] n	蛤蜊
shrimp [ʃrɪmp] n	蝦子	**scallop** [ˋskɑləp] n	扇貝

052

④ appearance 外觀；外顯

lively [ˋlaɪvlɪ] ⓐ ──────── 活潑的

dead [dɛd] ⓐ ──────── 死的

transparent [trænsˋpɛrənt] ⓐ ⋯ 透明的

fresh [frɛʃ] ⓐ ──────── 新鮮的

⑤ negative 負面的

influence [ˋɪnfluəns] ⓝ ⋯⋯ 作用；影響

poison [ˋpɔɪzn̩] ⓐ ──────── 有毒的

diarrhea [ˌdaɪəˋriə] ⓝ ──────── 腹瀉

smell [smɛl] ⓝ ──────── 臭味

disgusting [dɪsˋgʌstɪŋ] ⓐ ⋯ 令人作噁的

vomit [ˋvɑmɪt] ⓥ ──────── 嘔吐

dehydration [ˌdihaɪˋdreʃən] ⓝ ⋯ 脫水

stale [stel] ⓐ ──────── 不新鮮的

rotten [ˋrɑtn̩] ⓐ ──────── 發臭的、腐敗的

expire [ɪkˋspaɪr] ⓥ ──────── 過期

6 cooking 烹飪

deal with ph ························ 處理
sauté [soˋte] v ········ 嫩煎（或炒、煸）
roast [rost] v ··················· 烤；炙；烘
stir-fry [ˋstɝ͵fraɪ] v ··················· 炒
sashimi [saˋʃimɪ] n ············· 生魚片

7 fish tail 魚尾

fish eye ph ··········· 魚眼　　**fin** [fɪn] n ··········· 魚鰭
fish mouth ph ······· 魚嘴　　**vent** [vɛnt] n ········ 排氣孔
gill [gɪl] n ··················· 鰓

Daily Q&A

〔會話一〕

Q▸ **How would you like your crab to be cooked?**
你希望你的螃蟹怎麼烹調？

A▸ **I would like it to be steamed.**
我想用蒸的。

〔會話二〕

Q▸ **Do you like seafood?**
你喜歡海鮮嗎？

A▸ **Not really.**
還好。

〔會話三〕

Q▸ **How does the fish taste?**
這些魚嚐起來如何？

A▸ **They taste fantastic!**
嚐起來非常美味！

Proverbs & Idioms 道地諺語與慣用語｜讓句子更錦上添花

happy as a clam 〉 快樂

Since he has been in a university, he is happy as a clam.
因為他已經在大學了，他很快樂。

clam up 〉 閉嘴

He promised not to tell anyone the secret, so when people asked him about the thing, he just clammed up.
他保證不會告訴任何人這個祕密，所以只要有人問到這件事，他就閉嘴。

shut up like a clam 〉 突然閉口不提

I was chatting happily with Jeremy. However, he shut up like a clam when I asked him something about his trip to Japan.
我正快樂的和傑瑞米聊天，然而，我一問到關於他這次到日本的旅行時，他卻突然閉口不提。

a fish out of water 〉 不適應新地方，如魚沒有水

After having lived in Taipei for almost all his life, he is like a fish out of water when staying in New York.
在他花了一生大部份的時間住在台灣之後，他真的不太適應紐約的新環境，就好像魚出了水一般。

fish tale 〉 謊言

Kelly is a master at the fish tale. She should be a politician.
凱莉真的很擅長說謊，她很適合當一個政客。

fish around 〉 在某處到處找尋

The boy fished around his pocket for some coins.
那男孩在他的口袋裡到處找尋硬幣。

fish in troubled waters 〉 混水摸魚

Pay more attention to the class. Don't try to fish in troubled waters.
上課專心一點。不要老是混水摸魚。

Go to an American Restaurant 美式餐廳

A Welcome to American Classic Restaurant. Did you make a reservation?
歡迎來到經典美式餐廳。你們有訂位嗎？

B Nope. Can we have a table for two?
沒有。我們可以要一個兩人的座位嗎？

A Let me check. Yes, there is a table for two by the window. Just follow me. I will lead you to the table.
讓我看看。有的，有一個靠窗的兩人座位。跟著我，我帶你們到座位。

B Thank you very much.
非常謝謝你。

A Here is the menu. What would you like to order?
這是菜單。你們想要點什麼？

B We would like to order two set meals.
我們想要兩份套餐。

Additional Vocabulary & Phrases ｜ 補充單字 & 片語

- **reservation** n 預定
  We've made a reservation for a table at that restaurant.
  我們已經在那間餐廳訂了一桌位子。

- **follow** v 跟隨
  The dog followed the cat to the garden.
  那隻狗跟著那隻貓去到了花園。

- **lead** v 引領、領（路）
  She led us the way to the library.
  她帶著我們去到圖書館。

- **menu** n 菜單
  Can you ask the waiter to bring us the menu?
  你能請服務生幫我們送一下菜單嗎？

Chapter 1
Chapter 2
Chapter 3
Chapter 4
Chapter 5
Chapter 6
Chapter 7
Chapter 8
Chapter 9
Chapter 10

Daily Sentences 超高頻率使用句｜一分鐘學一句不怕不夠用
02-17

- Does the main course come with **soup or salad**[★1]?

  主餐有附湯和沙拉嗎？

- How do you like your steak? Medium-rare, medium, medium-well or well-done?

  你的牛排要幾分熟？三分、五分、七分或全熟？

- Can I have some **pepper and salt**[★2]?

  可以給我一些胡椒和鹽嗎？

- What do you feel like eating for the **starter**[★3]?

  你前菜要吃什麼？

- I would like to have two salads.

  我想要兩份沙拉。

- I would like to have one roast chicken and one steak.

  我想要一份烤雞腿和一份牛排。

- We would like to have **coffee**[★4] for drinks.

  我們飲料想要喝咖啡。

- I would like my steak medium-well.

  我想要我的牛排七分熟。

- Do you want anything to drink?

  你們想要點什麼飲料嗎？

★ 換個單字說說看｜用單字累積句子的豐富度，讓句子更漂亮！

soup or salad[★1] 可以替換：

| appetizer 開胃菜 | dessert and drink 甜點和飲料 | wine 紅酒 |

Does the main course come with

_____?

主餐有附_____ 嗎？

pepper and salt[★2] 可以替換

| napkin 餐巾紙 | chili sauce 辣醬 | water 水 |

Can I have some_____?

可以給我一些_____ 嗎？

starter[★3] 可以替換

| salad 沙拉 | main course 主餐 | side dish 副菜 |

What do you feel like eating for the

_____?

你_____ 想吃什麼？

coffee[★4] 可以替換

| lemonade 檸檬汁 | mineral water 礦泉水 | iced tea 冰紅茶 |

We would like to have _____ for drinks.

我們飲料想要喝_____ 。

1 atmosphere 氣氛

cheerful [ˈtʃɪrfəl] a	興高采烈的
noisy [ˈnɔɪzɪ] a	吵雜的
quiet [ˈkwaɪət] a	安靜的
elegant [ˈɛləgənt] a	雅緻的
graceful [ˈgresfəl] a	典雅的
relax [rɪˈlæks] a	輕鬆的
comfortable [ˈkʌmfətəbl̩] a	舒適的

2 table manners 餐桌禮儀

politeness [pəˈlaɪtnɪs] n	有禮貌
slurp [slɝp] v	出聲地吃（或喝）
pass [pæs] v	傳遞
order [ˈɔrdɚ] v	點（餐）
elegant [ˈɛləgənt] a	優雅的

3 cutlery 餐具

silverware [ˈsɪlvɚˌwɛr] n	銀器	**steak knife** ph	牛排刀
fork [fɔrk] n	叉子	**butter knife** ph	奶油刀
spoon [spun] n	湯匙	**pastry fork** ph	甜點叉

④ appetizer 開胃菜

aperitif [aperiˋtif] n ·················· 開胃酒　　　**finger food** ph ·················· 手抓小食品

chicken wing ph ·················· 雞翅　　　**refined** [rıˋfaınd] a ·················· 精緻的

nachos [ˋnætʃoz] n （墨西哥人食用的）烤乾酪辣味玉米片

⑤ main dish 主菜

steak [stek] n ·················· 牛排

pork [pork] n ·················· 豬肉

chicken [ˋtʃıkın] n ·················· 雞肉

beef [bif] n ·················· 牛肉

lamb chop ph ·················· 羊小排

barbecue [ˋbɑrbıkju] n ·················· 烤肉

⑥ pasta 義大利麵

lasagna [ləˋzanjə] n ·················· 千層麵

spaghetti [spəˋgɛtı] n ·················· 義大利麵條

rigatoni [ˌrıgəˋtoni] n ·················· 通心粉

capellini n ·················· 天使麵

ravioli [ˌrævıˋolı] n ·················· 義大利餃

7 **fruit 水果**

dragon fruit ph	火龍果
honeydew [ˈhʌnɪˌdju] n	白蘭瓜
bell-apple ph	蓮霧
star fruit ph	楊桃
kiwi [ˈkiwɪ] n	奇異果

8 **dessert 甜點**

Éclair [eˈklɛr] n	閃電泡芙	**chocolate fondant** ph	熔岩巧克力
soufflé n	舒芙蕾	**crème brûlée** ph	烤布蕾
panna cotta ph	奶酪		

Daily Q&A

〔會話一〕

Q▸ What do you feel like eating?
你想吃什麼？

A▸ I feel like eating steak.
我想吃牛排。

〔會話二〕

Q▸ What is your favorite type of pasta?
你最喜歡哪種義大利麵？

A▸ I like ravioli the best!
我最喜歡義大利餃！

〔會話三〕

Q▸ What do you want for dessert?
你甜點想要吃什麼？

A▸ I would like to have the panna cotta.
我想要奶酪。

Proverbs & Idioms **道地諺語與慣用語** | 讓句子更錦上添花

beef something up 〉 加強

Let's beef up the music project with more money.
讓我們增加更多的預算到那個音樂的計畫裡。

beef about 〉 抱怨

Stop beefing about Helen. She didn't do that on purpose.
不要再抱怨海倫了,她不是故意那麼做的。

have a beef with someone/something 〉 認為某事或某人需要改變

I have a beef with those bad programs on TV.
我認為那些電視上不好的電視節目需要改善。

pork out 〉 暴飲暴食

I am overweight now. I wish I had not porked out all the time for the past three weeks.
我現在超重了,我真希望我過去三週以來,沒有暴飲暴食。

like a lamb to the slaughter 〉 如待宰的羔羊

The young solider went to the army like a lamb to the slaughter. Little did he know there was something dangerous waiting for him.
那個年輕的軍人,服兵役就像待宰的羔羊一般,他不知道一些危險的事情正在等著他。

Where's the beef? 〉 實際的方法在哪裡

That's really clever and appealing, but where's the beef? There's no substance in this proposal.
那真的是很聰明又吸引人,但是實際的方法在哪裡?這企劃書中沒有一個實際的執行方法。

make lemonade out of lemons 〉 苦中作樂

Since I've lost my job, I plan on making lemonade out of lemons. I want to start my own business!
既然我丟了工作,我打算苦中作樂。我想要開始我的事業!

Go to a Chinese Restaurant 中國餐廳

A I know a good Chinese restaurant around here. Let's go there.
我知道這附近有一間很棒的中國餐廳，我們去那邊吃點東西吧。

B That is a really good idea.
那真是一個好主意

A Let's order some food for lunch.
我們點一些食物當午餐吧。

B Would you like rice with minced meat?
你想要吃滷肉飯嗎？

A I am more interested in eating oyster noodle thread.
我對蚵仔麵線比較有興趣。

B Then, I will order a rice with minced meat. For the drink, I want the rice and peanut milk.
那麼，我會點滷肉飯，至於喝的，我要點米漿。

A Good. I want the soy bean milk.
好。那麼我想要豆漿。

Additional Vocabulary & Phrases | 補充單字 & 片語

- **mince** v 切碎、剁碎
  We have some minced beef in the freezer.
  我們有一些碎牛肉在冷凍庫裡。

- **interested in** ph 對…有興趣
  I am really interested in this movie.
  我對這部電影非常有興趣。

- **thread** n 線、線狀物
  There's a piece of thread on your hair.
  你的頭髮上有一小條線。

- **soy bean** ph 黃豆
  Tofu is made from soy beans.
  豆腐是黃豆做的。

Daily Sentences 超高頻率使用句 ｜ 一分鐘學一句不怕不夠用 02-20

- Can you eat with chopsticks?
  可以用筷子吃飯嗎？

- Can you recommend some delicious dishes?
  你可以推薦我一些好吃的菜餚嗎？

- Do you have **Peking duck**★1 on the menu?
  你們的菜單上有北京烤鴨嗎？

- What dish is popular in your restaurant?
  你們餐廳裡，哪些菜餚受歡迎？

- Can I share the table with other people?
  我可以和別人共用桌子嗎？

- Can I have some chili sauce and vinegar?
  可以給我一些辣椒和醋嗎？

- Let's sit around the table and ask the waiter to come and serve us.
  我們圍著桌子坐，請服務生來替我們服務。

- My tummy is grumbling. I would like to have a **scallion pancake**★2.
  我的肚子餓得呱呱叫。我想吃些蔥油餅。

- There are so many people in the restaurant. I think we have to share the table with the couple over there. Otherwise, it may take ages for us to get a table.
  餐廳裡面真的好多人，我想我們要跟那邊的夫妻共用一張桌子，要不然我們要花上一輩子等座位。

★ 換個單字說說看 ｜ 用單字累積句子的豐富度，讓句子更漂亮！

Peking duck★1 可以替換：

General Zhou chicken 左宗棠雞	cashew chicken 腰果雞丁	chow mein 炒麵

Do you have _____on the menu?
你們的菜單上有_____嗎？

scallion pancake★2 可以替換：

plate of stinky tofu 一盤臭豆腐	glass of bubble tea 一杯珍珠奶茶	bowl of beef noodle 一碗牛肉麵

I would like to have a _____.
我想吃_____。

Additional Vocabulary & Phrases ｜ 補充單字 & 片語

- **chopstick** n 筷子
  Many westerners don't know how to use chopsticks.
  很多西方人不知道怎麼用筷子。

- **serve** v 為…服務、供應
  The waiter served me a glass of water.
  那個服務生為我上一杯水。

- **grumble** v 發轟隆聲、發出咕嚕聲
  She's grumbling about the bad weather.
  她正因為糟糕的天氣發出咕嚕聲。

- **otherwise** ad 否則
  You need to go to bed early; otherwise you will get tired tomorrow. 你要早點上床睡覺，否則你明天會很累。

① table 餐桌

round [raʊnd] ⓐ		圓的
square [skwɛr] ⓝ		正方的
rectangle [rɛk`tæŋgl̩] ⓝ		長方形
rotate [`rotet] ⓥ		旋轉
together [tə`gɛðɚ] ⓐ		一起；共同
menu [`mɛnju] ⓝ		飯菜；菜單

② tea 茶

Woolong tea ⓟʰ		烏龍茶
osmanthus tea ⓟʰ		桂花茶
puer tea ⓟʰ		普洱茶
Biluochun ⓝ		碧螺春
Long Jing Tea ⓟʰ		龍井茶
Tieguanyin ⓝ		鐵觀音

③ staple 主食

rice [raɪs] ⓝ		米飯
noodle [`nudl̩] ⓝ		麵
sliced noodles ⓟʰ		刀削麵
fried rice ⓟʰ		炒飯
fried noodles ⓟʰ		炒麵
ramen ⓟʰ		拉麵
beef noodles ⓟʰ		牛肉麵

4 Dimsum 港式點心

dumpling [ˋdʌmplɪŋ] n	水餃
spring roll ph	春捲
sweet and sour pork ph	糖醋排骨
hot and sour soup ph	酸辣湯

5 walnut paste 核桃糊

sesame paste ph	芝麻糊
red bean soup ph	紅豆湯
green bean soup ph	綠豆湯
tapioca [ˌtæpɪˋokə] n	西谷米

6 hot pot 火鍋

broths [brɔθs] n	湯頭
rice noodle ph	米粉
green bean noodle ph	冬粉
tofu [ˋtofu] n	豆腐
hot and spicy hot pot ph	麻辣火鍋

7 **oyster omelet** 蚵仔煎

scallion pancake [ph] ·············· 蔥油餅

rice with minced meat [ph] ····· 滷肉飯

oyster noodle thread [ph] ···· 蚵仔麵線

pig's blood rice pudding [ph] 豬血糕

8 **breakfast** 早餐

Chinese omelet [ph] ·············· 蛋餅

fried leek dumpling [n] ········· 韭菜盒

steamed bun [ph] ·················· 饅頭

steamed dumpling [ph] ·········· 蒸餃

rice ball [ph] ······················· 飯糰

rice congee [ph] ···················· 粥

deep-fried Chinese donut [ph] ·· 油條

sesame flat bread [ph] ············· 燒餅

soybean milk [ph] ·················· 豆漿

rice and peanut milk [ph] ········· 米漿

Daily Q&A

〔會話一〕

Q▶ **Can I have a pot of Woolong tea?**
我可以點一壺烏龍茶嗎？

A▶ **Just a moment, please.**
請等一下。

〔會話二〕

Q▶ **Do you fancy some sesame paste?**
你想吃芝麻糊嗎？

A▶ **Sure.**
好啊。

〔會話三〕

Q▶ **What would you like to have for breakfast?**
你想要吃什麼當早餐？

A▶ **I would like to have a scallion pancake with an egg and a soy bean milk.**
我想要蔥油餅加蛋，和一杯豆漿。

Proverbs & Idioms 道地諺語與慣用語｜讓句子更錦上添花

strike it lucky 〉 有突然來的好運

She struck it lucky with her first book which became an immediate best-seller.

她突如其來的好運，讓她的第一本書馬上就成為暢銷書。

thank one's lucky stars 〉 感謝某人的幸運星

I thanked my lucky stars. I studied the right things for the test.

我感謝我的幸運星，我都剛好讀到考試要考的東西。

lucky dog 〉 幸運的人

You won the lottery?! You lucky dog!

你中樂透了嗎？你這個幸運的人！

it is better to be born lucky than rich 〉 出生富裕不如出生幸運

Maybe your family is not rich. But you are still lucky. You know it is better to be born lucky than rich.

你的家庭可能不富有，但你還是很幸運的。你要知道，出生富裕不如出生幸運。

lucky at cards, unlucky in love 〉 牌運亨通情場失利

Jack always won lots of money in the card games. However, it is always said that lucky at cards, unlucky in love. I think God is fair on everything.

傑克總是在玩牌時贏得很多錢，然而俗話說「牌運亨通，情場就失利」，我想上天總是公平的。

like the white on rice 〉 就像白色在米上面沒有什麼差別

Those two colors are really close—like the white on rice.

那兩個顏色真的很相近，沒有什麼差別。

noodle around 〉 到處晃晃

I couldn't find the signs so I noodled around until I found the right address.

我無法找到指標所以只好到處晃晃直到我找到正確的地址。

You cannot get blood from a turnip. 〉 徒勞無功或無濟於事的事

The government can't increase taxes any further—nobody has the money! You can't get blood from a turnip.

政府沒辦法再徵收更多的稅 — 沒有人有錢繳稅！你不能做無濟於事的事。

Go to a Coffee Shop 咖啡店

02-22

A I'll go find a place for us. Can you order an iced latte and a waffle with honey?
我去找我們的座位。你可以幫我點一杯冰拿鐵和蜂蜜比利時鬆餅嗎？

B Sure. I think I will have a cappuccino and some pancakes.
當然，我想要一杯卡布奇諾和一些美式鬆餅。

A It did not take a long time waiting for the food.
食物上來得很快。

B That is true. Their service is very fast. Do you want to read a magazine or newspaper?
的確，他們的上菜速度很快。你想看一些雜誌或報紙嗎？

A Yup. I had better catch up on the latest news, or I will become really outdated.
當然，我最好跟上一些最新的消息，否則我會落伍的。

B Me too. It's been three days. I did not have enough time to read the news. I needed to finish my report this morning.
我也是。我已經有三天沒有時間好好看一下新聞了，我今天早上需要完成我的報告。

A Let's enjoy our coffee and reading!
讓我們享受我們的咖啡和閱讀吧！

Additional Vocabulary & Phrases | 補充單字 & 片語

- **honey** n 蜂蜜
  I'd like to have some hot tea with honey.
  我想要喝些熱茶加蜂蜜。

- **catch up** ph 跟上、趕上
  I am really behind on my class. I need to catch up.
  我在班上真的很落後了，我得趕緊跟上進度。

- **outdated** a 過時的
  That outfit is really outdated.
  那件衣服真的很過時。

- **report** n 報告
  I have a final report to finish.
  我有一份期末報告要完成。

Daily Sentences 超高頻率使用句│一分鐘學一句不怕不夠用 MP3 02-23

- Is the coffee shop self-catering or does it have clerks to wait on the customers?

  這間咖啡店是自助式的,還是店員會服務客人?

- Do you want some **sugar**★1 in your coffee?

  你想要加一些糖到你的咖啡裡嗎?

- We have a beef bagel special and salmon bagel special. All the specials are served with **an boiled egg and a regular coffee**★2.

  我們有牛肉貝果特餐、鮭魚貝果特餐。所有的特餐都附有一顆白煮蛋,和一杯中杯咖啡。

- I prefer strong coffee to weak coffee.

  我喜歡濃咖啡勝於淡咖啡。

- Cake usually tastes better with coffee.

  蛋糕配咖啡會更好吃。

- Would you like to sit inside or outside the coffee shop?

  你喜歡坐在咖啡店裡頭,還是外面?

- I am a coffee lover. I cannot live without drinking coffee.

  我是一個咖啡愛好者,我不喝咖啡不能活。

- I can never resist the aroma of coffee.

  我永遠無法抗拒咖啡的香味。

★ 換個單字說說看│用單字累積句子的豐富度,讓句子更漂亮!

sugar★1 可以替換			**an boiled egg and a regular coffee**★2 可以替換		
cinnamon powder 肉桂粉	**vanilla syrup** 香草糖漿	**rose syrup** 玫瑰糖漿	**breakfast tea** 早餐茶	**rye bread and juice** 裸麥麵包和果汁	**toast and milk** 土司和鮮奶

Do you want some _____ **in your coffee?**
你想要加一些 _____ 到你的咖啡裡嗎?

All the specials are served with _____.
所有特餐都有附_____。

Additional Vocabulary & Phrases │ 補充單字 & 片語

- **self-catering** a 自助式的
  This restaurant is self-catering.
  這間餐廳是採自助式的。

- **boiled** a 煮沸的
  The water is boiled. Don't touch it!
  那水已經煮沸了。別碰它!

- **prefer** v 寧可;更喜歡…
  I prefer not to think about the past.
  我寧可不去想過去的事情。

- **resist** v 抗拒、拒絕
  I cannot resist the temptation of chocolate.
  我無法抗拒巧克力的誘惑。

1 **coffee** 咖啡

coffee latte ph ························· 拿鐵
cappuccino [͵kɑpə'tʃino] n 卡布奇諾
mocha ['mokə] n ················· 摩卡咖啡
espresso [ɛs'prɛso] n ·········· 濃縮咖啡
iced coffee ph ····················· 冰咖啡

2 **coffee mill** 咖啡豆研磨機

espresso machine ph ···· 義式咖啡機
brew [bru] v ···················· 煮（咖啡）
grind [graɪnd] v ··· 磨（碎）；磨（成）
pour-over iced coffee brewer ph
···························· 冰滴咖啡機
coffee press ph ·········· 咖啡濾壓壺

3 **taste** 嚐

caffeine ['kæfiin] n ··········· 咖啡因
aroma [ə'romə] n ·············· 香味

acidity [ə'sɪdətɪ] n ············· 酸度
body ['bɑdɪ] n ·················· 濃度

4 coffee bean 咖啡豆

roast spectrum ph ⋯⋯⋯⋯ 烘焙色譜	**medium roast** ph ⋯⋯⋯⋯ 中度烘焙
blonde roast ph ⋯⋯⋯⋯ 黃金淺培	**dark roast** ph ⋯⋯⋯⋯ 深度烘焙

5 preference 偏愛

condense [kən`dɛns] v ⋯⋯⋯⋯ 濃縮

mixed [mɪkst] a ⋯⋯⋯⋯ 參雜的

decaffeinated [dɪ`kæfˌnetɪd] a
⋯⋯⋯⋯ 無咖啡因的

low-fat milk ph ⋯⋯⋯⋯ 低脂牛奶

milk foam ph ⋯⋯⋯⋯ 奶泡

6 flavors 味道

syrup [`sɪrəp] n ⋯⋯⋯⋯ 糖漿

caramel [`kærəml] n ⋯⋯⋯⋯ 焦糖

cinnamon [`sɪnəmən] n ⋯⋯⋯⋯ 肉桂

vanilla [və`nɪlə] n ⋯⋯⋯⋯ 香草

cocoa [`koko] n ⋯⋯⋯⋯ 可可

peppermint [`pɛpɚˌmɪnt] n 胡椒薄荷

7 sandwich 三明治

bagel [ˋbeɡəl] n ⋯⋯⋯⋯⋯⋯⋯⋯⋯⋯⋯ 貝果

roast beef croissant ph ⋯ 烤牛肉可頌

tuna sandwich ph ⋯⋯⋯⋯ 鮪魚三明治

egg salad sandwich ph 蛋沙拉三明治

8 tiramisu 提拉米蘇

donut [ˋdoˌnʌt] n ⋯⋯⋯⋯⋯⋯⋯ 甜甜圈

muffin [ˋmʌfɪn] n ⋯⋯⋯⋯⋯⋯⋯⋯ 馬芬

madeleine [ˋmædəˌlɛn] n ⋯ 瑪德蓮蛋糕

cinnamon bun ph ⋯⋯⋯⋯⋯⋯⋯ 肉桂捲

waffle [ˋwɑfl] n ⋯⋯⋯⋯⋯⋯⋯⋯⋯ 鬆餅

puff [pʌf] n ⋯⋯⋯⋯⋯⋯⋯⋯⋯⋯⋯⋯ 泡芙

mousse [mus] n （多泡沫的）奶油甜點

pudding [ˋpudɪŋ] n ⋯⋯⋯⋯⋯⋯⋯ 布丁

sundae [ˋsʌnde] n ⋯⋯⋯⋯⋯ 聖代冰淇淋

pancake [ˋpænˌkek] n ⋯⋯⋯⋯⋯⋯ 煎餅

Daily Q&A

〔會話一〕

Q▶ What kind of coffee would you like to have?

你想要喝哪一種咖啡？

A▶ I would like to have a double espresso.

我想要一杯雙倍濃縮咖啡。

〔會話二〕

Q▶ Do you want to have some room for the milk?

你要留一些空間加牛奶嗎？

A▶ Yes, please.

是的。

〔會話三〕

Q▶ Do you want some sugar in your coffee?

你想要加一些糖到你的咖啡裡嗎？

A▶ No, thanks. I like black coffee without sugar.

不，謝謝，我喜歡黑咖啡，不加糖。

Proverbs & Idioms 道地諺語與慣用語｜讓句子更錦上添花

not someone's cup of tea ＞ 不是某人的菜，不是某人所喜愛的東西
Reading books is really not my cup of tea. I prefer doing sports.
閱讀實在不是我喜歡的事情，我喜歡運動。

be in one's cup ＞ 酒醉時
When Jerry is in his cup, he would sit there and do nothing but laugh.
傑瑞喝醉的時候，會坐在那裡什麼事都不做，只會傻笑。

wake up and smell the coffee ＞ 注意並著手進行
The parents had better wake up and smell the coffee. It is very obvious that their children have got some serious problems.
這對父母親最好要開始做一些事情了。很明顯的，他們的孩子有一些嚴重的問題。

the flavor of the mouth ＞ 暫時或目前普遍流行
The first music album of the rap artist just released and it suddenly became the flavor of the mouth.
這位饒舌歌手的第一張音樂專輯才剛發行，就馬上變成目前最流行的音樂。

it's no use crying over spilled milk ＞ 木已成舟，於事無補
I know you do not like your new hairstyle, but you can't change it since it is no use crying over spilled milk.
我知道你不喜歡新髮型，但是你沒有辦法改變，因為木已成舟，於事無補。

milk a duck ＞ 替鴨子擠牛奶（做不可能的事）
It is just like milking a duck. I can't do it!
這好像替鴨子擠牛奶。 我不會！

land of milk and honey ＞ 像聖經中的應許之地。
Many people came to the United States thinking it was the land of milk and honey.
很多人來到美國以為它是塊應許之地，十分美好。

milk someone for something ＞ 索求
The thief milked me for 3,000 dollars.
那個小偷向我索求 3,000 元。

Chapter 1
Chapter 2
Chapter 3
Chapter 4
Chapter 5
Chapter 6
Chapter 7
Chapter 8
Chapter 9
Chapter 10

MP3
02-25

A Gee… I am so hungry. I want to get something to eat at the convenience store.
天哪！我好餓，我想到便利商店找一些東西吃。

B I know they now have some special offers.
我知道他們現在有特價。

A Do you want to come with me?
你想跟我一起去嗎？

B Why not? I need some stationery. I ran out of paper and ball point pens.
好呀！我想買一些文具用品。我的紙和原子筆都沒有了。

A I want to buy a hot dog, a tea egg and some oden.
我想買一份熱狗、一個茶葉蛋和一些關東煮。

B Do you want me to get a drink for you? The stationery section is right next to the fridge.
你要我幫你拿些喝的嗎？文具區就在冰箱隔壁。

A OK. I want a bottle of coke.
好呀！我要一瓶可樂。

Additional Vocabulary & Phrases｜補充單字 & 片語

- **convenience** n 方便、合宜
  Do you think Jane is making a convenience of Lily?
  你有覺得珍在利用莉莉嗎？

- **offer** v 給予、提供
  She offered me a cup of hot tea.
  她給我一杯熱茶。

- **run out of** ph 用完、耗盡
  We've ran out of toilet paper.
  我們的衛生紙用完了。

- **bottle** n 瓶子
  There's a bottle of water over there.
  那邊有一瓶水。

Daily Sentences 超高頻率使用句｜一分鐘學一句不怕不夠用 MP3 02-26

- What kind of stationery is there at a convenience store?

  便利商店有賣哪些文具？

- What things are on special sale?

  哪種東西正在特價？

- The convenience store offers newspapers, glue, white-out, paper clips and even scissors.

  這間便利商店有報紙、膠水、立可白、迴紋針，甚至剪刀。

- I bought something online. I would like to collect my goods here.

  我在網路上買一些東西。我想要在這裡取這些商品。

- The ice cream is buy two get one free.

  冰淇淋買二送一。

- I usually buy my groceries at the convenience store.

  我通常在便利商店買雜貨。

- All drinks are buy one get the second 40% off.

  所有的飲料買一件，第二件六折。

- Can you get a pack of **cigarettes** ★1 for me?

  你可以拿一包香煙給我嗎？

- I want to pay my **telephone bill** ★2.

  我想繳電話費。

★ 換個單字說說看｜用單字累積句子的豐富度，讓句子更漂亮！

cigarettes★1 可以替換：

| potato chips 洋芋片 | chocolate 巧克力 | chewing gum 口香糖 |

Can you get a pack of _____ for me?
你可以幫我拿一包 _____ 嗎？

telephone bill★2 可以替換：

| tuition 學費 | insurance 保險費 | credit card bill 信用卡費 |

I want to pay my _____.
我想要繳 _____。

Additional Vocabulary & Phrases ｜補充單字 & 片語

- **white-out** ph 修正液

  I've run out of white-out.
  我修正液用完了。

- **goods** n 商品、貨物

  She sells handmade goods.
  她賣手工商品。

- **grocery** n 食品雜貨

  We need to buy some groceries this weekend.
  這個周末我們需要添購一些食品雜貨。

- **pack** n 一包（盒，箱，袋）

  She gave me a pack of candy.
  她給我一包糖果。

① daily necessity 日常必需品

tissue paper ph	衛生紙
razor [ˋrezɚ] n	刮鬍刀
soap [sop] n	肥皂
hand moisturizer ph	護手霜
cleansing foam ph	洗面乳
shower gel ph	沐浴乳
shampoo [ʃæmˋpu] n	洗髮精
hair conditioner ph	護髮乳

② canned food 罐頭食品

potato chips ph	洋芋片
vinegar [ˋvɪnɪgɚ] n	醋
soy sauce ph	醬油
instant noodles ph	泡麵
dried bean curd ph	豆乾
expiration date ph	保存期限

③ stationery 文具

knife [naɪf] n	刀片	**ink pens** ph	簽字筆
scissors [ˋsɪzɚz] n	剪刀	**glue** [glu] n	膠水
envelope [ˋɛnvəˏlop] n	信封		

4 delicatessen 熟食

oden [n]	關東煮	
hot dog [ph]	熱狗	
tea egg [ph]	茶葉蛋	
onigiri [n]	三角飯糰	
rice balls/fan tuan [ph]	中式飯糰	

5 counter 櫃臺；櫃臺式長桌

cashier [kæˋʃɪr] [n] ·········· 收銀員
telephone bill [ph] ·········· 電話帳單
gas bill [ph] ·········· 瓦斯費帳單
utility bill [ph] ·········· 電費帳單
water bill [ph] ·········· 水費帳單

6 cigarettes 香煙

beer [bɪr] [n] ·········· 啤酒
wine [waɪn] [n] ·········· 紅酒
sparkling wine [ph] ·········· 氣泡酒
champagne [ʃæmˋpen] [n] ·········· 香檳酒
rice wine [ph] ·········· 米酒

7 beverage 飲料

juice [dʒus] n ⸺⸺⸺⸺⸺⸺ 果汁
milk [mɪlk] n ⸺⸺⸺⸺⸺⸺ 鮮奶
green tea ph ⸺⸺⸺⸺⸺⸺ 綠茶
soda [ˋsodə] n ⸺⸺⸺⸺⸺⸺ 汽水
bottled water ph ⸺⸺⸺⸺⸺⸺ 瓶裝水

8 magazine 雜誌

newspaper [ˋnjuzˌpepɚ] n ⸺⸺ 報紙
comic books ph ⸺⸺⸺⸺⸺⸺ 漫畫

catalog [ˋkætəlɔg] n ⸺⸺⸺⸺ 型錄
flyer [ˋflaɪɚ] n ⸺⸺⸺⸺⸺⸺ 廣告傳單

Daily Q&A

〔會話一〕

Q▸ Can I pay my telephone bill here?
我可以在這裡付電話費嗎？

A▸ Sure.
當然。

〔會話二〕

Q▸ Do you sell cigarettes?
你們有賣香煙嗎？

A▸ Yes. We sell a variety of cigarettes.
有的，我們有賣各式各樣的香煙。

〔會話三〕

Q▸ Can I have some hot water?
我可以要些熱水嗎？

A▸ Here you are.
這給你。

7天就能用英文
行遍全世界！ ——②—○—○—○—○—○

Chapter 1
Chapter 2
Chapter 3
Chapter 4
Chapter 5
Chapter 6
Chapter 7
Chapter 8
Chapter 9
Chapter 10

Proverbs & Idioms 道地諺語與慣用語｜讓句子更錦上添花

foot the bill 付帳單

My boss took me out for lunch and the company footed the bill.
我的老闆請我吃飯，公司會付帳。

sell someone a bill of goods 欺騙

What your mom tells you is always true. She will never sell you a bill of goods.
你媽媽告訴你的都是真的。她從來不會欺騙你。

a clean bill of health 被證明公司營運良好或一個人身體健康

⇨ Jason got a clean bill of health from his doctor. He can live longer than 100.
傑森被醫生證明身體健康，他可以活到一百歲。

⇨ Burger Ding got a clean bill of health from the government. They have good and stable profits every year.
Ding 漢堡被政府查出營運良好，他們每年有好又穩定的收入。

fit the bill 到達所需標準或資格

If you want some exciting entertainments, the amusement park in Taichung will fit the bill.
如果你想要一些較刺激的娛樂，台中的一家遊樂園會符合你的標準。

a whale of a bill 很大一筆金額的帳單

We went to a luxury French restaurant. We ran up a whale of bill at the restaurant.
我們到一間豪華的法式餐廳，我們最後要付很大的一筆錢給餐廳。

pay the water bill 上廁所

I will be right back with you as soon as I pay the water bill.
我上完廁所馬上回來。

billie 紙鈔

Do you have any billies on you?
你身上有一些紙鈔嗎？

Everyday Sentences 語言學校獨家傳授必備好用句

- I would like to copy something. Can you turn on the copy machine?
  我想要影印一些東西。可以幫我把影印機打開嗎？

- I love the meal boxes at QK. They come in different types of food, such as oden, rice balls, sushi, sandwiches, congee and so on.
  我喜歡在 QK 買餐盒。他們有不同種類的食物，例如：關東煮、飯糰、壽司、三明治和粥等。

- I really like BK convenience store.
  我真的很喜歡 BK 便利商店。

- They offer a variety of sweets and delicatessen. I really want a hot dog and some oden.
  他們有各式各樣的甜食和熟食，我真的很想吃一份熱狗和一些關東煮。

- Welcome to BK convenience store.
  歡迎光臨 BK 便利商店。

- You can go to the aisle next to the snack section. There is some basic stationery. Go look whether you can find anything you want.
  你可以去零食區旁邊的走道，那裡有一些基本的文具。看看有沒有你想要的文具。

- I will get you a pack of cigarettes when I check out at the counter.
  我去櫃台結帳的時候會順便幫你買包菸。

- What do you want for breakfast?
  你早餐想吃什麼？

- I'd like a large latte.
  我要一杯大杯拿鐵。

- Can I have some ketchup please?
  能給我些番茄醬嗎？

MEMO

From AM-PM 從早到晚都用得到的必備好用句

- Be careful. The coffee is very hot.
  小心！這咖啡很燙。

- What kind of dumplings do they have?
  他們有哪種水餃？

- I'd rather not eat anything too spicy.
  我不想吃太辣的食物。

- I think I'll pass on the chicken feet.
  我想我跳過鳳爪不吃好了。

- Is pig's blood good?
  豬血好吃嗎？

- Do they serve pearl milk tea here?
  他們這有珍珠奶茶嗎？

- They serve "family style" meal here.
  這裡提供「家庭式」的食物。

- Do you know how to use chopsticks?
  你知道怎麼用筷子嗎？

- I don't know how to use chopsticks. Do they have forks?
  我不會用筷子，他們有叉子嗎？

- I eat fast food all the time.
  我一直都是吃速食。

- This hamburger is so juicy!
  這個漢堡肉汁好多！

MEMO

- Does this fast food restaurant have a drive-through?
  這家速食店有得來速嗎？

- I'm on a diet. I can't eat fast food.
  我在減肥，不能吃速食。

- These shoes are not very comfortable.
  這些鞋子穿起來不是很舒適。

- I need to buy a present for my mom.
  我要買禮物給我媽。

- I'm shopping for a present.
  我在採買禮物。

- Ohh…My stomach doesn't feel good after eating that.
  喔！吃完那個東西之後我的胃不太舒服。

- What did I just eat?
  我剛剛吃了什麼？

- What is this drink made from?
  這飲料是用什麼做的？

- Put your toys away.
  把你的玩具收好。

- Clean the floor, please.
  請把地板清乾淨。

- Mom, let me help you.
  媽媽，讓我來幫妳。

MEMO

_____

_____

_____

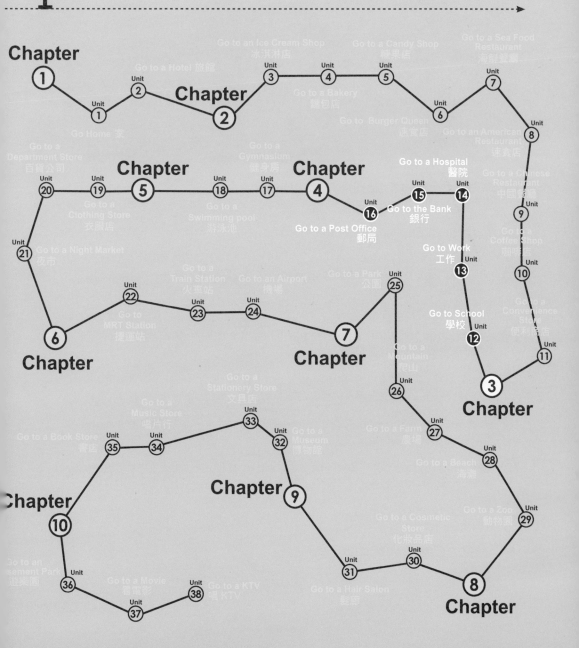

Chapter 3

Institutions , School & Work
辦正經事的地方

Chapter **1**

Unit **1**
Go Home 家

Unit **2**
Go to a Hotel 旅館

Chapter **2**

Unit **2**

Unit **3**
Go to an Ice Cream Shop 冰淇淋店

Unit **4**
Go to a Bakery 麵包店

Unit **5**
Go to a Candy Shop 糖果店

Unit **6**
Go to Burger Queen 速食店

Unit **7**
Go to a Sea Food Restaurant 海鮮餐廳

Unit **8**
Go to an American Restaurant 速食店

Unit **9**
Go to a Chinese Restaurant 中國餐廳

Go to a Department Store 百貨公司

Chapter **5**

Unit **20**
Unit **19**
Go to a Clothing Store 衣服店

Unit **18**
Go to a Swimming pool 游泳池

Unit **17**
Go to a Gymnasium 健身房

Chapter **4**

Unit **16**
Go to a Post Office 郵局

Unit **15**
Go to the Bank 銀行

Unit **14**
Go to a Hospital 醫院

Go to a Coffee Shop 咖啡店

Unit **10**
Go to a Convenience Store 便利商店

Unit **21**
Go to a Night Market 夜市

Unit **22**
Go to a Train Station 火車站

Unit **23**
Go to an MRT Station 捷運站

Unit **24**
Go to an Airport 機場

Unit **25**
Go to a Park 公園

Go to a Mountain 爬山

Unit **13**
Go to Work 工作

Unit **12**
Go to School 學校

Unit **11**

Chapter **3**

Chapter **6**

Unit **7**

Chapter **7**

Unit **26**

Unit **27**
Go to a Farm 農場

Unit **28**
Go to a Beach 海灘

Go to a Stationery Store 文具店

Go to a Music Store 唱片行

Unit **33**
Go to a Museum 博物館

Unit **32**

Unit **35**
Go to a Book Store 書店

Unit **34**

Unit **9**

Unit **29**
Go to a Zoo 動物園

Chapter **9**

Chapter **10**

Unit **10**

Go to an Amusement Park 遊樂園

Unit **36**

Unit **37**
Go to a Movie 看電影

Unit **38**
Go to a KTV 唱KTV

Unit **31**

Go to a Cosmetic Store 化妝品店

Unit **30**
Go to a Hair Salon 髮廊

Unit **8**

Chapter **8**

Daily Conversation 日常對話 | 快速融入超擬真的日常對話

A Hi, Jenny. Are you going to school now?
嗨，珍妮。妳現在要去上學嗎？

B Yup. I have English at 9 in the morning.
是啊！我早上九點有英文課。

A I plan to look for some important books and study at the library. Do you want to join me?
我想在圖書館讀書並找一些書。你要一起來嗎？

B Sure. I need to return some books. They are due today.
好啊！我也要還書。我的書今天到期。

A Great. We can go to the swimming pool in the gymnasium after that.
太好了。我們之後可以去體育館裡的游泳池。

B That sounds like a good idea. We can chill out a little in this hot weather.
很不錯。我們可以在炎炎夏日中消暑一下。

A I am running late now. See you after class in front of the library then. Bye!
我快遲到了。那麼下課後圖書館前見。再見囉！

B See you then.
到時候見。

Additional Vocabulary & Phrases | 補充單字 & 片語

● **due** a 到期的
The report is due next Monday.
這份報告下周一到期截止。

● **chill out** ph 冷靜；讓人放鬆的
This music can really chill me out.
這個音樂真的能令我放鬆。

Daily Sentences 超高頻率使用句｜一分鐘學一句不怕不夠用
03-02

- What is your major?
  你主修什麼？

- Who is the **president** ★1 of this school?
  這間學校的校長是哪一位？

- Excuse me. Where and how can I apply for a library card? I would like to borrow some books.
  不好意思。我可以在哪裡並如何申請一張圖書館卡？我想借一些書。

- What is the due date of these library books? I need to return them by the due date, or I will need to pay the fine.
  這些書幾號到期？我要在到期前還書，不然我就得付罰金。

- At school, we need to follow the school regulations. We shall not violate those rules. Otherwise, we will be detained.
  在學校我們要遵守校規。我們不能違規，不然會被留校查看。

- I'm majoring in **Chemistry** ★2.
  我主修化學。

- When do you finish your class?
  你何時上完課？

- Please hand in your homework on time every day.
  請每天準時繳交作業。

★ 換個單字說說看｜用單字累積句子的豐富度，讓句子更漂亮！

president★1 可以替換：

vice president 副校長	chief secretary 主任祕書	school nurse 學校護士

Who is the _____ of this school?
學校的 _____ 是哪一位？

Chemistry★2 可以替換：

English and Literature 英文和文學	psychology 心理	philosophy 哲學

I'm majoring in _____.
我主修 _____。

Additional Vocabulary & Phrases ｜ 補充單字 & 片語

- **apply** v 申請
  I want to apply for the graduate program at Ohio State University.
  我想要申請俄亥俄州立大學的碩士課程。

- **fine** n 罰金、罰款
  I need to pay for a $500 dollar fine.
  我需要繳一筆 500 元的罰金。

- **regulation** n 規章、規則
  We need to follow the regulation.
  我們必須遵守規則。

- **violate** v 違反、違背；侵犯
  The company was fined because they violated its customer's privacy.
  那間公司因為侵犯顧客的隱私而被罰款。

① classroom 教室

blackboard [`blæk͵bord] n		黑板
whiteboard [`hwaɪtbord] n		白板
eraser [ɪ`resɚ] n		板擦
chalk [tʃɔk] n		粉筆
desks and chairs ph		課桌椅
wastepaper basket ph		廢紙簍
bell [bɛl] n		鐘聲

② sports field 操場

track and field ph		田徑
badminton [`bædmɪntən] n		羽毛球
football [`fut͵bɔl] n		美式足球
dodge ball ph		躲避球
track [træk] n		運動跑道

③ playground 遊戲場

swing [swɪŋ] n		鞦韆	**jungle gym** ph	鐵方格
seesaw [`si͵sɔ] n		翹翹板	**sand play area** ph	沙坑
the bars ph		單槓		

4 library 圖書館

bookshelf [`bʊkˌʃɛlf] n ⋯⋯⋯⋯ 書櫃
library card ph ⋯⋯⋯⋯ 借書證
overdue [`ovɚˋdju] a ⋯⋯⋯⋯ 逾期的
solemn silence ph ⋯⋯⋯⋯ 保持肅靜
novel [`nɑvl̩] n ⋯⋯⋯⋯ 小說

journal [`dʒɝn̩l] n ⋯⋯⋯⋯ 期刊
quarterly publication ph ⋯⋯⋯⋯ 季刊
weekly publication ph ⋯⋯⋯⋯ 週刊
monthly publication ph ⋯⋯⋯⋯ 月刊

5 curriculum 學校全部課程大綱

mathematics [ˌmæθəˋmætɪks]
= math [mæθ] n ⋯⋯⋯⋯ 數學
history [`hɪstərɪ] n ⋯⋯⋯⋯ 歷史
English [`ɪŋglɪʃ] n ⋯⋯⋯⋯ 英文
Chinese [`tʃaɪˋniz] n ⋯⋯⋯⋯ 國文
chemistry [`kɛmɪstrɪ] n ⋯⋯⋯⋯ 化學
physics [`fɪzɪks] n ⋯⋯⋯⋯ 物理

science [`saɪəns] n ⋯⋯⋯⋯ 科學
literature [`lɪtərətʃɚ] n ⋯⋯⋯⋯ 文學
biology [baɪˋɑlədʒɪ] n ⋯⋯⋯⋯ 生物
art [ɑrt] n ⋯⋯⋯⋯ 美術
P.E. = Physical Education ph ⋯ 體育
geography [`dʒɪˋɑgrəfɪ] n ⋯⋯⋯⋯ 地理

⑥ gymnasium 體育館

swimming pool ph 游泳池	**baseball field** ph 棒球場
gymnastics [dʒɪmˋnæstɪks] n 體操	**football field** ph 足球場
basketball court ph 籃球場	**golf course** ph 高爾夫球場
tennis court ph 網球場	

⑦ faculty 教職員

staff [stæf] n 行政人員

professor [prəˋfɛsɚ] n 教授

associate professor ph 副教授

assistant professor ph 助理教授

instructor [ɪnˋstrʌktɚ] n 講師

teaching assistant ph 教學助理

chair professor ph 講座教授

chair [tʃɛr] n 系主任

Daily Q&A

〔會話一〕

Q▸ **Are you good at playing golf?**
你擅長打高爾夫球嗎？

A▸ **Yes, I am good at playing it.**
是的，我很會打。

〔會話二〕

Q▸ **What time does your school start?**
你學校幾點開始上課？

A▸ **It starts at 7:00 am.**
早上七點開始。

〔會話三〕

Q▸ **Which subject do you like the most?**
你最喜歡那一科？

A▸ **I like English the most.**
我最喜歡英文。

Proverbs & Idioms 道地諺語與慣用語｜讓句子更錦上添花

cut class/cut school 〉 翹課
Jane was punished because she cut school in order to join the party.
珍因為翹課去派對而被處罰了。

from the old school 〉 老派的
Aunt Helen is from the old school. She loves to wear a colorful long skirt.
海倫阿姨很老派。她喜歡穿彩色的長裙。

school of hard knocks 〉 從艱苦中習得經驗
Jeff did not go to school, but he went to the school of hard knocks. He learned things by his experience.
傑夫沒有上過學，但是他從他的困難中學習成長。

tell tales out of school 〉 散佈謠言和秘密
Don't trust what Jimmy says. He never stops telling tales out of school.
別相信吉米說的話。他從沒停止散佈不實的話和消息。

the old school tie 〉 學校所認識的人脈
The old school tie still has enormous power when you work in some big companies.
當你到大公司工作時，學校所認識的人脈有著很重大的影響。

schoolboy humor 〉 幼稚的笑話
Come on! The joke is not funny at all. That is really schoolboy humor.
拜託！這個笑話一點也不好笑。真的是個幼稚的笑話。

pass with flying colors 〉 高分通過考試
Greg studied really hard and he passed the final exam with flying colors.
桂格很用功讀書。他高分通過期末考。

teacher's pet 〉 善於取悅老師的人
Frank is definitely teacher's pet. He always knows what to say to make our teacher happy.
法蘭克當然是老師的寵兒。他總是知道說什麼來取悅老師。

03-04

A Good morning, Mr. Smith.
早安，史密斯先生。

B Good morning, Jamie. What time is it now?
早安，潔咪。現在幾點了？

A It is 9 o'clock now.
現在九點整。

B I see. What is today's schedule?
我知道了。今天的行程是什麼呢？

A You have two meetings today. One is at 10 am, and the other is at 2 pm.
你今天有兩個會議。一個在早上十點，另一個在下午兩點。

B OK. Can you prepare things for the meeting in the conference room? Make enough copies of the handouts.
好。妳可以替我在會議室準備會議所需要的物品嗎？準備足夠的提綱影本。

A No problem. 沒問題。

Additional Vocabulary & Phrases | 補充單字 & 片語

- **schedule** n 行程表、課程表
  What is your class schedule next semester?
  你下學期的課表是什麼？

- **prepare** v 準備
  Can you prepare some apple juice for your sister?
  你能幫你姐姐準備一些蘋果汁嗎？

- **conference** n 會議、討論會
  The professor will give a speech at the annual conference.
  那位教授會在年度討論會上演講。

- **handout** n 講課題綱、講義
  Please make 30 copies of handouts for the class.
  這堂課請準備 30 份的講義。

Daily Sentences 超高頻率使用句｜一分鐘學一句不怕不夠用
MP3
03-05

- Can you fax this to Mr. Chen by 9 o'clock?

  你可以在 9 點前把這份文件傳真給陳先生嗎？

- Hello, can you make a phone call to Mr. Brown and set up the meeting time?

  哈囉，你可以打電話給布朗先生並訂下會議時間嗎？

- We are going to have a meeting about the contract with BMY at 9 am.

  我們將在早上 9 點和 BMY 進行關於合約的會議。

- Excuse me, can you tell me where the **copy machine**★¹ is?

  不好意思，可以請你告訴我影印機在哪裡嗎？

- Those are used documents. Please destroy them by using the paper shredder because they contain some important information.

  那些都是用過的資料。請用碎紙機銷毀，因為那些資料含有重要資訊。

- BMY is a very big company. There are 200,000 employees in this company.

  BMY 是一間很大的公司。這家公司有 200,000 名員工。

- In the meeting, I want to briefly show my ideas by using the OHP.

  在這次會議中，我想要用投影機簡單的展示我的想法。

- Can you put those **files**★² in the cabinet over there?

  你可以將這些文件放置在那邊的櫃子中嗎？

- Please ask the receptionist to wait for an important customer at the reception counter.

  請叫接待員在接待處等候重要的貴賓。

★ 換個單字說說看｜用單字累積句子的豐富度，讓句子更漂亮！

copy machine★¹ 可以替換：			files★² 可以替換：		
scanner 掃描機	**fax machine** 傳真機	**puncher** 打洞器	**ring binders** 環裝資料夾	**copy paper** 影印紙	**folders** 資料夾

Can you tell me where the ＿＿＿＿＿＿ is ?
可以請你告訴我 ＿＿＿＿＿＿ 在哪裡嗎？

Can you put those ＿＿＿＿＿＿ in the cabinet over there?
你可以將這些 ＿＿＿＿＿＿ 放置在那邊的櫃子中嗎？

① **office** 辦公室

reception counter ph	⋯⋯⋯	服務台
receptionist [rɪˈsɛpʃənɪst] n	⋯⋯	接待員
meeting room ph	⋯⋯⋯	會議室
meeting table ph	⋯⋯⋯⋯	會議桌
office cubicle ph	⋯⋯⋯⋯	辦公室隔間

② **boss** 老闆

secretary [ˈsɛkrəˌtɛrɪ] n	⋯⋯⋯	祕書
assistant [əˈsɪstənt] n	⋯⋯⋯	助手
employee [ˌɛmplɔɪˈi] n	⋯⋯⋯	員工
staff [stæf] n	⋯⋯⋯⋯	員工
customer [ˈkʌstəmə] n	⋯⋯⋯	顧客

③ **facsimile(fax) machine** 傳真機

傳真機內的功能鍵：

stop [stɑp] v	⋯⋯	停止	**hold** [hold] v	⋯⋯	暫停
exit [ˈɛksɪt] v	⋯⋯	退出	**caller ID** ph	⋯⋯	使用者身份
search [sɝtʃ] v	⋯⋯	尋找	**quick-scan** ph	⋯⋯	快速掃瞄
speed dial ph	⋯⋯	快速撥號	**receive mode** ph	⋯⋯	接收模式

④ photocopier 影印機

resolution [ˌrɛzəˈluʃən] n ········ 解析度	**telephone** [ˈtɛləˌfon] n ·········· 電話機
time recorder ph ········· 打卡機	**laminating machine** ph ········ 護貝機
paper cutter ph ········· 裁紙機	**laminator film** ph ········ 護貝膜
shredder [ˈʃrɛdɚ] n ········· 碎紙機	**overhead projector (OHP)** ph ··· 投影機

⑤ filing cabinet 資料櫃

stapler [ˈsteplɚ] n ················· 訂書機
file folder ph ················· 資料夾
paper clip ph ················· 迴紋針
glue [glu] n ················· 膠水
correction pen/tape ph ··· 立可白 / 帶
rubber [ˈrʌbɚ] n ················· 橡皮擦

⑥ drinking fountain 飲水機

soda fountain ph ···餐廳的汽水飲料機
water dispenser ph ················· 飲水機
vending machine ph ··· 自動販賣機
lunch break ph ················· 午餐休息時間

7 salary 薪水

promotion [prə`moʃən] n ········· 升等
absent [`æbsn̩t] a ················· 缺席的
sick leave ph ····················· 病假
vacancy [`vekənsɪ] n ············· 職缺
layoff [`le͵ɔf] n ··················· 臨時解僱

8 computer 電腦

mouse [maʊs] n ················· 滑鼠
printer [`prɪntɚ] n ·············· 印表機
computer virus ph ·············· 電腦病毒
memory disc ph ················· 隨身碟
CD burner ph ···················· 燒錄機

Internet [`ɪntɚ͵nɛt] n ··········· 網際網路
wireless [`waɪrlɪs] n ·········· 無線網路
modem = modulator - demodulator
ph ····························· 數據機
software [`sɔft͵wɛr] n ········· 電腦軟體

Daily Q&A

〔會話一〕

Q▶ **What time is the meeting?**
會議是什麼時候呢？

A▶ **10 o'clock.**
10 點鐘。

〔會話二〕

Q▶ **What is this meeting about?**
這會議是關於什麼呢？

A▶ **It's about our new CEO.**
是關於我們新的執行長。

〔會話三〕

Q▶ **Do you need the OHP for the meeting?**
你開會時要用到投影機嗎？

A▶ **Yes.**
是的。

Proverbs & Idioms 道地諺語與慣用語 | 讓句子更錦上添花

All work and no play makes Jack a dull boy. > 工作與休閒要並重

Don't always sit at the computer and think about work only. All work and no play makes Jack a dull boy. Have fun sometimes!

不要整天只想工作並坐在電腦前。工作與休閒要並重。有時候要做一些有趣的事。

Many hands make light work. > 很多人的協助可使一份工作輕鬆完成

Cleaning the room will not take long if we all help. You know, many hands make light work.

如果我們幫忙的話，打掃房間不會花很久的時間。你知道的，有很多人的協助可使一份工作輕鬆完成。

work like a dog > 忙碌工作中

Jack needs money to buy a house. He works like a dog every day.

傑克需要錢買一間房子。他每天都像狗一樣的忙碌工作。

A little hard work never hurt/killed anyone. > 達成目標之前都一定努力

Don't be afraid of difficulties. A little hard work never hurt/killed anyone. Just do your best!

別害怕困難。達成目標前都一定要努力。只要盡力就好！

donkey work/hard work > 困難的工作

Why do I have to do all the donkey work and you can just sit there and enjoy your TV?

為什麼我必須作所有困難的事而你只需要坐在那看你的電視？

show someone who's the boss. > 讓某人知道誰才是做決定的人

If you want to have the power in this group, you should show them who the boss is first. Therefore, they will listen to you.

如果你想要在這個團隊中有影響力，你必須讓他們知道誰才是做決定的人。如此，他們才會聽你的。

work your fingers to the bone > 賣力工作

I will work my fingers to the bone for you.

我會為你賣力工作。

Daily Conversation 日常對話 | 快速融入超擬真的日常對話

MP3
03-07

A Did you eat anything that was not fresh yesterday?
你昨天有吃什麼不新鮮的食物嗎？

B Well, I couldn't recall having eaten anything that was not fresh. Besides, I have a fever up to 38 ℃ .
嗯，我實在想不起來吃了什麼不新鮮的東西。還有，我現在發燒到三十八度。

A Let me take your temperature. I will use my stethoscope to check the sound of your heart beat and breath.
讓我量一下你的體溫。我用我的聽診器聽聽看你的心跳和呼吸的聲音。

B Doctor, will I need to stay here and have my health checkup?
醫生，我要待在這裡做健康檢查嗎？

A I will prescribe you some medicine first. If the pain still doesn't go away today, I am afraid you will have to come back and have your health checked.
我會先給你一些藥，如果今天之內疼痛還是沒有減輕的話，我想你恐怕要再回來做健康檢查。

Additional Vocabulary & Phrases | 補充單字 & 片語

- **stethoscope** n 聽診器
  Almost every doctor needs a stethoscope.
  幾乎每個醫生都需要一個聽診器

- **prescribe** v 為…開藥方、開醫囑
  The doctor prescribed me some pain killers.
  醫生開一些止痛藥給我。

Daily Sentences 超高頻率使用句｜一分鐘學一句不怕不夠用
MP3
03-08

● Can I make an appointment with Dr. Chen?
我可以和陳醫生預約嗎？

● Can I take your **blood pressure** ★¹?
我可以量你的血壓嗎？

● Let me measure your height and weight.
讓我量一下你的身高和體重。

● The doctor prescribed me some **medicine** ★².
醫生開了一些藥給我。

● I have a headache, a stomachache, a runny nose, a stuffy nose and a fever.
我有頭痛、胃痛、流鼻水、鼻塞和發燒。

● I do not feel well and I feel dizzy all the time.
我不太舒服而且一直覺得頭暈。

● I have a sore throat and my muscles are sore.
我有喉嚨痛，還有我肌肉痠痛。

● Did you eat anything that was not fresh yesterday? Or do you think your symptom are more like a cold?
你昨天有吃什麼不新鮮的食物嗎？或者你覺得你的症狀比較像是感冒？

★ 換個單字說說看｜用單字累積句子的豐富度，讓句子更漂亮！

blood pressure★¹ 可以替換：			**medicine**★² 可以替換：		
temperature 體溫	**heartbeat** 心跳	**pulse** 脈搏	**vitamin C** 維他命 C	**antibiotics** 抗生素	**cough syrup** 咳嗽糖漿

Can I take your _____?
我可以量你的_____嗎？

The doctor prescribed me some _____.
醫生開了一些 _____ 給我。

Additional Vocabulary & Phrases ｜補充單字 & 片語

● **measure** ⓥ 測量
We measured the length of the wall.
我們測量了那面牆的長度。

● **dizzy** ⓐ 頭暈目眩的
I felt very dizzy.
我感覺頭暈目眩的。

● **sore** ⓐ 痠痛的
My arms are really sore.
我的手臂很痠痛。

● **symptom** ⓝ 症狀
What are the symptoms of lung cancer?
肺癌會有些甚麼樣的症狀？

1 hospital 醫院

ward [wɔrd] n	病房
emergency room ph	急診室
ambulance [ˈæmbjələns] n	救護車
pharmacy [ˈfɑrməsɪ] n	藥局

2 patient 病人

fever [ˈfivɚ] n	發燒
cough [kɔf] n	咳嗽
cold [kold] n	感冒
dizzy [ˈdɪzɪ] a	頭暈
stomachache [ˈstʌməkˌek] n	胃痛

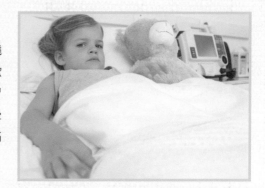

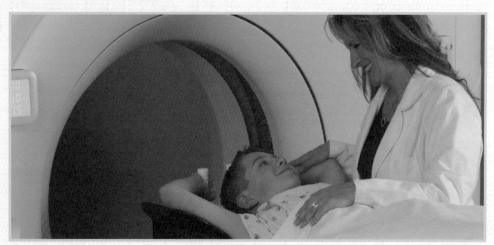

3 cancer 癌症

tumor [ˈtjumɚ] n	腫瘤	**ache** [ek] v	疼痛
chemotherapy [ˌkɛmoˈθɛrəpɪ] n	化療	**pulse** [pʌls] n	脈搏
diagnose [ˈdaɪəgnoz] v	診斷		

098

④ doctor 醫生

dentist [ˋdɛntɪst] n ⋯⋯⋯⋯⋯⋯⋯ 牙醫師

pediatrician [ˏpidɪəˋtrɪʃən] n 小兒科醫師

obstetrician [ˏɑbstɛˋtrɪʃən] n 婦產醫師

ophthalmologist [ˏɑfθælˋmɑlədʒɪst] n ⋯⋯⋯⋯⋯⋯⋯⋯⋯⋯⋯⋯⋯ 眼科醫師

internist [ɪnˋtɝnɪst] n ⋯⋯⋯⋯⋯ 內科醫師

surgeon [ˋsɝdʒən] n ⋯⋯⋯⋯⋯ 外科醫師

⑤ operating room 手術室

tweezers [ˋtwizɚz] n ⋯⋯⋯⋯⋯⋯ 鑷子

face mask ph ⋯⋯⋯⋯⋯⋯⋯⋯⋯⋯⋯ 口罩

syringe [ˋsɪrɪndʒ] n ⋯⋯⋯⋯⋯⋯⋯ 針筒

cotton ball ph ⋯⋯⋯⋯⋯⋯⋯⋯⋯⋯ 棉球

blood transfusion ph ⋯⋯⋯⋯⋯⋯ 輸血

bandage [ˋbændɪdʒ] n ⋯⋯⋯⋯⋯ 紗布

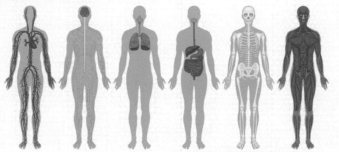

⑥ body 身體

head [hɛd] n ⋯⋯⋯⋯⋯⋯⋯⋯⋯⋯⋯⋯⋯ 頭

chest [tʃɛst] n ⋯⋯⋯⋯⋯⋯⋯⋯⋯⋯ 胸部

abdomen [ˋæbdəmən] n ⋯⋯⋯⋯ 腹部

heart [hɑrt] n ⋯⋯⋯⋯⋯⋯⋯⋯⋯⋯ 心臟

stomach [ˋstʌmək] n ⋯⋯⋯⋯⋯⋯⋯ 胃

intestines [ɪnˋtɛstɪn] n ⋯⋯⋯⋯⋯⋯ 腸

liver [ˋlɪvɚ] n ⋯⋯⋯⋯⋯⋯⋯⋯⋯⋯⋯⋯ 肝

lung [lʌŋ] n ⋯⋯⋯⋯⋯⋯⋯⋯⋯⋯⋯⋯⋯ 肺

Chapter 1 2 3 4 5 6 7 8 9 10

7 **pill** 藥丸

tablet [ˋtæblɪt] n ·········· 藥片
dragee [drɑˋʒe] n ·········· 糖衣錠
capsule [ˋkæpsl̩] n ·········· 膠囊
eye drops ph ·········· 眼藥水
cough syrup ph ·········· 咳嗽糖漿

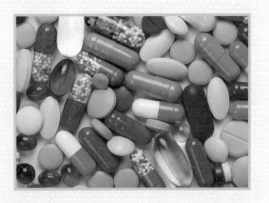

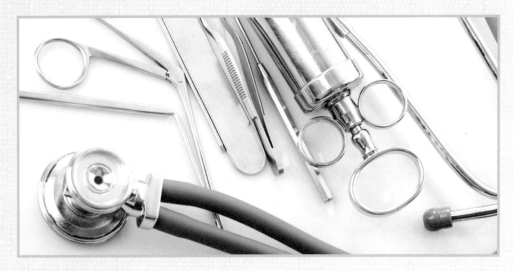

8 **medical** 醫學的；醫術的；醫療的

stretcher [ˋstrɛtʃɚ] n ·········· 擔架
crutch [krʌtʃ] n ·········· 拐杖
ear thermometer ph ·········· 耳溫槍

sling [slɪŋ] n ·········· 三角巾
stethoscope [ˋstɛθəˏskop] n ·· 聽診器

Daily Q&A

〔會話一〕

Q▶ What symptoms do you have?
你有什麼症狀？

A▶ I have a sore throat.
我喉嚨痛。

〔會話二〕

Q▶ Do you have a headache or a cold?
你有頭痛還是感冒嗎？

A▶ I have a headache.
我有頭痛。

〔會話三〕

Q▶ Can I take your temperature?
我可以量你的體溫嗎？

A▶ Absolutely!
當然！

Proverbs & Idioms　道地諺語與慣用語｜讓句子更錦上添花

---

an apple a day keeps the doctor away 〉 一天一顆蘋果，醫生遠離你

If you want to prevent yourself from getting a bad cold, always remember that "an apple a day keeps the doctor away."

如果你想避免得到重感冒，你一定要記得「一天一顆蘋果，醫生遠離你」。

---

a spin doctor 〉 統籌決策的人；軍師

He needs a good spin doctor to help him win the election.

他需要一個好軍師來幫忙他贏得選戰。

---

doctor someone up 〉 快速給予他人第一時間的醫療治療

That man is seriously injured. Give me a minute to doctor him up, and then we can send him to the hospital.

那個男人受傷很嚴重，讓我幫他急救一下，然後再把他送到醫院。

---

just what the doctor ordered 〉 所期望並想要的事

An evening with lots of surprises is not just what the doctor ordered.

一個晚上發生這麼多出乎意料的事，實在不是令人想要的事。

---

doctor's orders 〉 醫生的命令

I have to be on a vegetable diet. That is doctor's orders and I don't like it.

我只能吃蔬菜，這是醫生的命令，但是我不喜歡。

---

a bitter pill to swallow 〉 不能不做的苦差事，不得不忍受的屈辱

Losing the championship was a bitter pill to swallow for Jim who was used to winning every year.

對每年會贏的吉姆而言失去冠軍頭銜是不得不忍受的屈辱。

---

do drugs 〉 吸毒

Sam doesn't do drugs, and he doesn't drink.

山姆不吸毒也不喝酒。

---

rush someone to the hospital 〉 把某人快速送到醫院

We rushed him to the hospital after he complained of a serious chest pain.

在他痛苦地說他胸很痛之後我們快速地將他送到醫院。

---

a clean bill of health 〉 身體健康的消息

Johnson was given a clean bill of health by his doctors in the beginning of this month.

強森這個月初被醫生告知身體健康的消息。

A Hi, Jenny. You look like you are in a hurry to go somewhere. Where are you going?
嗨，珍妮。妳看起來好像趕著去那裡一樣。妳要去哪裡？

B I am going to the bank. I need to cash some checks.
我要去銀行。我要將支票兌換成現金。

A That's great. We can go to the bank together.
那太好了！我們可以一起去銀行。

B Why are you going there? 為什麼你要去那裡？

A I will go to Japan on business for five days next Tuesday. I want to exchange some Japanese yen.
我下星期二會去日本出差五天。我想換一些日幣。

B I see. Will you bring a lot of money with you? 我瞭解了。你會帶很多錢去嗎？

A Not really. I plan to bring some cash and withdraw money at the ATM in Japan. 不會。我計畫帶點現金，到日本再用提款機領錢。

Additional Vocabulary & Phrases │ 補充單字 & 片語

- **in a hurry** ph 匆忙地
  She ate in a hurry.
  她匆忙地吃完東西。

- **exchange** v 交換、兌換
  I'd like to exchange some Thai bahts for dollars.
  我想要用些泰銖換美金。

- **plan** v 計畫、打算
  I plan to go to New York next week.
  我計畫下星期去紐約。

- **withdraw** v 抽回、提取
  Mom withdrew some money at the bank.
  媽媽在銀行領了一些錢。

7天就能用英文
行遍全世界！ ③

Chapter 1
Chapter 2
Chapter 3
Chapter 4
Chapter 5
Chapter 6
Chapter 7
Chapter 8
Chapter 9
Chapter 10

Daily Sentences 超高頻率使用句│一分鐘學一句不怕不夠用 MP3 03-11

- To open an account, you need a personal stamp, your identification card and some money.

  開一個戶頭，你需要印章、身分證和一些錢。

- Do you want to apply for a Visa or Master card?

  你想申請 Visa 或 Master 卡嗎？

- To apply for a credit card, you need to have a copy of the bank statement which lists your income for the last three months.

  申請一張信用卡需要有一份列有你最後三個月的收入證明。

- I would like to rent a safe in your bank to store some of my valuable things.

  我想租一個你們銀行的保險箱來存放我的貴重物品。

- I want to buy a house. I need to apply for a mortgage.

  我想買一棟房子。我想申請貸款。

- Can I transfer money to my son's account in Japan?

  我可以匯款到我兒子日本的戶頭嗎？

- What is the US dollar to **New Taiwan dollar**★1 exchange rate now?

  現在一元美金對新台幣是多少？

- The security guard is paying full attention to the cash in the armored truck.

  這位警衛正全神貫注在這輛運鈔車上。

- Do you have a **bank card**★2 in Japan?

  你在日本有提款卡嗎？

★ 換個單字說說看│用單字累積句子的豐富度，讓句子更漂亮！

New Taiwan dollars★1 可以替換：

euro 歐元	Korean Won 韓國元	Philippine Peso 菲律賓比索

What is the US dollar to _____ exchange rate now?

現在一元美金對_____是多少

bank card★2 可以替換：

debit card 現金卡	credit card 信用卡	loyalty card 忠誠卡

Do you a _____ in Japan?

你在日本有 _____ 嗎？

Additional Vocabulary & Phrases │ 補充單字 & 片語

- **identification** n 身分證明、認出
  She uses her health insurance card as identification.
  她用健保卡當作身分證明。

- **income** n 收入、所得
  She doesn't have any income.
  她沒有任何收入。

- **valuable** a 有價值的、值錢的
  This vase is really valuable.
  這個花瓶非常的值錢。

- **transfer** v 轉換、調動；改變
  Judi was transferred to a better school.
  茱蒂轉去另一所更好的學校。

① counter 櫃臺，櫃臺式長桌

teller [ˋtɛlɚ] n	銀行行員
cashier [kæˋʃɪr] n	出納員
manager [ˋmænɪdʒɚ] n	銀行經理
security guard ph	警衛
customer [ˋkʌstəmɚ] n	顧客

② bill 匯票，單據

cash [kæʃ] n	現金 v 把…兌現
currency exchange ph	兌幣
fund [fʌnd] n	資金
check [tʃɛk] n	支票（美國）

③ account 帳戶，客戶

account [əˋkaunt] n	現金帳戶
deposit [dɪˋpazɪt] v	把錢存放
credit [ˋkrɛdɪt] n	銀行存款（帳戶餘額）
currency [ˋkɝənsɪ] n	流通貨幣
check book ph	支票簿

④ credit card 信用卡

personal stamp ph	圖章，私章
identification card ph	身分證件
National Health Insurance Card ph	健保卡

automatic teller machine ph	ATM 自動櫃員機
bank card ph	提款卡

⑤ business 事務

withdraw [wɪðˋdrɔ] v	提款
savings [ˋsevɪŋz] n	儲蓄存款
borrow [ˋbaro] v	借款
loan [lon] n	貸款
transfer [ˋtrænsfɝ] v	匯款

⑥ savings and loan association 信用合作社

interest [ˋɪntərɪst] n	利息，股份…股權
mortgage [ˋmɔrgɪdʒ] n	抵押契據，抵押借款
save [sev] v	儲存
pay into ph	把（錢）存銀行
stock [stɑk] n	股票，國債（英）
share [ʃɛr] n	股票，股份

7 **vault** 金庫，保管庫

alarm [əˋlɑrm] n	警報器
safe [sef] n	保險箱
safe-deposit box ph	保險櫃
surveillance camera ph	監視器
coin [kɔɪn] n	硬幣
armored truck ph	運鈔車

8 **commercial bank** 商業銀行

industrial development bank ph
　　　　　　　　　　　　開發工業銀行
federal bank ph ………… 聯邦銀行
mortgage bank ph ………… 抵押銀行
land development's bank ph
　　　　　　　　　　　　土地發展銀行

indigenous bank ph ………… 國家銀行
saving bank ph ………… 儲蓄銀行
exchange bank ph ………… 外匯銀行
internet bank ph ………… 網路銀行
offshore bank ph ………… 境外金融銀行

Daily Q&A

〔會話一〕

Q▸ Can I open an saving account?
我可以開一個存款帳戶嗎？

A▸ Sure. Please fill out the form first.
當然。請先把表格填好。

〔會話二〕

Q▸ How much money would you like to save for the first time?
你第一次想先存多少錢？

A▸ I would like to save about 2,000 dollars.
我想存大約 2,000 元

〔會話三〕

Q▸ Do you also want to take out money with a bank card?
你想用提款卡提領一些錢出來嗎？

A▸ Yes, please.
好啊，麻煩你。

Proverbs & Idioms 道地諺語與慣用語｜讓句子更錦上添花

break the bank 〉 用完所有的錢

Buying a new pair of shoes at a discount price won't break the bank.
用折扣後的價格買一雙鞋不會用完所有的錢。

bank on something 〉 信賴某事

I'll pay back all the money. You can bank on me.
我會還清所有錢。你可以相信我。

laugh all the way to the bank 〉 對已賺取的錢感到高興

He may not be the greatest singer, but he is popular and can laugh all the way to the bank.
他可能不是最棒的歌手，但是他很受歡迎並且很滿意自己所賺得的錢。

cry all the way to the bank 〉 對已賺取的錢感到失望

The movie sucks. Many people feel disappointed after seeing it. I think people who make the movie are crying all the way to the bank.
這部電影很爛。很多人在看過電影之後感到失望。我認為製作這部電影的人會對自己賺取的錢感到失望。

can take it to the bank 〉 可證明所說的是真的

What I am telling you is the truth. You can take it to the bank.
我所說的都是真的。你可以去求證。

be broke 〉 沒錢、窮光蛋

Jack is broke. He can't even afford to buy a cup of coffee.
傑克是個窮光蛋。他甚至沒法負擔買一杯咖啡。

a loan shark 〉 放高利貸的人

That man was beaten because he was late to pay money back to a loan shark.
那個男人被打是因為他延遲還錢給高利貸。

be strapped (for cash) 〉 缺錢

I seem to be a bit strapped. Can you lend me some money?
我好像有一點缺錢。 你可以借我一些錢嗎？

03-13

A Excuse me, Ma'am. I would like to mail this package door to door via air mail to London. It is a very important package and has to be sent within three days.
不好意思，小姐。我想用航空掛號郵寄這件包裹到倫敦，這是一件很重要的包裹，必須於三天內寄到。

B No problem. But the postage is much higher than that for the regular package.
沒問題。但是郵資會較一般包裹貴出很多。

A That's fine with me. I am willing to pay for it as long as you can guarantee me the package can arrive in time.
那沒關係。我很願意支付，只要你保證我的包裹可以準時寄到。

B OK. All the registered air mail packages will be received in 5 working days.
好的。所有掛號的航空包裹可在五個工作天內寄達。

A I see. How much do I need to pay in total for this package?
我知道了。這件包裹總共需要多少郵資？

B It's 500 dollars.
共 500 元。

Additional Vocabulary & Phrases | 補充單字 & 片語

● **via** prep 經由、透過
Jonathan flew to America via Thailand.
強納生經過泰國飛到美國。

● **guarantee** v 保證、擔保
Cynthia guaranteed me this product is organic.
辛西亞和我保證這個產品是有機的。

Daily Sentences 超高頻率使用句｜一分鐘學一句不怕不夠用
03-14

● Excuse me. I would like to send this letter by air mail.
不好意思，我想寄封航空郵件。

● Excuse me. Can I send the file by **express**[*1]?
不好意思。我可以用快遞寄送這份文件嗎？

● Please put the file in this paper box and seal it.
請將文件放入紙盒中，並把盒子封好。

● How much is it to mail a registered package?
寄一封掛號包裏要多少錢？

● I am collecting **postcards**[*2].
我有收集明信片。

● You can buy a set of commemorative postcards published by the post office. They just came out last week.
你可以買一套郵局發行的紀念明信片。它們上星期才發行。

● Where do I put the sender's and the receiver's address?
我要在哪裡填寫寄件人和收件人的住址？

● How many days does it take to send a letter to Japan by surface mail?
海運郵件到日本要多少天？

● What you need to do is to put a stamp with enough postage and mark the cover with "By Air Mail".
你只要貼足夠的郵資，並在上面註明「航空郵件」即可。

★ **換個單字說說看**｜用單字累積句子的豐富度，讓句子更漂亮！

express[*1] 可以替換：

Express 快捷	**sea mail** 海運	**prompt delivery mail** 限時郵件

Can I deliver the file by_____?
我可以用_____寄送這份文件嗎？

postcards[*2] 可以替換：

stamps 郵票	**commemorative stamps** 紀念郵票	**postmarked stamps** 蓋郵戳的郵票

I am collecting _____.
我有收集_____。

Additional Vocabulary & Phrases ｜補充單字 & 片語

● **seal** [v] 密封
Please seal this envelope.
請將這個信封密封好。

● **register** [v] 登記、註冊
Have you registered for the piano class?
你有登記要上鋼琴課了嗎？

● **publish** [v] 發行、出版
This book will be published next month.
這本書將在下個月發行

● **mark** [v] 做記號、記下
Can you mark an "X" here in the corner?
你能在角落這邊記下一個「X」的記號嗎？

❶ mailman 郵差

mail [mel] n ⸻⸻⸻ 郵政，郵件
express [ɪk`sprɛs] n ⸻⸻⸻ 快遞
mailbox [`mel͵baks] n ⸻ 郵筒，私人信箱
postbox [`post͵baks] n ⸻⸻⸻ 郵箱
deliver [dɪ`lɪvɚ] v ⸻⸻⸻ 投遞

❷ package 包裹

postage [`postɪdʒ] n ⸻⸻⸻ 郵資
international parcel ph ⸻ 國際包裹
EMS (Express Mail Service) ph
⸻⸻⸻ 快捷郵件
prompt delivery mail ph ⸻ 限時郵件
value-declared mail ph ⸻ 報值郵件

❸ address 地址

zip code ph ⸻⸻⸻ 郵遞區號
return address ph ⸻⸻⸻ 寄件人地址
recipient's address ph ⸻ 收件人地址
revenue stamp ph ⸻⸻⸻ 印花稅票
zone [zon] n ⸻⸻⸻ 區域

4 postmark 郵戳

commemorative stamp ph ⋯⋯⋯ 紀念郵票

stamp [stæmp] n ⋯⋯⋯⋯⋯⋯⋯ 郵票

stamp tax ph ⋯⋯⋯⋯⋯⋯⋯ 印花稅

canceled stamp ph ⋯⋯⋯⋯⋯⋯ 蓋銷票

stamp machine ph ⋯⋯⋯⋯⋯ 打印機

5 postal 郵政的

postal clerk ph ⋯⋯⋯⋯⋯⋯ 郵政辦事員

postal money order ph ⋯ （郵）匯票

insurance [ɪnˋʃʊrəns] n ⋯⋯⋯⋯ 保險

post office box ph ⋯⋯⋯⋯ 郵政專用信箱

6 letter 信件

personal mail ph ⋯⋯⋯⋯⋯⋯ 私人信件

air mail ph ⋯⋯⋯⋯⋯⋯⋯⋯ 航空郵件

surface mail ph ⋯⋯⋯⋯⋯⋯⋯ 海運

registered letter ph ⋯⋯⋯⋯ 掛號信

printed material ph ⋯⋯⋯⋯⋯ 印刷品

7 envelope 信封

letter paper ph ·············· 信紙
post card ph ·············· 明信片
box [bɑks] n ·············· 紙箱
letterhead [ˈlɛtəˌhɛd] n 印在信紙的信頭
bulk mail ph ·············· 大宗函件

8 postal savings 郵政儲金

remittances [rɪˈmɪtn̩s] n ·············· 匯兌
life insurance ph ·············· 壽險
agency services ph ·············· 代理

postal account withdrawal ph 劃撥提款
financial calculator ph ·············· 理財試算

Daily Q&A

〔會話一〕

Q▶ **Where can I buy commemorative stamps?**
哪裡可以買到紀念郵票呢？

A▶ **Go to counter No. 12, please.**
請到第 12 號櫃台。

〔會話二〕

Q▶ **Can I apply for a personal mail box at the post office?**
我可以申請一個郵局的私人信箱嗎？

A▶ **Sure!**
當然！

〔會話三〕

Q▶ **I need 3 postcards.**
我需要三張明信片。

A▶ **OK! They cost 30 dollars.**
好的，總共 30 元。

Proverbs & Idioms 道地諺語與慣用語 ｜ 讓句子更錦上添花

snail mail 紙筆信件，用以區分電子郵件

It is outdated to send snail mails. Almost all the people send emails nowadays.
寄送紙筆信已過時了，大部分的人現在都寄送電子郵件。

junk mail 垃圾信

It seems to be unlikely not to receive any junk mail when you check your email. What you can do is to delete it with patience.
當你收電子郵件時，沒有垃圾郵件似乎是不太可能發生的事。你能做的只有耐心的把它刪掉。

by return mail 回覆信

Since the bill is overdue, would you please send us your check back by return mail?
由於這張帳單過期未繳，能否請你用回函寄回你的支票呢？

best things come in small packages 麻雀雖小，五臟俱全

Jenny always hates to be so short and tiny. However, her mother always says to her that best things come in small packages.
珍妮很討厭自己又矮又小，但是她媽媽總是告訴她，麻雀雖小，五臟俱全。

a dear John letter 分手信

Susan doesn't love her boyfriend any more. She plans to send him a dear John letter.
蘇珊不再愛她的男朋友了，她計劃寫封分手信給他。

bread and butter letters 追蹤信

Karen just had the meeting with Mr. and Mrs. Brown. After she went back to the office, she spent some time writing bread and butter letters to them.
凱倫剛剛和伯朗夫婦開會，回到公司後，她花了一些時間寫追蹤信給他們。

go postal 抓狂、變的超級生氣

My boyfriend will go postal if he sees me hang out with Jason.
我男朋友如果看到我和傑森出去會抓狂。

- You put the sender's address on the top left corner, and the receiver's address in the center.

  你要在左上角寫寄件人的住址，並在中間寫收件人住址。

- Read the note carefully and follow the steps on the note. I am sure you can retrieve your letter.

  仔細閱讀通知並遵照上面的步驟。我想你一定可以收到你的信。

- The postage depends on the weight of the package. The more it weighs, the more you pay.

  郵資要視包裹重量而定。重量愈重價格就愈貴。

- I missed an important letter when I went out this afternoon. All I have is a note left by the postman.

  我今天下午出門時錯過了一封重要郵件。我只收到一張郵差留下的通知。

- Do I need to include my zip code in the address?

  需要在住址中加上我的郵遞區號嗎？

- Thank you very much. Here is 500 dollars.

  非常謝謝你。這是 500 元。

- Here is your receipt. Contact us if your friend still doesn't receive the package after 5 work days.

  這是你的收據。如果你的朋友在五個工作天內沒收到包裹的話，可聯絡我們。

- You had better include the zip code on the letter because it is easier for the mailman to find the correct mailing place.

  最好加上郵遞區號，這樣郵差較易找到正確的郵寄地址。

- How may I help you?

  我能為你服務嗎？

- What do you recommend?

  你有什麼建議呢？

MEMO

From AM-PM 從早到晚都用得到的必備好用句

Chapter 1
Chapter 2
Chapter 3
Chapter 4
Chapter 5
Chapter 6
Chapter 7
Chapter 8
Chapter 9
Chapter 10

- I can mop the floor.
  我可以拖地。

- I can sweep the floor.
  我可以掃地。

- I need to prepare my lunchbox for tomorrow.
  我得準備明天的便當。

- It is time to start preparing to go to bed.
  該準備上床了。

- Hang up the phone and get into bed.
  掛掉電話去睡覺。

- We're not allowed to have guests over after 12 am.
  晚上 12 點後，我們是禁止會客的。

- I'm tired.
  我好累。

- If you finish your homework, you can watch TV for one hour.
  如果你功課做完了，你可以看一小時電視。

- May I use the computer?
  我可以用電腦嗎？

- You are allowed to use the computer after finishing your homework.
  你寫完功課之後可以使用電腦。

- I can't sleep!
  我睡不著！

MEMO

- I want to sleep, but I can't.

  我很想睡，但睡不著。

- Do you have any suggestions for my insomnia?

  對於我的失眠問題，你有什麼建議嗎？

- I'm really a bad singer.

  我唱歌很難聽。

- Don't worry. KTV is just a place to relax and have fun.

  不要擔心啦！KTV 只是個讓你放鬆快樂的地方。

- I love singing!

  我喜歡唱歌！

- Shilin night market has some of the best food stands in Taipei.

  士林夜市有台北最棒的小吃攤。

- You can buy pearl milk tea at this drink stand.

  你可以在這飲料攤買珍珠奶茶。

- How do you eat chicken feet?

  雞腳要怎麼吃？

- I love trying all types of snacks.

  我喜歡嘗試各種不同的小吃。

- I don't know what to get for him.

  我不知道要買什麼給他。

- I hope he likes this present.

  我希望他喜歡這份禮物。

MEMO

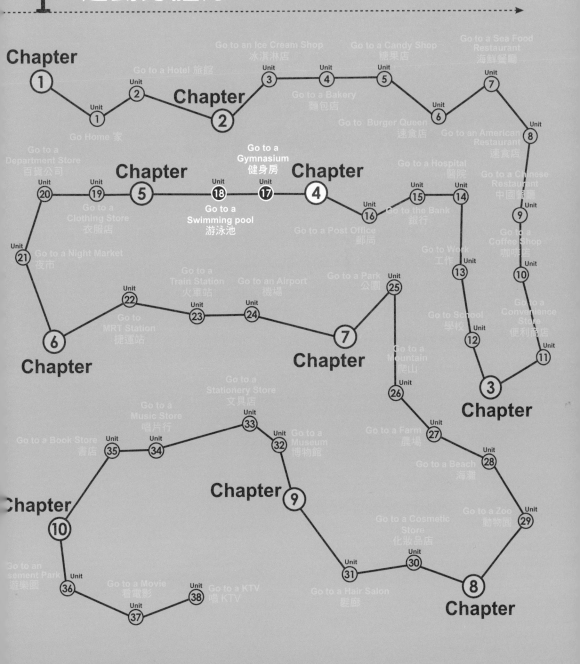

Chapter 4

Exercising
運動身體好

Go to a Gymnasium 健身房

A I bet you will like this gym. It is the best in town.
我打賭你會喜歡的,這間健身房是這城市中最好的。

B Look at my beer belly. It is disgusting. Can you offer me some ways to make it disappear?
看看我的啤酒肚,真令人討厭!你可以建議我一些方法讓它消失嗎?

A Sure. You can try the sit-up bench. You can train your abdominals.
當然,你可以試試仰臥起坐台。你可以訓練你的腹部。

B I also want to train my arms. It's like I am always carrying two meaty bags with me.
我也想訓練我的手臂。我看起來好像掛了兩個肉袋。

A You can try using the dumbbells to train your arm muscles.
你可以用啞鈴訓練你的肌肉。

B Well, sounds like I have some hard work to do.
好吧,聽起來我還有好長一段路要走。

Additional Vocabulary & Phrases | 補充單字 & 片語

- **belly** n 肚子
  Sherri has a big belly.
  雪莉有一個大肚子。

- **disgusting** a 令人作嘔的、十分討厭的
  The dirty warehouse is really disgusting.
  那個骯髒的倉庫真的很噁心。

- **disappear** v 消失、不見
  The magician made the bird disappear.
  魔術師把小鳥變不見了。

- **abdominals** n 腹部、腹肌
  I want to train my abdominals.
  我想要訓練我的腹肌。

Daily Sentences 超高頻率使用句｜一分鐘學一句不怕不夠用 MP3 04-02

- How can I become your member?
  要如何才能成為你們的會員呢？

- If I want to train my thighs and back, what equipment should I use?
  如果我想訓練我的大腿和背肌，要用什麼器材呢？

- What facilities do you have?
  你們有什麼設備？

- Can I hire a personal coach to teach me how to train my abdominals?
  我可以請一個私人教練教我訓練我的腹部嗎？

- You can ask for more information at the information desk.
  你可以在詢問處詢問更多相關訊息。

- How much do I need to pay for a membership for one year?
  我要為一年會員資格付多少錢？

- When is the **yoga**★1 class?
  瑜珈課是什麼時候？

- Excuse me, can you show me how to use the **pedometer**★2?
  不好意思，你可以使用計步器給我看嗎？

- You can use the treadmill and the back extension bench over there.
  你可以使用那邊的跑步機和背部伸展機。

★ 換個單字說說看｜用單字累積句子的豐富度，讓句子更漂亮！

yoga★1 可以替換：

aerobic dance 有氧舞蹈	pilates 皮拉提斯	Judo 柔道

When is the ＿＿＿＿＿＿＿ class?
＿＿＿＿＿＿＿課是什麼時候？

pedometer★2 可以替換：

cable crossover 雙臂交叉訓練機	triceps pushdown 三角肌擴拉器	treadmill 跑步機

Can you show me how to use the＿＿＿＿＿＿?
你可以使用＿＿＿＿＿＿給我看嗎？

Additional Vocabulary & Phrases｜補充單字 & 片語

- train ⓥ 訓練、培養
  Cynthia was trained to be an excellent nurse.
  辛西亞被培養成為一個優秀的護士。

- hire ⓥ 雇用
  We need to hire another assistant.
  我們需要雇用另一個助手。

- personal ⓐ 個人的、私人的
  This is my personal notebook.
  這是我私人的筆記本。

- extension ⓝ 伸展、身長
  We asked our professor for a two-day extension to the final report.
  我們請求教授期末報告再給我們延長兩天。

① fitness 健康

yoga [ˋjogə] n	瑜珈
aerobic dance ph	有氧舞蹈
pilates n	皮拉提斯
boxing [ˋbɑksɪŋ] n	拳擊
Judo [ˋdʒudo] n	柔道

② kinesiology 人體運動學

coach [kotʃ] n	教練
shape up ph	減肥
training [ˋtrenɪŋ] n	訓練、鍛鍊
goal [gol] n	目標
energy [ˋɛnɚdʒɪ] n	活力、精力

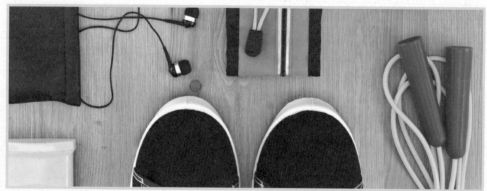

③ gloves 拳擊手套

wraps [ræpz] n	護腕	**towel** [ˋtauəl] n	毛巾
weightlifting belt ph	舉重帶	**sneaker** [ˋsnikɚ] n	運動鞋
wrist straps ph	手腕帶		

7天就能用英文
行遍全世界！ ◯─◯─**3**─◯─◯─◯─◯

Chapter 1
Chapter 2
Chapter 3
Chapter **4**
Chapter 5
Chapter 6
Chapter 7
Chapter 8
Chapter 9
Chapter **10**

4 **energy drink** 能量飲料

mineral water ph		礦泉水
bottled water ph		瓶裝水
vitamin [ˋvaɪtəmɪn] n		維他命
electrolyte [ɪˋlɛktrəˌlaɪt] n		電解質

5 **muscle** 肌；肌肉

biceps [ˋbaɪsɛps] n		二頭肌	**chest** [tʃɛst] n		胸大肌
triceps [ˋtraɪsɛps] n		三頭肌	**abdominals** [æbˋdɑmɪnəlz] n		腹肌
shoulders [ˋʃoldɚs] n		三角肌	**thighs** [θaɪz] n		腿肌
traps [træpz] n		斜方肌	**back** [bæk] n		背肌

6 **sauna** 蒸汽浴；桑拿浴

steam sauna chamber ph		蒸氣室
sauna cabinet ph		烤箱
infrared ray radiation sauna ph		紅外線烤箱
jacuzzi [dʒəˋkuˑzɪ] n		按摩浴池
massage cha.r ph		按摩椅
locker [ˋlɑkɚ] n		置物櫃

7 cycling 騎腳踏車

dancing [ˈdænsɪŋ] n ⸺ 跳舞
ice-skating ph ⸺ 溜冰
hiking [haɪkɪŋ] n ⸺ 健行
skiing [ˈskiɪŋ] n ⸺ 滑雪
hockey [ˈhɑkɪ] n ⸺ 冰上曲棍球

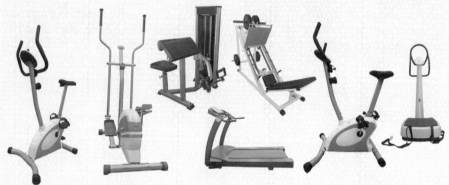

8 gymnasium 體育館；健身房

back extension bench ph 背部伸展機
cable crossover ph 雙臂交叉訓練機
climber [ˈklaɪmə] n ⸺ 登山踏步機
dumbbell [ˈdʌmˌbɛl] n ⸺ 啞鈴
pedometer [pɪˈdɑmətə] n ⸺ 計步器
recumbent bike ph ⸺ 斜式健身車
Roman chair ph ⸺ 羅馬椅訓練機

rotary torso ph ⸺ 轉體機
seated row ph ⸺ 坐式划船機
sit-up bench ph ⸺ 仰臥起坐台
stepper [ˈstɛpə] n ⸺ 踏步機
triceps pushdown ph 三角肌擴拉器
treadmill n ⸺ 跑步機

Daily Q&A	〔會話一〕	〔會話二〕	〔會話三〕
	Q▶ Can I have the timetable of the dance classes of your gym?	**Q▶ Where is the jacuzzi?**	**Q▶ Where can I put my bags?**
	我可以要一張你們健身房舞蹈課程的時刻表嗎？	按摩浴缸在哪裡？	我可以把袋子放在哪裡呢？
	A▶ Sure. There you go.	**A▶ Go ahead to the end and turn left.**	**A▶ You can put your bags in the locker.**
	當然，在這裡。	直走到底左轉。	你可以把包包放入置物櫃裡。

7天就能用英文
行遍全世界！ ───○───○─ 3 ─○───○───○

Chapter 1
2
3
Chapter 4
Chapter 5
Chapter 6
Chapter 7
Chapter 8
Chapter 9
Chapter 10

Proverbs & Idioms | 道地諺語與慣用語 | 讓句子更錦上添花

muscle (someone) out of (something) > 迫使某人不參與某事

Tommy tries to muscle Jack out of the job because he doesn't like Jack's ideas.

湯米迫使傑克不參與這項工作，因為他不喜歡傑克的主意。

muscle in on (something) > 強迫更換或佔有別人的財產、感情或興趣

Don't try to muscle in on my project. If you do, you will be facing big trouble.

不要試著強迫更換我的計劃，如果你這樣做的話，你會有大麻煩。

pull a muscle > 肌肉拉傷

I pulled a muscle in my arm and can't play tennis today.

我拉傷了手臂的肌肉，今天沒辦法打網球了。

flex your muscles > 用行動讓對方知道自己的能力

This poor country began to flex its muscles as the biggest producer in wine industry.

這個貧窮國家開始以成為最大的酒品製造商的方式，讓大家知道它的實力。

not move a muscle > 保持不動

I am worn out. I can't move a muscle after climbing the mountains for a whole day.

我累死了。在爬完一整天的山之後，我動彈不得。

blind-sided > 沒看到

Tim blind-sided the ball was thrown across the field.

提姆沒看到橫跨球場丟來的球。

the ball is in your court > 自己要做的決定或責任

Remember that the ball is in your court whenever you have doubts in life.

記得每當你生命有困惑時那是自己要做的決定或責任。

Daily Conversation 日常對話 | 快速融入超擬真的日常對話

MP3
04-04

A I used to be on my school team when I was a high school student.
我還是高中生的時候，曾經是游泳校隊。

B Wow, I never heard you mention about it. Do you know how to do the freestyle?
哇，我從來沒聽你提起過。你知道怎麼游自由式嗎？

A Sure, it's easy. You just wave one of your arms to the front and the other one to the back and flip your two feet regularly in the water.
當然，非常簡單。你只要將你其中一隻手臂往前划，另一隻手臂往後划，並且規律的在水裡用腳拍水就可以了。

B I see. I still need floats to help me stay on top of the water. I am so afraid of sinking.
我知道了。我還需要游泳圈讓我浮在水面上，我真的很害怕沉下去。

A You should try to do it without using any floats. You can learn faster that way.
你應該試著不要用游泳圈游游看。這樣會比較快學會。

B Let's jump into the water and start swimming now.
我們下水開始游吧。

Additional Vocabulary & Phrases | 補充單字 & 片語

● **mention** ⓥ 提到、說起
Emily mentioned something about her friends.
艾蜜莉提到一些關於她朋友的事情

● **sink** ⓥ 下沉
The stone sank into the water.
石頭沉到水裡了。

Daily Sentences 超高頻率使用句｜一分鐘學一句不怕不夠用
MP3
04-05

- How many laps do you swim every time you go swimming?
  你每次游泳可以游幾圈？

- Can you do the **breaststroke**[1]？
  你會游蛙式嗎？

- When doing the breaststroke, you need to put your two arms in the front and bend your knees a bit and kick in the water.
  游蛙式的時候，你只需要把兩隻手放在前面，並把膝蓋彎曲在水中踢水就可以了。

- It's very dangerous to swim in the sea.
  在海裡游泳很危險。

- What do I need to wear when I go swimming?
  我游泳的時候要穿什麼？

- Do you know how to breathe properly when swimming?
  你知道在游泳時怎麼正確地換氣嗎？

- How can I apply for a membership at this swimming pool?
  我要怎麼申請加入這個游泳池的會員？

- Remember to do some warm-up exercises before you swim.
  游泳前記得要做暖身運動。

- I can teach you how to **dog paddle**[2].
  我可以教你怎麼游狗爬式。

★ **換個單字說說看**｜用單字累積句子的豐富度，讓句子更漂亮！

breaststroke[1] 可以替換：			dog paddle[2] 可以替換：		
freestyle 自由式	backstroke 仰式	butterfly stroke 蝶式	fin swimming 蹼式	dolphin stroke 海豚式	floating 漂浮

Can you do the ＿＿＿＿＿＿＿＿?
你會游＿＿＿＿＿＿嗎？

I can teach you how to do ＿＿＿＿＿＿＿＿.
我可以教你怎麼游＿＿＿＿＿＿。

Additional Vocabulary & Phrases｜補充單字 & 片語

- **bend** v 使彎曲、折彎
  Adonis was so strong that he could bend the metal bar.
  阿多尼斯強壯到可以把金屬棍子折彎。

- **kick** v 踢
  Mom! He just kicked me!
  媽！他剛剛踢我！

- **dangerous** a 危險的
  It's dangerous to walk alone at night.
  晚上獨自一個人走是很危險的。

- **warm-up** ph 暖身
  It's important to do warm-up before doing exercise.
  運動前暖身是很重要的。

1 swimsuit 泳裝

swimming trunks ph	⋯⋯	泳褲
swimming cap ph	⋯⋯	泳帽
bikini [bɪ`kinɪ] n	⋯⋯	比基尼
goggles [`gɑglz] n	⋯⋯	蛙鏡
earplugs [`ɪr͵plʌgz] n	⋯⋯	耳塞

2 breaststroke 蛙式

freestyle [`fri͵staɪl] n	⋯⋯	自由式
backstroke [`bæk͵strok] n	⋯⋯	仰式
butterfly stroke ph	⋯⋯	蝶式
dog paddle ph	⋯⋯	狗爬式
floating [`flotɪŋ] a	⋯⋯	漂浮的

3 swimming pool 游泳池

poolside [`pulsaɪd] a	⋯⋯	游泳池邊的
hot tub ph	⋯⋯	熱水池
wave pool ph	⋯⋯	海浪池

depth [dɛpθ] n	⋯⋯	深度
lane [len] n	⋯⋯	泳道

4 changing room 更衣室

shower [`ʃaʊɚ] [n]	淋浴	**locker room** [ph]	置物櫃間
get dressed [ph]	換裝	**spin dryer** [ph]	脫水機
dry off [ph]	擦乾		

5 cannonball 抱膝跳水

diving [`daɪvɪŋ] [n]	跳水
figure [`fɪgjɚ] [n]	花式
belly flop [ph]	腹部朝下，身體平著入水跳水法
shallow dive [ph]	淺潛
lap [læp] [n]	一圈（來回游泳池）

6 lifeguard 救生員

ladder [`lædɚ] [n]	梯子
diving board [ph]	跳水板
lounge chair [ph]	躺椅
life ring [ph]	游泳圈
life jacket [ph]	救生衣

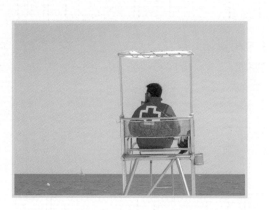

Chapter 1
Chapter 2
Chapter 3
Chapter 4
Chapter 5
Chapter 6
Chapter 7
Chapter 8
Chapter 9
Chapter 10

7 **brush** 梳子

sunscreen [ˋsʌn͵skrin] n ········· 防曬乳

kickboard [kɪkbord] n ············· 浮板

waterproof bag ph ············· 防水包包

floaties n ························· 手套式游泳圈

swim fins ph ····················· 蛙鞋

8 **profession** 專業

Synchronized swimming ph 水上芭蕾

timekeeper [ˋtaɪm͵kipɚ] n
·················· （比賽中的）計時員

contestant [kənˋtɛstənt] n
···················· 參加競賽者；角逐者

cardiopulmonary resuscitation ph
···················· CPR 心肺復甦術

land drill ph ····················· 陸上練習

long distance ph ············· 長距離游泳

middle distance ph ········· 中距離游泳

short distance ph ··········· 短距離游泳

swimming committee ph ··· 游泳協會

Daily Q&A

〔會話一〕

Q▶ Do you know how to do the breaststroke?
你會游蛙式嗎？

A▶ No, I don't.
我不會。

〔會話二〕

Q▶ Can you help me put some sunscreen on?
你能幫我上點防曬乳嗎？

A▶ Sure!
當然！

〔會話三〕

Q▶ Where are you going?
你要去哪裡？

A▶ I'm going to the swimming pool.
我要去游泳池。

Proverbs & Idioms 道地諺語與慣用語｜讓句子更錦上添花

sink or swim 〉 沉或浮；成功或失敗

Newcomers are given no training. They are simply left to sink or swim.
新來的人不會有訓練，就讓他們自生自滅吧。

swim against the tide 〉 持相反意見

He always swims against the tide of public opinions.
他總是和大家持相反的意見。

swim in something 〉 充滿很多⋯⋯

Every meal at my home swims in grease. How can I not become fatter?
我們家每次吃飯都吃得很油，我怎麼能不變胖啊？

out of the swim of things 〉 沒有參與事務

I have been out of the swim of things for a few weeks. Please bring me up-to-date.
我已經好幾週沒有插手管事，請告訴我最新的進度。

make someone's head swim 〉 使困擾頭暈

All the numbers make my head swim.
所有的數字都讓我頭暈。

still waters run deep 〉 深藏不露；水深不可測

He's quiet and shy. But still waters run deep.
他很安靜和害羞。但是這樣的人是深藏不露的。

in deep water 〉 危險的處境

Bill got in deep water in math class. The class is too difficult for him, and he's almost failing.
比爾在他的數學課裡處境危險。這堂課對他來說太難了，而且他快被當了。

keep one's head above water 〉 避開麻煩

Try to keep your head above water when there are economy crises.
有經濟危機時你要試著避開麻煩。

pour cold water on something 〉 澆冷水

John poured cold water on the whole project by refusing to participate.
約翰用拒絕加入來表示對整個計畫澆冷水。

- Look at the water ballet dancers over there. They can do the figure stroke up and down the water.
  看那邊的水上芭蕾舞者，他們可以在水中做花式動作，游上又游下。

- I swim about twenty laps.
  我大約可以游二十圈。

- You need to find a place where you see a lifeguard on the shore when swimming in the sea.
  在海裡游泳的時候必須找一個可以看到岸邊有救生員的地方。

- You need to wear a swimming cap, a swim suit, ear plugs and goggles when swimming.
  游泳的時候你要帶泳帽、泳衣、耳塞和蛙鏡。

- You should do CPR on the people who drown.
  你應該對溺水的人做心肺復甦術。

- When your leg cramps, you need to stretch it for a second until the feeling disappears.
  當你的腳抽筋時，你要把腳伸直一下，直到抽筋的感覺消失為止。

- Where can I put my clothes and bags at this swimming pool?
  在游泳池時，我可以把衣服和包包放在哪裡？

- I have a swimming class this afternoon. Do you want to go with me?
  我今天下午有游泳課，你要一起來嗎？

- I am getting fatter and fatter. I need to do some exercise to lose some weight.
  我愈來愈胖了，我需要運動一下來減肥。

- Can you swim? I am still learning how to breathe in the water.
  你會游泳嗎？我還在學怎麼在水中換氣。

MEMO

From AM-PM 從早到晚都用得到的必備好用句

- This is the perfect present for him!
  這禮物最適合他了！

- What's your best offer?
  你能給的最好價格是多少？

- Can I get a special discount?
  我能有些優惠嗎？

- Your price is outrageous!
  你的價錢太誇張了！

- These t-shirts are on sale.
  這些 T 恤在特價。

- All winter clothing is now 30% off.
  冬季服飾現在打七折。

- What's your size?
  您穿幾號呢？

- Do you have this dress in size 8?
  你這件洋裝有八號的嗎？

- I'm afraid we don't have your size.
  我恐怕已經沒有您的尺寸了。

- Would you like to see a movie tonight?
  你晚上要不要看電影？

- What movie do you want to watch?
  你想看哪一部電影？

MEMO

- What movies are in theater now?
  現在上映的電影有什麼？

- What's your favorite clothing brand?
  你最喜歡哪一牌的衣服呢？

- Which dress do you think I should buy?
  你覺得我該買哪一件洋裝？

- I don't look good in stripes.
  我穿條紋不好看。

- What material is this T-shirt made of?
  這件 T 恤的材質是什麼？

- I can't decide which shirt to buy.
  我沒辦法決定該買哪一件襯衫。

- What shade of lipstick matches my skin tone?
  哪種顏色的口紅適合我的膚色？

- I want to try this blush on my cheeks.
  我想在臉頰上試擦這個腮紅。

- How do I remove this make up?
  我該如何卸妝？

- Making yourself beautiful may cost a lot.
  讓自己變美是很花錢的。

- How long do you spend putting make up on?
  妳化妝要花多久時間啊？

MEMO

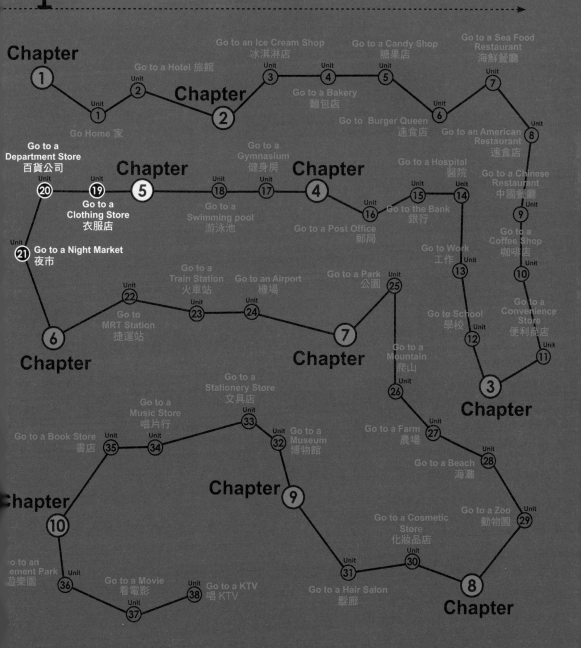

Chapter 5

Shopping
逛街好心情

Chapter

Go to an Ice Cream Shop 冰淇淋店
Go to a Candy Shop 糖果店
Go to a Sea Food Restaurant 海鮮餐廳
Go to a Hotel 旅館

Chapter

Go to a Bakery 麵包店
Go to Burger Queen 速食店
Go to an American Restaurant 速食店

Go Home 家

Go to a Department Store 百貨公司

Chapter

Go to a Gymnasium 健身房

Chapter

Go to a Hospital 醫院
Go to a Chinese Restaurant 中國餐廳

Go to a Clothing Store 衣服店

Go to a Swimming pool 游泳池
Go to a Post Office 郵局
Go to the Bank 銀行

Go to a Coffee Shop 咖啡店

Go to a Night Market 夜市

Go to Work 工作

Go to a Train Station 火車站
Go to an Airport 機場
Go to a Park 公園

Go to School 學校
Go to a Convenience Store 便利商店

Go to MRT Station 捷運站

Chapter

Chapter

Go to a Mountain 爬山

Chapter

Go to a Stationery Store 文具店
Go to a Museum 博物館
Go to a Farm 農場

Go to a Music Store 唱片行

Go to a Beach 海灘

Go to a Book Store 書店

Chapter

Go to a Cosmetic Store 化妝品店
Go to a Zoo 動物園

Go to an ___ement Park 遊樂園

Go to a Movie 看電影
Go to a KTV 唱 KTV

Go to a Hair Salon 髮廊

Chapter

Go to a Clothing Store 服飾店

05-01

A Hmm, what should I wear today?
嗯，我今天要穿哪一件衣服？

B Come on, you think about what to wear almost every day. There are thousands of clothes in your wardrobe.
拜託，你幾乎每天都在想要穿哪一件？你的衣櫃裡頭有數以千計的衣服了。

A Well, haven't you ever heard people say that there is always one piece of clotheing missing from a women's wardrobe?
哎唷，你沒聽過人家說「女人的衣櫃總是少一件衣服」嗎？

B I do and I can prove that is 100 % true for you.
有啊，而且我可以從你身上百分之百證明是真的。

A Loving to look beautiful is women's nature. In fact, I am thinking about going to my favorite clothing shop today.
愛漂亮是女人的天性，事實上，我在想今天要去一間我最喜歡的服飾店。

B No kidding! Again?! You just went shopping yesterday. You really are a shopaholic.
別開玩笑了！又來了！你昨天才買衣服，你真的是一個購物狂。

Additional Vocabulary & Phrases | 補充單字 & 片語

- **wardrobe** n 衣櫃
  We have a wooden wardrobe in our room.
  我們有一個木衣櫃在房間裡。

- **prove** v 證明
  I'll prove you are wrong!
  我會證明你是錯的！

- **nature** n 自然、天性
  I like to be close to nature.
  我喜歡接近大自然。

- **shopaholic** n 購物狂
  You are really a shopaholic.
  你真的是一個購物狂。

Daily Sentences 超高頻率使用句｜一分鐘學一句不怕不夠用　05-02

- Do you have this **shirt**[*1] in a bigger size?
  你這件襯衫有大一號的尺寸嗎？

- What other **colors**[*2] does this T-shirt come in?
  這款 T 恤還有哪些顏色？

- When will you have a big sale?
  你們什麼時候有大拍賣？

- Our store usually has a big sale in July and January. All the prices are up to 70% off.
  我們店通常在七月和一月的時候有大拍賣，所有的商品都打三折。

- How much does the bag cost after the discount?
  這個袋子打折後是多少錢？

- Can I try on these clothes?
  我可以試穿這些衣服嗎？

- Does this scarf come in yellow?
  這條圍巾有黃色的嗎？

- Excuse me, the skirt is too loose. Do you have a smaller one?
  不好意思，這裙子太鬆了，你們有小一號的嗎？

- I think the hat does not fit me. Do you have it in other styles?
  我想那個帽子不適合我，你們有其他款式的嗎？

★ 換個單字說說看｜用單字累積句子的豐富度，讓句子更漂亮！

shirt[*1] 可以替換：

| sweater 毛線衣 | hoodie 帽 T | turtleneck sweater 套頭毛衣 |

Do you have this ＿＿＿＿＿＿ in a bigger size?
你這件＿＿＿＿＿＿有大一號的尺寸嗎？

colors[*2] 可以替換：

| sizes 尺寸 | patterns 花色 | materials 材質 |

What other ＿＿＿＿＿＿ does this T-shirt come in?
這款 T 恤還有哪些 ＿＿＿＿＿＿ ？

Additional Vocabulary & Phrases ｜ 補充單字 & 片語

- **sale** [n] 賣、拍賣
  They have a garage sale tomorrow.
  他們明天會有一個舊物拍賣。

- **price** [n] 價錢
  The price of the dress is too high.
  那件洋裝的價錢太高了。

- **discount** [n] 折扣
  Can you give me some discount?
  你能給我打一些折扣嗎？

- **loose** [a] 鬆的、寬的
  These pants are too loose.
  這件褲子太鬆了。

135

1 catalogue 目錄

clothes [kloz] n	衣服
model [`madl] n	模特兒
style [staɪl] n	款式
colorful [`kʌləfəl] a	鮮艷的
simple [`sɪmpl̩] a	簡單的
popular [`papjələ] a	流行的
fashionable [`fæʃənəbl̩] a	時髦的
noble [`nobl̩] a	顯貴的

2 fitting room 試穿間

size [saɪz] n	尺寸
fitting [`fɪtɪŋ] n	試穿
wear [wɛr] v	穿、戴
fit [fɪt] v	（衣服）使…合身
coordinate [ko`ɔrdn̩et] v	搭配

3 top 上衣

T-shirt [`ti.ʃɜt] n	T 恤
dress [drɛs] n	洋裝
shirt [ʃɜt] n	襯衫
blouse [blauz] n （婦女、兒童等的）短上衣、短衫	
coat [kot] n	外套；大衣
jumper [`dʒʌmpɚ] n 毛線衣；（背心連褲的）娃娃服	
sweater [`swɛtɚ] n	毛衣
jacket [`dʒækɪt] n	夾克
tank top ph	無袖背心

④ pants 褲子；長褲

slacks [slæks] n	寬鬆的長褲
trousers [ˋtrauzɚz] n	長褲
shorts [ʃɔrts] n	寬鬆運動短褲
jeans [dʒinz] n	牛仔褲
skirt [skɝt] n	裙子
pantskirt [ˏpæntsˋkɝt] n	褲裙

⑤ hat 帽子

baseball cap ph	棒球帽
balmoral [bælˋmɔrəl] n	蘇格蘭無邊圓頂帽
beret [bəˋre] n	貝雷帽
boonie hat ph	登山帽
fedora [fɪˋdorə] n	紳士軟呢帽
top hat ph	紳士高禮帽

⑥ scarf 圍巾；領帶

belt [bɛlt] n	腰帶	**bow** [bo] n	蝴蝶領解
necktie [ˋnɛkˏtaɪ] n	領帶；領結	**neckerchief** [ˋnɛkɚtʃɪf] n	領巾
sock [sɑk] n	襪子		

7 jewelry 首飾

earrings [ˈɪrˌrɪŋz] n .... 耳環
ring [rɪŋ] n .... 戒指
necklace [ˈnɛklɪs] n .... 項鍊
bracelet [ˈbreslɪt] n .... 手觸
jewel [ˈdʒuəl] n .... 寶石
accessory [ækˈsɛsərɪ] n .... 配件
trinket [ˈtrɪŋkɪt] n ...... 小裝飾物；廉價首飾
glasses [ˈglæsɪz] n .... 眼鏡

8 underwear 內衣

undergarment [ˈʌndəˌgarmənt] n ......
.... 內衣褲
briefs [brifs] n .... 三角褲
panties [ˈpæntɪz] n .... 內褲
thong [θɔŋ] n .... 丁字褲
bra [brɑ] n .... 胸罩

corset [ˈkɔrsɪt] n .... 馬甲
front closure ph .... 前扣式胸罩
nursing bra ph .... 哺乳用胸罩
seamless bra ph .... 無痕內衣
sports bra ph .... 運動胸罩
bustier [ˈbʌstɪr] n .... 調整型內衣

Daily Q&A

〔會話一〕

Q▶ How much are a blouse and a pair of pants in total?
一件女用上衣和一件褲子總共多少錢？

A▶ They are 3000 dollars.
它們總共是三千元。

〔會話二〕

Q▶ Good morning, sir. How can I help you?
早安，先生。我能為你效勞嗎？

A▶ No, thanks. I am just browsing around.
不用，我只是到處看看。

〔會話三〕

Q▶ Where is the fitting room?
試衣間在哪裡？

A▶ It is at the end of the aisle.
在走道的最後面。

Proverbs & Idioms 道地諺語與慣用語｜讓句子更錦上添花

give someone the shirt off one's back ＞ 盡全力幫助別人

You can depend on Jack when you are in trouble. He would give you the shirt off his back.

你有麻煩的時候可以依靠傑克，他會盡全力的幫助你。

keep your shirt on! ＞ 等一下、耐心點

Keep your shirt on! I will be right back with you in a minute.

耐心點！我馬上就回來。

lose one's shirt ＞ 輸錢

I almost lost my shirt on that investment. Luckily, I also invested my money on some other things.

我幾乎在那項投資裡輸掉所有的錢，但很幸運的，我也有投資一些別的東西。

wear several hats ＞ 身兼數職

Tina needs money. She now wears several hats to make her ends meet.

緹娜需要錢，她現在身兼數職，賺取生活所需的錢。

I'll eat my hat if ... ＞ ⋯⋯如果（一件不可能的事發生），我就把我的頭剁下（帽子吃掉）

I'll eat my hat if the sun rises from the west.

如果太陽從西邊出來，我的頭就剁下來給你。

dress to the nines ＞ 穿著華麗，盛裝

Lena dressed to the nines to the party. She wanted to impress her boyfriend.

莉娜穿著華麗出席派對。她想要讓她的男朋友印象深刻。

keep something zipped ＞ 保守秘密

Will broke up with her girlfriend. He hasn't let anyone know. Let's keep the news zipped.

威爾和她的女朋友分手了。他還沒讓任何人知道。讓我們先保守這個秘密。

Go to a Department Store 百貨公司

A Tiffany, look at the long line in front of the department store. I think they are having their annual sale again.

蒂芬妮，看看百貨公司前面排隊的那些人，我想百貨公司週年慶又到了。

B Really? Then, how can I miss such a great timing to buy some cheap facial treatment product.

真的嗎？那我怎麼能夠錯失買便宜保養品的好時機呢？

A Are you sure? It's really crowded inside. I can hardly breathe ever time I go there during the annual sales.

妳確定？裡頭真的很擠耶，每次我週年慶的時候到那裡，幾乎都沒辦法呼吸。

B But, everything is really on special discount.

但是，所有東西真的都有特別的折扣。

A You are right. But, we had better look at the catalog and make a shopping list first. I do not want to waste my time.

對呀，但是我們最好先看一下目錄，然後列一下購物清單，我不想浪費我的時間。

B That is a good idea.

這是個好主意。

Additional Vocabulary & Phrases | 補充單字 & 片語

- **annual** [a] 一年一次的、年度的
  Kevin's annual income is $NT 3 million dollars.
  凱文的年收入是新台幣三百萬元。

- **treatment** [n] 治療、處理
  Dr. Wu suggested me to try a new treatment for my skin.
  吳醫師建議我試試一個新的皮膚治療。

- **crowded** [a] 擁擠的
  The new restaurant is always crowded.
  那間新的餐廳總是擠滿很多人。

- **hardly** [ad] 簡直不、幾乎不
  I can hardly eat anything today.
  我今天幾乎吃不下任何東西。

Chapter 1
Chapter 2
Chapter 3
4
Chapter **5**
Chapter 6
7
Chapter 8
9
Chapter 10

Daily Sentences **超高頻率使用句**｜一分鐘學一句不怕不夠用　🎧MP3 05-05

- Alice, are you free to go to the department store with me this afternoon?
  愛麗絲，妳今天下午有空跟我一起到百貨公司嗎？

- I need to buy some make-up.
  我需要買一些化妝品。

- Where is the information desk?
  詢問處在哪裡？

- The **shoe shop**★1 is in the center of the ground floor.
  鞋店在一樓中間。

- Which floor sells appliances?
  哪一層樓有賣家電用品？

- The **new Italian restaurant**★1 is on the 10th floor.
  新的義大利餐廳在十樓。

- Do you accept credit cards?
  你們接受信用卡嗎？

- Can I get a special discount?
  我可以有特別折扣嗎？

- Is there a book store in this building?
  這棟樓有書店嗎？

- Do you offer any free delivery service?
  你們有提供免費送貨的服務嗎？

★ **換個單字說說看**｜用單字累積句子的豐富度，讓句子更漂亮！

shoe shop★1 可以替換：

bag store 包包店	**jewelry store** 珠寶店	**bedding store** 寢具店

The _____ is in the center of the ground floor.
_____在一樓中間。

new Italian restaurant★2 可以替換：

coffee shop 咖啡廳	**ice cream store** 冰淇淋店	**food court** 美食區

The_____ is on the 10th floor.
新的_____在十樓。

Additional Vocabulary & Phrases ｜ 補充單字 & 片語

- **ground floor** ph 一樓
  The ice cream shop is on the ground floor of the mall.
  冰淇淋店在購物商場的一樓。

- **accept** v 接受
  I accept your apology.
  我接受你的道歉。

① department store 百貨公司

shopping mall ph ⸺⸺ 購物中心
plaza [`plæzə] n ⸺⸺ 購物廣場
outlet [`aʊtˌlɛt] n ⸺⸺ 暢貨中心
community mall ph ⸺ 社區購物中心
neighborhood center ph 里鄰型購物中心

② service 服務

information desk ph ⸺⸺ 服務台
customer service ph ⸺⸺ 顧客服務
flyer [`flaɪɚ] n ⸺⸺ 廣告單
parking lot ph ⸺⸺ 停車場
branch [bræntʃ] n ⸺⸺ 分店

③ customers 顧客

clerk [klɝk] n ⸺⸺ 店員
attendant [ə`tɛndənt] n ⸺⸺ 服務員
assistant [ə`sɪstənt] n ⸺⸺ 助理

manager [`mænɪdʒɚ] n ⸺⸺ 經理
elevator operator ph ⸺ 電梯服務員

4 pay 付錢

check [tʃɛk] n	支票	
cash [kæʃ] n	現金	
note [not] n	鈔券	
coin [kɔɪn] n	硬幣	

card machine ph	信用卡讀卡機
credit card ph	信用卡
debit card ph	現金卡
loyalty card ph	忠誠卡

5 casual wear 休閒服飾

jeans [dʒinz] n	牛仔服飾
swim suit ph	泳裝
tailor [ˋtelɚ] n	男裝
boutique [buˋtik] n	女裝精品
shoe shop ph	鞋店
bedding [ˋbɛdɪŋ] n	寢具
housewares [ˋhaʊsˏwɛrz] n	家庭用品

6 activity 活動

annual sale ph	周年慶
discount [ˋdɪskaʊnt] n	打折
on sale ph	拍賣
special offer ph	特賣
go window-shopping ph	櫥窗購物

7 floor 樓層

floor guide [ph] 樓層介紹
elevator [ˈɛləˌvetɚ] [n] 電梯
escalator [ˈɛskəˌletɚ] [n] 手扶梯
stairway [ˈstɛrˌwe] [n] 樓梯
basement [ˈbesmənt] [n] 地下室

8 merchandise 商品

brand [brænd] [n] 品牌
fashion [ˈfæʃən] [n] 時尚
consume [kənˈsjum] [n] 消費
shopping [ˈʃɑpɪŋ] [n] 購物
perfume [ˈpɝˈfjum] [n] 香水
cosmetic [kɑzˈmɛtɪk] [n] 化妝品

skin care product [ph] 保養品
packsack [ˈpækˌsæk] [n] 皮製包
jewelry [ˈdʒuəlrɪ] [n] 珠寶
purse [pɝs] [n] 女用手提提包
wallet [ˈwɑlɪt] [n] 錢包

Daily Q&A

〔會話一〕

Q▸ Where is the food court?
美食街在哪裡？

A▸ It is in the basement.
在地下室。

〔會話二〕

Q▸ Where are the tights?
褲襪在哪裡？

A▸ They are on the 5th floor next to the escalator.
在五樓手扶梯旁。

〔會話三〕

Q▸ Where can I exchange some free gifts?
我可以在哪裡兌換免費商品？

A▸ Go to the top floor and turn left.
到頂樓左轉。

7天就能用英文
行遍全世界！

④

Chapter 1
Chapter 2
Chapter 3
Chapter 4
Chapter 5
Chapter 6
Chapter 7
Chapter 8
Chapter 9
Chapter 10

Proverbs & Idioms 道地諺語與慣用語 | 讓句子更錦上添花

five finger discount 〉 偷竊

Peter got the diamond ring by five finger discount.
彼得偷了一個鑽戒。

up for sale 〉 可以購買

The CD will be up for sale in late December. You can not find one in the store now.
在十二月底的時候，這片 CD 就能購買到了。現在你沒辦法在店裡找到。

garage sale 〉 車庫拍賣 （在自己家的車庫販賣二手物品）

Jenny has so many things she doesn't need. She plans to have a garage sale to clean out something she has not used them for ages and earn some money.
珍妮有太多不想要的東西了，她計畫舉辦一個車庫拍賣，把她多年不用的東西賣掉，順便換一點現金。

close the sale 〉 成功賣掉某物

Fiona just took out the computer the customer looked for and closed the sale.
費歐娜才剛把顧客要找的電腦拿出來，就成功的賣出去了。

elevator music 〉 電梯音樂 （在公共場合裡所播放的愉悅但單調的音樂）

In some shopping mall you can never get away some elevator music.
在一些購物中心，你永遠沒有辦法擺脫電梯音樂。

gift-wrap something 〉 包裝成禮盒

I bought this watch as my boyfriend's birthday gift. Can you please gift-wrap it for me?
我買這隻手錶當作我男朋友的生日禮物。可以請你幫我包裝成禮盒嗎？

clearance sale 〉 清倉大拍賣

It's the end of the year. A lot of clothing stores are having their clearance sale.
現在是年終。很多服飾店正在清倉大拍賣。

A Let's go to DingDing night market. I miss the taste of stinky tofu and Taiwanese fried chicken.
我們去頂頂夜市吧！我想念臭豆腐和鹽酥雞的味道。

B Me too. When people talk about night markets, the snack food which first comes across my mind is the oyster omelet.
我也是。每次人們提到夜市，在我腦中浮現的小吃是蚵仔煎。

A Oh, my mouth is watering now. Let's set out for the night market.
喔，我開始流口水了。我們現在出發到夜市去吧！

B Today is Monday. It is usually not very busy on weekdays.
今天是星期一，工作日裡逛夜市的人都不會太多。

A I like that. I don't like to walk in the crowds in summer. It makes me sweat all the time.
我喜歡這樣。在夏天裡，我不喜歡和很多人一起擠。那總是會讓我滿身大汗。

B I am thirsty. Look at the sign across from the Tempura stand. It says the papaya milk is buy one get one free. It's cheap!
我好渴喔。看看天婦羅攤對面的那個招牌，上面寫說，木瓜牛奶買一送一耶，真便宜！

Additional Vocabulary & Phrases | 補充單字 & 片語

- **stinky** [a] 臭的
  Your socks are stinky!
  你的襪子真臭！

- **papaya** [n] 木瓜
  My favorite fruit is papaya.
  我最喜歡的水果是木瓜。

- **set out** [ph] 出發
  They set out at six o'clock to the airport.
  他們六點鐘出發去機場。

- **sweat** [v] 出汗
  Dan was sweating due to the hot temperature.
  丹因為溫度太高而一直出汗。

Daily Sentences 超高頻率使用句│一分鐘學一句不怕不夠用
MP3 05-08

- Taiwan is famous for a great variety of snack food.
  台灣以各式各樣的小吃聞名，

- Can you tell me where I can find the **stinky tofu** ★1 stand?
  你可以告訴我，哪裡可以找到臭豆腐攤嗎？

- It is so crowded here. I am lost.
  這裡好擠喔，我迷路了。

- Can you recommend some delicious Taiwanese traditional snacks to me?
  你可以推薦我一些好吃的台灣傳統小吃嗎？

- What time do the stands usually come out? What time do they usually finish their business for today?
  這些小攤販什麼時候出來？他們什麼時候會結束當天的營業？

- What do you like to do at a night market?
  你喜歡在夜市做什麼？

- Can you show me the meat ball stand shown in my guide book at this night market?
  你可以告訴我，這本旅遊書上介紹這個夜市的這家肉圓攤在哪嗎？

- Have you ever played **net fish** ★2?
  你玩過撈魚嗎？

★ 換個單字說說看│用單字累積句子的豐富度，讓句子更漂亮！

stinky tofu★1 可以替換：			net fish★2 可以替換：		
chicken claw 雞爪	**Pig's blood rice pudding** 豬血糕	**oyster omelet** 蚵仔煎	**crane games** 夾娃娃機	**marble** 彈珠遊戲	**water ball** 水球

Can you tell me where I can find the _____ stand?
你可以告訴我，哪裡可以找到_____攤嗎？

Have you ever played _____?
你玩過_____嗎？

Additional Vocabulary & Phrases │ 補充單字 & 片語

- **variety** n 多樣化、種類
  Sandy has a variety of interests.
  辛蒂有很多種不同的嗜好。

- **stand** n 攤子
  This shaved ice stand is very famous.
  這間刨冰攤很有名。

- **recommend** v 推薦
  Can you recommend me some books to read?
  你能推薦我一些書嗎？

- **guide** n 嚮導、指南
  Katy is an experienced tour guide.
  凱蒂是一位很有經驗的導遊。

1 **Taiwanese fried chicken** 鹹酥雞

stinky tofu [ph] ···································· 臭豆腐

tempura [ˋtɛmpʊrə] [n] ·················· 天婦羅

meat ball [ph] ································· 肉圓

hot dog [ph] ································· 熱狗

delicacy [ˋdɛləkəsɪ] [n] ········· 美味；佳餚

2 **sausage** 香腸

roasted corn on the cob [ph] · 烤玉米

chicken claw/feet [ph] ··············· 雞爪

pig's blood rice pudding [ph] 豬血糕

oyster omelet [ph] ···················· 蚵仔煎

oyster vermicelli [ph] ··········· 蚵仔麵線

3 **Taiwanese sausage with sticky rice** 大腸包小腸

fish ball soup [ph] ···················· 魚丸湯

hot and sour soup [ph] ·········· 酸辣湯

salted chicken [ph] ················· 鹽水雞

three-cup chicken [ph] ··········· 三杯雞

Tamsui Agei [ph] ···················· 淡水阿給

④ wheel pie 車輪餅

cream [krim] n		奶油
red bean ph		紅豆
sesame [`sɛsəmɪ] n		芝麻
taro [`tɑro] n		芋頭

peanut [`pinʌt] n		花生
dried/pickled radish ph		蘿蔔乾
dried/pickled cabbage ph		高麗菜

⑤ watermelon juice 西瓜汁

sugar cane juice ph		甘蔗汁
plum juice ph		酸梅汁
pearl milk tea ph		珍珠奶茶
star fruit juice ph		楊桃汁
papaya milk ph		木瓜牛奶
fruit stand ph		水果攤

⑥ ice 冰

shredded ice ph		刨冰
snowflake ice ph		雪花冰
ice cream ph		冰淇淋
soybean pudding ph		豆花
shaved ice mountain ph		刨冰山

❼ vendor 小販

stand [stænd] n ……………… 路邊攤
decoration [ˌdɛkəˈreʃən] n ……… 裝飾品
characteristic [ˌkærəktəˈrɪstɪk] n … 特色
traditional [trəˈdɪʃənl̩] a …………… 傳統的
cultural [ˈkʌltʃərəl] a ……………… 文化的

❽ crane games 夾娃娃機

marbles [ˈmɑrbl̩z] n ……… 彈珠遊戲
water ballons ph ……… 水球
darts [dɑrtz] n ……… 飛鏢

net fish ph ……………… 撈魚
dolls [dɑlz] n ……………… 娃娃
mahjong n ……………… 麻將

Daily Q&A

〔會話一〕

Q▶ Sir, I would like to have a large papaya milk with less sugar and ice.
先生,我想要一杯大杯的木瓜牛奶,少糖少冰。

A▶ No problem.
沒問題。

〔會話二〕

Q▶ Would you like some chili sauce on the side of your plate?
你要在盤子旁邊放一些辣椒醬嗎?

A▶ Sure.
好啊!

〔會話三〕

Q▶ Would you like some shaved ice?
你想要來點刨冰嗎?

A▶ No, thanks.
不了,謝謝!

Proverbs & Idioms 道地諺語與慣用語｜讓句子更錦上添花

a drug on the market 充斥市場
Right now, small computers are a drug in the market.
現在，迷你電腦充斥整個市場。

like a blind dog in a meat market 失控
The kids played around the museum like blind dogs in a meat market, touching everything they were not supposed to touch.
那些小孩在博物館裡玩到失控，碰了他們不應該碰的所有東西。

a cattle market 酒池肉林的場所
The nightclub is actually a cattle market. You can always see some sexy bikini girls dance on the stage.
那間夜店事實上是個聲色場所，你總是可以看到一些性感的比基尼女郎在舞台上跳舞。

on the market 出售
Kelly put her car on the market last month.
凱莉上個月把她的車賣掉了。

in the market for something 有興趣購買
I am in the market for a new cell phone. My old one is not working.
我想購買一個新的手機，我舊的手機已經壞了。

price sb. or sth. out of the market 用價格壟斷市場淘汰某人或某事
The discount prices posted by the chain store were meant to price us out of the market.
連鎖店刊登的優惠價格注定壟斷市場讓我們被市場淘汰。

corner the market on something 讓某物市場獨佔
The company sought to corner the market on their new cellphones.
那公司尋求讓他們的新手機市場獨佔。

crowd together 聚集在一起
Many food stands crowded together to sell delicious food to customers who came to the night market for good food.
很多小吃攤聚集一起販賣美味的食物給那些來夜市吃美食的客人。

語言學校獨家傳授必備好用句

- Can you name some famous snack food in this night market?
  你可以説出這個夜市一些有名的小吃嗎？

- My favorite Taiwanese snacks are stinky tofu, oyster omelet, and pearl milk tea.
  我最喜歡的台灣小吃是臭豆腐、蚵仔煎和珍珠奶茶。

- The fruit stand is in the middle next to a shredded ice stand.
  水果攤在夜市中間，剉冰攤的旁邊。

- Don't be panic. Just follow the crowds and they will lead you to the next exit.
  不要慌，只要跟著人群走，他們會帶你到下一個出口。

- It is usually not easy to get a place to eat some popular snack food like stinky tofu.
  要吃像臭豆腐一樣的小吃也很難有位子。

- Look at the Tampura stand over there. You are not possible to eat it on the weekends since it is recently reported to be the most delicious stand in this night market.
  看那邊那個天婦羅攤位。假日時，你是不可能吃到天婦羅的，因為它最近被報導為這個夜市裡最好吃的小吃攤。

- What is the smell coming from? It smells so good.
  那個味道是從哪裡來的？好好聞喔！

- I love roasted corn on a cob.
  我超喜歡烤玉米。

- Do you see the old lady standing over there? She can make the most delicious pig's blood rice pudding in Taiwan.
  你看到正站在那邊的老婦人嗎？她會做台灣最好吃的豬血糕喔！

MEMO

7天就能用英文
行遍全世界！

4

Chapter 1
Chapter 2
Chapter 3
Chapter 4
Chapter 5
Chapter 6
Chapter 7
Chapter 8
Chapter 9
Chapter 10

From AM-PM 從早到晚都用得到的必備好用句

- I want a dress that's shorter.
  我想要買短一點的洋裝。

- I'm looking for some running shoes.
  我想找找慢跑鞋。

- Do you know your shoe size?
  您知道您鞋子的尺寸嗎？

- Do you want to cook an egg in a pot?
  你想要把蛋打進鍋裡煮嗎？

- Eating hot pot is really good on cold days.
  冷天吃火鍋真是棒透了。

- This hot pot restaurant is all-you-can-eat.
  這家火鍋店是吃到飽的。

- Could we eat and watch TV at the same time?
  我們可以邊吃飯邊看電視嗎？

- Don't chew with your mouth open.
  嚼食物時嘴巴不要張開。

- You shouldn't be picky about what you eat.
  你不該挑食。

- The specialty here is Peking duck.
  這裡的招牌就是北京烤鴨。

- I need some coffee to wake me up.
  我需要一些咖啡來提神。

MEMO

- I prefer iced coffee over hot coffee.
  跟熱咖啡比起來，我比較想喝冰咖啡。

- Could I have extra cream for my coffee?
  可以幫我在咖啡裡多加一些奶油嗎？

- The coffee here is freshly brewed.
  這裡的咖啡是現煮的。

- Game time! Let's play games.
  遊戲時間！我們來玩遊戲吧。

- What's the progress on your assignment?
  你工作進度如何？

- Do you have any new updates for me?
  有新進展嗎？

- I think I caught a cold.
  我想我感冒了。

- Don't worry about work.
  不要擔心工作。

- Could someone turn on the air conditioner?
  誰能把空調打開？

- Put on your socks.
  穿上你的襪子。

- Comb your hair.
  把頭髮梳一梳。

MEMO

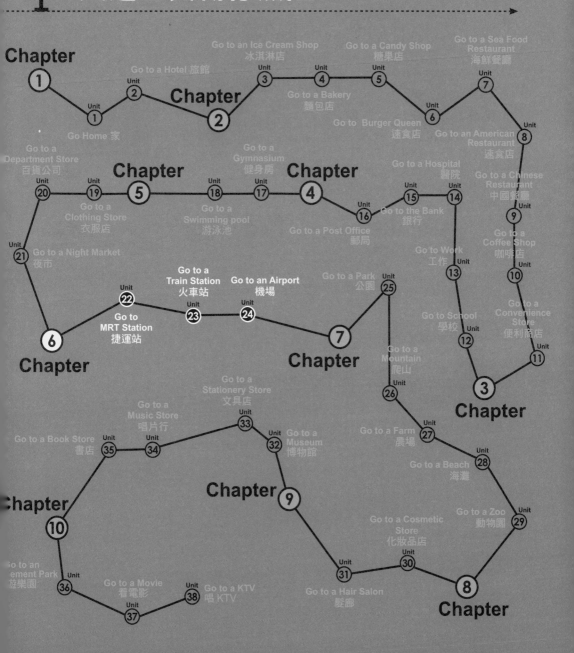

Chapter 6

Transportation
交通工具暢行無阻

Chapter 1
① Unit 1
Go Home 家

Unit 2
Go to a Hotel 旅館

Chapter 2
②

Unit 3
Go to an Ice Cream Shop 冰淇淋店

Unit 4
Go to a Bakery 麵包店

Unit 5
Go to a Candy Shop 糖果店

Unit 6
Go to Burger Queen 速食店

Unit 7
Go to a Sea Food Restaurant 海鮮餐廳

Unit 8
Go to an American Restaurant 速食店

Go to a Department Store 百貨公司
Unit 20

Unit 19

Chapter 5
⑤

Unit 18

Unit 17

Chapter 4
④

Unit 16
Go to the Bank 銀行

Go to a Post Office 郵局

Unit 15

Unit 14

Go to a Hospital 醫院

Go to a Chinese Restaurant 中國餐廳

Go to a Gymnasium 健身房

Go to a Clothing Store 衣服店

Go to a Swimming pool 游泳池

Unit 9
Go to a Coffee Shop 咖啡店

Unit 21
Go to a Night Market 夜市

Unit 13
Go to Work 工作

Unit 10

Go to a Convenience Store 便利商店

Unit 22
Go to MRT Station 捷運站

Go to a Train Station 火車站
Unit 23

Go to an Airport 機場
Unit 24

Go to a Park 公園
Unit 25

Chapter 6
⑥

Chapter 7
⑦

Go to School 學校
Unit 12

Unit 11

Chapter 3
③

Go to a Mountain 爬山
Unit 26

Go to a Stationery Store 文具店
Unit 33

Go to a Music Store 唱片行

Unit 32
Go to a Museum 博物館

Go to a Farm 農場
Unit 27

Go to a Book Store 書店
Unit 35

Unit 34

Unit 28

Go to a Beach 海灘

Chapter 10
⑩

Chapter 9
⑨

Go to a Cosmetic Store 化妝品店

Go to a Zoo 動物園
Unit 29

Go to an Amusement Park 遊樂園
Unit 36

Go to a Movie 看電影

Unit 38
Go to a KTV 唱 KTV

Unit 37

Unit 31
Go to a Hair Salon 髮廊

Unit 30

Chapter 8
⑧

Go to an MRT Station 捷運站

Daily Conversation 日常對話 | 快速融入超擬真的日常對話

A How should we go to Tamsui?
我們要怎麼去淡水？

B Let's take the MRT. It's faster and cheaper.
我們搭捷運好了，捷運又快又便宜。

A Which line should we take if we go to Tamsui?
我們要搭哪一條線到淡水？

B We should take the red line. Let's get the tickets at the automatic ticket vending machine.
我們應該搭紅線。我們到自動售票機買票吧！

A How much money should I insert in the slot?
我應該要投多少錢進去？

B 50 dollars. You have to place your ticket near the sensor.
五十元。等一下你必須把票放在靠近感應器的地方。

A I see.
我懂了。

Additional Vocabulary & Phrases | 補充單字 & 片語

- **automatic** [a] 自動的、自動裝置的
  This dish washer is automatic.
  這個洗碗機是全自動的。

- **insert** [v] 插入、嵌入
  Please insert your card here.
  請將卡片插入這裡。

- **slot** [n] 投幣孔
  You can insert coin into the slot.
  你可以將硬幣投入投幣孔。

- **place** [v] 放置、安置
  Please place your cup on the cupboard.
  請將你的杯子放在杯架上。

Daily Sentences 超高頻率使用句｜一分鐘學一句不怕不夠用
06-02

- How can I take the MRT?
  我該怎麼搭捷運呢？

- Elvis, put your **cola** ★¹ away before entering the MRT station.
  艾維斯，進捷運站前先把可樂喝完。

- Watch out! The train is coming. Stand behind the yellow line. It's dangerous.
  小心！火車要來了，你要站在黃線後面。這樣很危險！

- Which line should I take to get to **Taipei City Zoo** ★² by MRT?
  捷運哪一條線可以到台北市立動物園？

- Please yield your seats to the elderly, pregnant women and the handicapped.
  請讓座給老人、孕婦和行動不便者。

- You need to change the train at Taipei Main Station to go to Tamsui.
  你必須在台北車站換車到淡水。

- Look at the sign over there on the wall. It says "No drinking and eating behind the yellow line." If you do not follow the rules, you will be asked to pay a fine of up to 6,000 dollars.
  看看牆上那張標語。標語上寫著「黃線後禁止飲食」。如果你不遵守規定，將會被罰款六千元。

★ **換個單字說說看**｜用單字累積句子的豐富度，讓句子更漂亮！

cola★¹ 可以替換：			Taipei City Zoo★² 可以替換：		
drink 飲料	**tea** 茶	**coffee** 咖啡	**Taipei 101** 台北 101	**Eslite Bookstore** 誠品書店	**Shilin Night Market** 士林夜市

Put your _____ away before entering the MRT station.
進捷運站前先把_____喝完。

Which line should I take to get to _____ by MRT?
捷運哪一條線可以到_____？

Additional Vocabulary & Phrases｜補充單字 & 片語

- enter ⱽ 進入
  She just entered the building.
  她剛剛才進入大樓裡。

- yield ⱽ 讓於
  Please yield your seat to those in need.
  請讓位給需要的乘客。

- pregnant ᵃ 懷孕的
  Mia is pregnant.
  米雅懷孕了。

- handicapped ᵃ 有生理殘缺的
  The handicapped doesn't mean useless.
  有生理殘缺的人不代表沒有用。

❶ Mass Rapid Transit (MRT) 捷運

subway [ˋsʌbˌwe] n	地鐵
metro [ˋmɛtro] n	捷運
The Underground ph	英國地下鐵
The Tube ph	英國地下鐵
public transportation ph	大眾交通工具

❷ station 車站

terminal station ph	終點站
transfer station ph	轉乘站
regular station ph	一般車站
automatic platform gate ph	安全閘門
exit [ˋɛksɪt] n	出口

❸ ticket 票，券；車票；入場券

automatic ticket vending machine ph	自動售票機
scan the ticket ph	感應票卡
easy card ph	悠遊儲值卡
top up ph	儲值
sensor [ˋsɛnsɚ] n	感應器
single-journey ticket ph	單程票
unregistered [ʌnˋrɛdʒɪstɚd] a	沒記錄到

④ platform 月台

platform gap [ph] ⋯⋯ 月台與列車的間隙

elevator [`ɛləˌvetə] [n] ⋯⋯⋯⋯ 電梯

escalator [`ɛskəˌletə] [n] ⋯⋯⋯ 手扶梯

handrail [`hændˌrel] [n] ⋯⋯⋯⋯ 把手

prohibit [prə`hɪbɪt] [v] ⋯⋯⋯⋯ 禁止

food and drink [ph] ⋯⋯⋯⋯⋯ 飲食

⑤ car 車廂

priority seat [ph] ⋯⋯⋯⋯⋯⋯⋯ 博愛座

wheelchair accessible [ph] ⋯⋯ 無障礙空間

yield [jild] [v] ⋯⋯⋯⋯⋯⋯⋯⋯⋯ 禮讓

emergency fire extinguisher [ph]

⋯⋯⋯⋯⋯⋯⋯⋯⋯⋯⋯⋯⋯⋯⋯ 緊急滅火器

seat [sit] [n] ⋯⋯⋯⋯⋯⋯⋯⋯⋯⋯ 座位

grip [grɪp] [v] ⋯⋯⋯⋯⋯⋯⋯⋯⋯ 緊握

⑥ tourist 旅遊者，觀光者

route map [ph] ⋯⋯⋯⋯⋯ 路線圖

timetable [`taɪmˌtebl̩] [n] ⋯⋯ 時刻表

ticket fare [ph] ⋯⋯⋯⋯⋯ 車票費

bulletin board [ph] ⋯⋯⋯ 佈告欄

easy mall [ph] ⋯⋯⋯⋯⋯ 捷運地下街

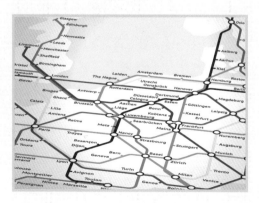

7 **passenger service** 乘客服務

information counter ph 服務台
station staff ph 車站站務人員
weekday [ˋwikˏde] n 平日；工作日
peak hour ph 尖峰時刻
off-peak hour ph 非尖峰時刻
holiday [ˋhɑləˏde] n 假日

8 **passenger** 乘客

elder [ˋɛldɚ] n 年長者
senior citizen ph 年長公民
pregnant woman ph 孕婦
indigenous people ph 低收入戶者

children [ˋtʃɪldrən] n 孩童
adult [əˋdʌlt] n 成人
restroom for the handicapped ph 無障礙廁所

Daily Q&A

〔會話一〕

Q▸ Excuse me. Which line should I take to get to Taipei Zoo by MRT?
請問一下，捷運哪一條線可以到動物園？

A▸ You should take the brown line.
你要搭棕線。

〔會話二〕

Q▸ How much is the ticket from Taipei Train Station to Tamsui?
從台北火車站到淡水票價多少？

A▸ It's 50 dollars.
五十元。

〔會話三〕

Q▸ Excuse me. Where can I buy the ticket?
不好意思，我在哪裡可以買到票？

A▸ You can buy it at the automatic ticket vending machine.
你可以在自動售票機買票。

Proverbs & Idioms 道地諺語與慣用語｜讓句子更錦上添花

hot ticket 熱門的人事

Singers who can dance now are a hot ticket right now.
現在會跳舞的歌手很熱門。

get one's ticket punched 死亡

Poor Greg! He got his ticket punched while he was waiting for a bus.
可憐的桂格！他等公車的時候去世了。

just a ticket 完美的事物

A bowl of hot soup is just a ticket in a freezing day.
在寒冷的日子裡來一碗熱湯是件完美的事。

round-trip ticket 來回票

A round-trip ticket is usually cheaper than a one-way ticket. If you want to go to Tainan by High Speed Railway, buy a round-trip ticket. You may have some discount.
來回票通常比單程票便宜。如果你要搭高鐵去台南，買張來回票吧！你可以有一些折扣。

big ticket 昂貴的物品

Not many people can afford buying big ticket items when the economy is bad.
不是所有人在經濟不景氣時都買得起昂貴物品。

a one-way ticket to something 無法避免的壞事

As far as I am concerned, being addicted to the drugs is a one-way ticket to misery and poor health.
就我來說有毒癮是一件無法避免的壞事，不但會帶來不幸也有害健康。

go off the rails 脫序的行為

That famous singer went off the rails again last weekend. He yelled at his fans and tried to attack them for no reason.
那位有名的歌手上周末又出現脫序的行為。他沒來由地對他的粉絲大吼並試圖攻擊他們。

off the beaten track 鮮少人出沒的地方

That restaurant is difficult to find. It is really off the beaten track.
那間餐廳很難被找到。它一定在鮮少人出沒的地方。

06-04

B Wow. There are so many passengers on this train.
哇！火車上好多乘客喔！

A There are. This is maybe because we have a long weekend. Many people want to take a trip to Hsinchu.
是啊！這是因為我們這週末有長假，很多人想去新竹玩。

B Well, maybe. Can you find our seats?
嗯，也許是。你找得到我們的位子嗎？

A Let me check our tickets… It says Row 12 A and B.
讓我查查我們的車票……上面寫著十二排 A 和 B。

B Look! Our seats are over there. 12 A is the window seat and 12 B is the aisle seat.
你看，我們的座位在那裡。12A 是靠窗的座位，12B 是靠走道的座位。

A Great! I like the window seat. It is more comfortable.
太好了！我喜歡靠窗的位子，比較舒服。

Additional Vocabulary & Phrases | 補充單字 & 片語

● **row** n 列、排
Which row do you seat?
你坐哪一排？

● **window** n 窗戶
Can you open the window?
可以請你開窗嗎？

● **aisle** n 通道、走道
Please do not block the aisle.
請不要阻擋通道。

● **comfortable** a 舒服的
It's so comfortable sitting on the sofa.
坐在沙發上真的很舒服。

Daily Sentences 超高頻率使用句｜一分鐘學一句不怕不夠用 06-05

● Excuse me. We would like a one-way ticket to **Taichung**★1.
不好意思，我們要一張到台中的單程車票。

● Would you be nice enough to find me a seat near the window? I am afraid of getting car sick.
你可不可以幫我安排一個靠窗的位子？我怕暈車。

● Look! There is a long line. Every one is lining up to buy tickets.
看！好長的隊伍，每個人都排隊買票。

● We should have bought the tickets online.
我應該網路購票的。

● Ma'am, I would like a round-trip ticket to Tainan.
女士，我要一張到台南的來回票。

● Look at the timetable. The train to Taoyuan departs at 6:20 and arrives at 6:45.
看看時刻表，到桃園的火車 6:20 離開，6:45 到達。

● Can I have a timetable for the High Speed Rail?
可以給我一張高鐵的車次表嗎？

● Where is the **ticket booth**★2?
售票亭在哪裡？

● Do you have your ticket with you? The train ticket puncher will punch the tickets before we get on the train.
你有帶你的票嗎？剪票員會在我們上火車時剪票。

★ 換個單字說說看｜用單字累積句子的豐富度，讓句子更漂亮！

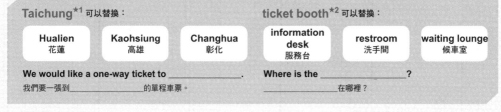

Taichung★1 可以替換：			ticket booth★2 可以替換：		
Hualien 花蓮	**Kaohsiung** 高雄	**Changhua** 彰化	**information desk** 服務台	**restroom** 洗手間	**waiting lounge** 候車室

We would like a one-way ticket to ＿＿＿＿＿＿.
我們要一張到＿＿＿＿＿＿＿的單程車票。

Where is the ＿＿＿＿＿＿?
＿＿＿＿＿＿＿在哪裡？

1 train 列車，火車

rail [rel] n	軌道
railroad [ˋrelˏrod] n	鐵路
railway [ˋrelˏwe] n	鐵路系統
track [træk] n	鐵軌
carriage [ˋkærɪdʒ] n	車廂

2 bullet train 子彈列車

express train ph	特快列車
high speed rail ph	高鐵列車
ordinary train ph	普通列車
local express ph	準急列車
limited express ph	特級列車

3 ticket window 售票處

convenience [kənˋvinjəns] n	方便
information desk ph	服務台
a long line ph	大排長龍

train ticket puncher ph	火車剪票員
waiting lounge ph	候車室

4 **timetable 時刻表**

passenger [ˋpæsn̩dʒɚ] n ········· 乘客

tourist [ˋturɪst] n ······ 旅遊者，觀光者

luggage [ˋlʌgɪdʒ] n ················· 行李

train announcer ph ········· 火車播音員

ticket gate ph ·················· 剪票口

5 **conductor 列車長**

train master compartment ph 列車長室

fare adjustment ph ······················ 補票

one way trip ph ························· 單程

round trip ph ····························· 來回

train staff ph ···················· 火車服務員

6 **seat number 座位號碼**

window seat ph ·············· 靠窗的座位

aisle seat ph ··············· 靠走道的座位

wheelchair accessible car ph
·································· 無障礙車廂

row [ro] n ···················· 一列，一排座位

smoking car ph ················ 吸菸車廂

unreserved seat ph ············· 自由座

reserved seat ph ··············· 對號座

7 **compartment** 火車包廂

food trolley ph .... 餐車
sales trolley ph .... 商品推車
first class ph .... 頭等艙
stateroom [`stet.rum] n
.... 火車單間臥舖
kitchenette [.kɪtʃɪn`ɛt] n .... 茶水間

8 **platform** 月台

locomotive [.lokə`motɪv] n ...... 火車頭
station master [`steʃən.mæstər] n
.... 火車站長
station attendant ph .... 站務員
direction [də`rɛkʃən] n .... 方向
main line ph .... 主幹線

time required ph .... 行車時間
destination [.dɛstə`neʃən] n ...... 終點
terminal [`tɝmənl] n .... 終點站
last train ph .... 末班車
first train ph .... 首班車

Daily Q&A

〔會話一〕

Q▸ **Excuse me! When will the train to Tainan depart?**
不好意思！到台南的車幾點離開？

A▸ **It'll leave for Tainan at 14:30.**
它將於 14:30 前往台南。

〔會話二〕

Q▸ **How much does the High Speed Rail ticket to Taoyun cost?**
到桃園的高鐵車票多少錢？

A▸ **It costs 200 dollars.**
約二百元。

〔會話三〕

Q▸ **Where is Platform 5?**
第五月台在哪裡？

A▸ **It's on the second floor. Walk up the stairs and turn right. It's on your right.**
在二樓。走上樓梯右轉，就在你右手邊。

Proverbs & Idioms 道地諺語與慣用語｜讓句子更錦上添花

the gravy train 〉 過奢華的生活

Many people think they can get on the gravy train by winning the lottery.
很多人以為他們可以靠著贏得樂透來過奢華的生活。

on the hot seat 〉 眾人批評的焦點

Kevin said something wrong in front of the ladies. He is on the hot seat now.
凱文在女士們面前說錯話了，他現在是眾人批評的焦點。

on the edge of one's seat 〉 跟隨表演情緒起伏

The play was so good. We sat on the edge of our seats of the whole play.
那齣戲劇真好看。我們的情緒跟隨著整齣戲的劇情而起伏。

in the driver's seat 〉 掌控主導某事

Tina can't wait to get into the driver's seat to do what she can turn things around.
蒂娜等不急掌控主導她可以扭轉乾坤的事。

in the catbird seat 〉 在主導控制的位子

I have all the power in deciding things. I am in the catbird seat.
我有決定的權力。我在主導控制的位子。

a train of thought 〉 一連串的思維

Don't interrupt my train of thought. I need to think this through with full concentration.
不要打斷我的思緒。我需要全神貫注的思考這件事。

depart for ...(place) 〉 前往……（地點）

When do we depart for New York?
我們何時前往紐約？

set in train 〉 開始某事

His protest in front of the presidential hall set in train the event which finally led to revolution.
他在總統府前的抗議最終導致一場革命。

Go to an Airport 機場

A The seats are pretty big although we are in the economy class section.
雖然我們是在經濟艙，座位還是蠻大的。

B Yup. The flight attendants are pretty and charming. That is why I love taking Taiwan Airline so much.
是呀！空中小姐都很漂亮、迷人。這就是為什麼我這麼喜歡搭乘台灣航空。

A Indeed. Every one of us has a personal TV. We can watch the programs we like without sharing with other people.
的確。每個人都有一台個人電視。我們可以看自己喜歡的電視而不用和別人共用電視。

B We are lucky. We are sitting near the lavatory right next to the emergency exit.
我們很幸運。我們就坐在靠近緊急逃生口的廁所旁邊。

A Yeah. I want a blanket and a pillow. Where are the earphones?
是呀！我想要一個毛毯和一個枕頭。耳機在哪裡呢？

B They are in the seat pocket in front of you.
就在你座位前方的袋子中。

Additional Vocabulary & Phrases | 補充單字 & 片語

- **charming** [a] 迷人的
  Sandy is a charming girl.
  仙蒂是一位迷人的女孩。

- **lucky** [a] 幸運的
  Violet was lucky that she won the lottery.
  薇莉特很幸運贏得彩券。

- **emergency** [a] 緊急的
  This was an emergency case.
  這是一個緊急的案件。

- **pillow** [n] 枕頭
  I need to buy a new pillow.
  我需要買一顆新枕頭。

7天就能用英文
行遍全世界！ ○─○─○─**4**─○─○
Chapter 1
Chapter 2
Chapter 3
Chapter 4
Chapter 5
Chapter 6
Chapter 7
Chapter 8
Chapter 9
Chapter 10

Daily Sentences 超高頻率使用句｜一分鐘學一句不怕不夠用 06-08

- Excuse me ma'am. I would like my luggage checked all the way to Japan. I will need to transfer at L.A. I don't want to claim my luggage and check in again. That is a tiring job.
  小姐，不好意思，我想把行李直接運送到日本。我必須在洛杉磯轉機，我不想把行李拿出又入關一次，那是一件很累人的事。

- Here are your **luggage claim tags**★1.
  這是你行李的條碼。

- Here is your boarding pass. Your flight is at Gate 12. Please arrive at the gate 30 minutes before take off.
  這是你的登機證。你的飛機在 12 號登機口。請於飛機起飛前三十分鐘到達登機門。

- We would like to look for the information desk and ask if there is a currency exchange desk in the airport.
  我想找詢問台，並詢問在這機場裡有沒有可以兌換貨幣的地方。

- Look at the catalogue for the online duty free shop. The LB bags come in 12 different colors. I definitely want one.
  看一下網路上免稅商店的型錄。LB 的袋子有十二種不同的顏色，我當然要一個。

- We will need to check in 3 hours ahead of the departure time.
  我會在起飛前三小時入關。

- Excuse me. I would like to get my tax refund at the airport. Where is the refund counter?
  不好意思，我想在機場退稅。退稅櫃檯在哪裡？

- Where can I find the carts at the airport? I need one to carry all my luggage.
  我可以在機場哪裡找到推車？我需要一台來推我的行李。

★ 換個單字說說看｜用單字累積句子的豐富度，讓句子更漂亮！

luggage claim tags★1 可以替換：

boarding pass 登機證	**passport** 護照	Here are your _____. 這是你的_____。

Additional Vocabulary & Phrases｜補充單字 & 片語

- **claim** v 要求、索取
  Where can I claim my baggage?
  我能到哪裡拿我的行李呢？

- **take off** ph 起飛
  The plane will be taken off in 30 minutes.
  飛機將在 30 分鐘後起飛。

- **refund** v n 退還、退款
  I need to get my refund.
  我需要拿到我的退款。

- **cart** n 推車
  Where are the carts?
  推車在哪呢？

① terminal 機場航廈

domestic terminal [ph]	國內航廈
departure lobby [ph]	出境大廳
information desk [ph]	詢問櫃檯
shuttle bus [ph]	機場巴士
currency exchange [ph]	外幣兌換處
insurance counter [ph]	保險櫃檯

② check-in counter 登機報到櫃檯

passenger [ˋpæsn̩dʒɚ] [n]	旅客
customer service [ph]	航空櫃檯人員
ground staff [ph]	地勤人員
airline service counter [ph]	航空公司服務櫃檯
luggage tag [ph]	行李吊牌
luggage scale [ph]	行李磅秤

③ baggage 行李

baggage claim [ph]	提領行李	**skycap** [ˋskaɪˌkæp] [n]	機場行李搬運員
baggage delivery [ph]	行李托運	**luggage carousel** [ph]	行李輸送台
carry-on bag [ph]	隨身行李		
luggage cart [ph]	行李推車		

④ customs 海關

x-ray machine ph ⋯⋯⋯ x 光檢測機	**security check** ph ⋯⋯⋯ 安全檢查
passport [`pæs,port] n ⋯⋯⋯ 護照	**immigration** [,ɪmə`greʃən] n ⋯ 出入境
metal detector ph ⋯⋯⋯ 金屬探測器	**duty-free shop** ph ⋯⋯⋯ 免稅商店

⑤ boarding 登機

boarding gate ph ⋯⋯⋯ 登機門
boarding pass ph ⋯⋯⋯ 登機證
delay [dɪ`le] n ⋯⋯⋯ 誤點
on time ph ⋯⋯⋯ 準時
departure n ⋯⋯⋯ 出境
greeting area ph ⋯⋯⋯ 到站等候區

⑥ airplane 飛機

runway [`rʌn,we] n ⋯⋯⋯ 跑道
control tower ph ⋯⋯⋯ 塔台
air bridge ph ⋯⋯⋯ 空橋
apron [`eprən] n ⋯⋯⋯ 停機坪
remote parking bay ph ⋯⋯ 接駁機坪

7 **cabin crew** 空服員

flight attendant ph	空服員
captain [`kæptɪn] n	機長
copilot [`ko‚paɪlət] n	副機長
first class ph	頭等艙
business class ph	商務艙
economy class ph	經濟艙

8 **in-flight meal** 飛機餐

tray [tre] n	機上餐桌	**window seat** ph	靠窗的座位
trolley [`tralɪ] n	餐車	**aisle seat** ph	靠走道的座位
call button ph	服務鈴	**overhead compartment** ph	
in-flight sale ph	機上免稅品販賣		艙頂置物櫃
window blinds ph	遮陽板	**lavatory** [`lævə‚torɪ] n	盥洗室
seat belt ph	安全帶	**emergency exit** ph	緊急出口

Daily Q&A

〔會話一〕

Q► Do you know where I can claim the luggage?
你知道在哪裡取回我們的行李嗎？

A► It's on the second floor.
在二樓。

〔會話二〕

Q► I would like to find the VIP Lounge
我想知道貴賓室在哪裡。

A► Just follow the red sign. You can find it.
只要跟著紅標走，你就會找到那個地方。

〔會話三〕

Q► Where is the duty free shop?
免稅商店在哪裡？

A► It's at Terminal 2.
在第二航廈。

Proverbs & Idioms **道地諺語與慣用語** | 讓句子更錦上添花

a flight of fantasy 〉 虛華不實的夢想

Do you mean you want to go cycling across the U.S.A.? Well, I think that is another flight of fantasy.

你是說你想騎腳踏車橫越美國？嗯，我想那是一個虛華不實的夢想。

in flight 〉 飛機航程中

A passenger had a heart attack in flight. The plane had to have an emergency landing in Mongolia.

有一個乘客在飛機上心臟病病發，飛機必須緊急迫降蒙古。

in full flight 〉 快速逃跑

The bank robber was in full flight before the bank manager called the police.

銀行的搶匪在銀行經理叫警察之前快速逃跑。

the top flight 〉 排名第一

Yankee is always the top flight among all the baseball teams in every season.

洋基隊一直以來在每一季所有棒球隊中排名第一。

depart from one place 〉 從（某處）離開

We will depart from Taipei on time. In a few hours, we will arrive in L.A.

我們將從台北準時離開。幾小時之後我們就會到達洛杉磯。

It's better to travel hopefully than to arrive. 〉 享受事情的過程

You should concentrate on enjoying your school life instead of getting a diploma or a degree. It's better to travel hopefully than to arrive.

你應該專注於享受你的學校生活，而不是獲得證書或文憑。要享受事情的過程。

on schedule 〉 按照行程計畫表走

The trains run pretty much on schedule except for the bad weather condition.

這些火車大多數按照行程計畫表行駛，除非天氣不佳。

behind schedule 〉 行程計畫延遲

The project is behind schedule because some workers are sick and have to take some days off.

這項計畫行程延遲，因為一些工人生病必須放幾天假。

- The customs need some time to examine every passenger in order to secure the flight safety.

  海關人員需要時間檢查每位乘客以確保飛行安全。

- You can find the duty-free shop next to the luggage claim section. But, I think you need some coins.

  你可以在行李取回處的旁邊找到免稅店。不過，我想你需要一些零錢。

- We would like to welcome you to take Taiwan Airline. Before the airplane takes off, please pay attention to a video clip about the flight security.

  歡迎搭乘台灣航空，在飛機起飛前，請注意看一段飛機安全事項的影片。

- Oh, we need to fasten our seat belt, turn off the mobile phone, put up your tray and put the seat in the upright position.

  喔，我們要繫緊安全帶，關掉手機，把餐盤收上，並把椅背拉直。

- I am almost ready to take a good rest on the plane.

  我幾乎已經完全準備好在飛機上好好休息了。

- The airplane is taking off in 5 minutes! We can do whatever we like after taking off.

  飛機再五分鐘就起飛了！我們可以在起飛後做任何想做的事。

- I think you need to prepare your passport when you shop at the duty-free shop.

  你在免稅店購物應該會需要你的護照。

- Where is the boarding gate?

  登機門在哪？

- What time does the plane take off?

  飛機幾點起飛？

- Our destination is Thailand.

  我們的目的地是泰國。

MEMO

174

From AM-PM 從早到晚都用得到的必備好用句

- I'll grab a bite to eat on the way to work.
  我會拿一點在上班路上吃。

- We're out of coffee. How about some milk instead?
  我們沒咖啡了，改喝牛奶好嗎？

- Wake up, sleepy head!
  起床了，貪睡蟲！

- Oh no! I overslept!
  喔不！我睡過頭了！

- I can't decide what to wear today.
  我無法決定今天要穿什麼。

- I had a weird dream last night.
  我昨晚做了個奇怪的夢。

- Let me wash my face first.
  讓我先洗臉。

- Drinking a glass of warm milk might help you sleep.
  喝一杯溫牛奶也許對你的睡眠有幫助。

- I might watch TV since I can't sleep.
  既然我睡不著，我不如看一下電視吧。

- Could you talk to me on the phone until I fall asleep?
  你能跟我講電話講到我睡著為止嗎？

- You look like you need some sleep.
  你看起來需要好好睡一下。

MEMO

- Why are you still awake?
  你怎麼還醒著？

- It's late! Go to bed!
  很晚了！去睡覺！

- Could you turn off the lights, please?
  請把燈關掉，好嗎？

- I need to take my contact lenses off before I go to sleep.
  我睡覺前得先拔掉隱形眼鏡。

- I want to finish reading my book before bedtime.
  我想在睡前把書看完。

- Could you please turn down the radio so I can study?
  能請你把收音機聲音關小，我才能唸書嗎？

- I like to play with my toys.
  我想玩我的玩具。

- Have you ever tried grilled squid?
  你吃過烤魷魚嗎？

- This night market is famous for snake soup.
  這夜市以蛇湯聞名。

- We can have some shaved ice here.
  我們可以在這裡吃刨冰。

- There are many night markets around Taipei city.
  台北市附近有很多夜市。

MEMO

_____

_____

_____

_____

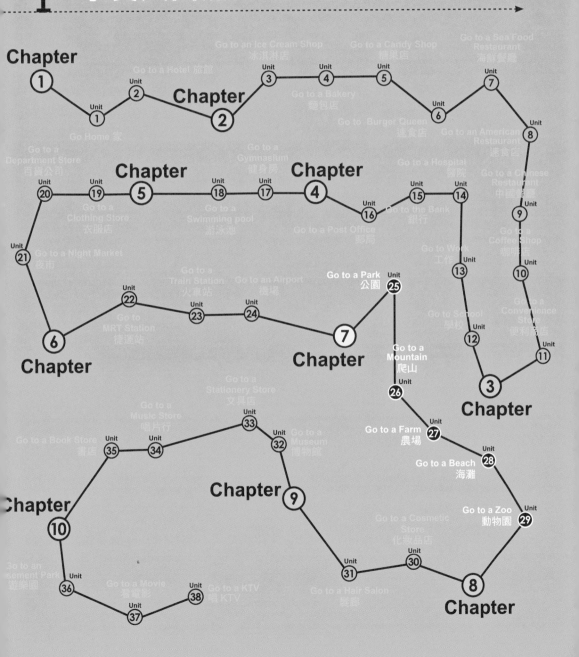

Go to a Park 公園

07-01

A It's a beautiful day! Let's play on those rides in the park.
天氣真好！我們去公園玩那些遊樂設施。

B Sounds like a good idea. I love to play on the jungle gym.
聽起來不錯。我超愛玩攀登架。

A Me too. I love to play on the swing as well. The swing is my favorite.
我也是。我還想想玩盪鞦韆。盪鞦韆是我的最愛。

B That's great. Then we won't fight about taking the same ride.
那太好了。那麼我們就不會搶同一個遊樂設施玩了。

A Look at the flowers over there. What are they?
看看那邊那些花。那些是什麼花呢？

B They are morning glories. They are cute, aren't they?
他們是牽牛花。他們很可愛，不是嗎？

A They are. We can find many kinds of flowers and insects in the park.
是啊！我們可以在公園裡找到不同種類的花和昆蟲。

Additional Vocabulary & Phrases | 補充單字 & 片語

- **jungle** n 叢林
  There are many animals in the jungle.
  在叢林裡有很多動物。

- **as well** ph 也
  I am going home and my sister is going as well.
  我要回家，我妹妹也是。

- **fight** v 打架、爭吵
  My girlfriend and I have never fought.
  我女友和我從未吵過架。

- **glory** n 燦爛、光榮
  Taipei 101 is the glory of our country.
  台北 101 是我們國家的光榮。

7天就能用英文
行遍全世界！ ─◯─◯─◯──❺─◯─◯

Chapter 1

2

3

4

Chapter 5

Chapter 6

Chapter 7

8

9

Chapter 10

Daily Sentences 超高頻率使用句│一分鐘學一句不怕不夠用
07-02

- There are so many **flies and mosquitoes**[*1] in the park.
  公園裡有很多蒼蠅和蚊子。

- You can apply some mosquito spray before you go there.
  你可以在去那兒之前抹一些防蚊液。

- What is the name of the insect?
  這昆蟲叫什麼名字？

- Didn't you see the sign? It says "Keep off the grass".
  你有看到這個標語嗎？上面寫著「請勿踐踏草坪」。

- Where is the restroom?
  廁所在哪裡？

- I am tired. Let's sit on the bench by the pond.
  我很累了。我們在池塘邊找一張板凳坐下來。

- I am hungry. Can we find something to eat?
  我好餓。我們可以找些東西吃嗎？

- Can we walk the dog in the park?
  我們可以在公園蹓狗嗎？

- This insect is a **beetle**[*2].
  這種昆蟲是金龜子。

★ 換個單字說說看│用單字累積句子的豐富度，讓句子更漂亮！

flies and mosquitoes[*1] 可以替換：

bees 蜜蜂	butterflies 蝴蝶	dragonflies 蜻蜓

There are so many_____ in the park.
公園裡有很多_____。

beetle[*2] 可以替換：

locust 蝗蟲	bumblebee 大黃蜂	silkworm 蠶寶寶

This insect is_____.
這種昆蟲是_____。

Additional Vocabulary & Phrases │補充單字 & 片語

- **apply** [v] 申請
  I want to apply for the graduate school in America.
  我想要申請美國的研究所。

- **mosquito** [n] 蚊子
  There's a mosquito on your arm!
  你的手臂上有一隻蚊子！

- **spray** [v] 噴、灑
  You can spray some water on the plant.
  你可以在植物上噴些水。

- **keep off** [ph] 遠離
  Please keep off that topic.
  請避開那個主題。

① botanical garden 植物園

fern [fɜn] n ·····················蕨類
morning glory ph ·············牽牛花
clover [ˋklovɚ] n ··············酢漿草
dandelion [ˋdændɪˏlaɪən] n ·····蒲公英
alfalfa [ælˏfælfə] n ···········紫花苜蓿

② grass 草

lawn [lɔn] n ·····················草坪
oak [ok] n ·······················橡樹
maple tree ph ··················楓樹
bamboo [bæmˋbu] n ···········竹子
banyan [ˋbænjən] n ············榕樹
bush [buʃ] n ····················灌木

③ pavilion 公園中的亭子

petunia [pəˋtjunjə] n ·········矮牽牛
shade [ʃed] n ··················樹蔭處
observatory [əbˋzɝvəˏtorɪ] n ···瞭望台

wooden [ˋwudn] a ·············木製的
tile [taɪl] n ·····················磁磚

④ pond 池塘

lake [lek] n		湖
wood [wʊd] n		樹林
swan [swɑn] n		天鵝
mandarin ducks ph		鴛鴦

mallard duck ph		綠頭鴨
feed [fid] v		餵食
pigeon [ˋpɪdʒɪn] n		鴿子

⑤ bench 長椅

path [pæθ] n		小徑
trash can ph		垃圾桶
fallen leaf ph		落葉
streetlamp [ˋstrit͵læmp] n		路燈
fence [fɛns] n		柵欄

⑥ insect 昆蟲

bee [bi] n		蜜蜂
beetle [ˋbitl] n		金龜子
ant [ænt] n		螞蟻
ladybug [ˋledɪ͵bʌg] n		瓢蟲
mosquito [məsˋkito] n		蚊子
fly [flaɪ] n		蒼蠅

⑦ walk the dog 遛狗

leash [liʃ] n ····· （拴狗的）皮帶、鍊繩
Labrador Retriever ph ····· 拉不拉多
husky [ˋhʌskɪ] n ····· 哈士奇
Golden Retriever ph ····· 黃金獵犬
shiba inu ph ····· 柴犬
chihuahua n ····· 吉娃娃

⑧ playground 遊樂場

ride [raɪd] n ····· 遊樂器材
slide [slaɪd] n ····· 滑梯
swing [swɪŋ] n ····· 鞦韆
seesaw [ˋsiˌsɔ] n ····· 翹翹板
bars [bɑrz] n ····· 單槓

jungle gym ph ····· 攀爬架
sports equipment ph ····· 運動器材
toddler [ˋtɑdlɚ] n ····· 剛學步的小孩
cycling [ˋsaɪklɪŋ] n ····· 自行車運動
roller-blades ph ····· 直排輪溜冰鞋

Daily Q&A

〔會話一〕

Q▶ Let's go to the park, shall we?
我們去公園好不好？

A▶ That sounds a good idea.
聽起來不錯。

〔會話二〕

Q▶ What do you like to play on in the park?
你要在公園玩什麼？

A▶ I like to play on the seesaw. It's fun.
我想玩翹翹板，很好玩耶。

〔會話三〕

Q▶ What is the name of the flower?
這朵花叫什麼名字？

A▶ It's morning glory.
這是牽牛花。

Proverbs & Idioms **道地諺語與慣用語｜讓句子更錦上添花**

a big frog in a small pond ＞ 大才小用

Tom is a big frog in a small pond. You need to force him to do something more challenging.

湯姆真的是大才小用。你要強迫他做一些有挑戰性的事情。

squirrel something away ＞ 偷藏東西

My father sometimes squirrels some money away before he gives his salary to my mom.

我爸爸有時會在將薪水交給我媽媽之前偷藏私房錢。

a stool pigeon ＞ 線民

The policeman got a stool pigeon. That is why he can always get the first-hand news.

那位警察有個線民。這就是為什麼他總有第一手消息的原因。

be somebody's pigeon ＞ 負責人

Accounting is not my pigeon. You should find Jack.

會計不是我負責的。你要找傑克。

put the cat among the pigeons ＞ 鬧得雞飛狗跳

If you tell them this shocking news, I believe that will put the cat among the pigeons.

如果你告訴他們這則驚人的新聞，我相信那將會鬧得雞飛狗跳。

a walk in the park ＞ 輕鬆有趣的事

Finishing that job is really like a walk in the park. There shouldn't be any problem to him.

完成那項工作是件輕鬆愉快的工作。這對他而言應該沒有問題。

a ballpark figure ＞ 幾近確切的數目

We don't know the actual cost, but a ballpark figure would be about five thousand dollars.

我不知道實際的數目，但是幾近確切的數目應是 5,000 元。

Go to a Mountain 爬山

MP3
07-04

A It's wonderful to be in the mountains after a hustle bustle week.
在忙碌的一週過後跑到山裡面是件美好的事。

B Indeed. I love the smell of the grass and trees. They certainly refresh my mind.
沒錯。我愛極了草和樹的味道。它們無庸置疑的洗淨了我的心靈。

A Can we stop here for a while? My backpack is very heavy.
我們可以在這裡停一下嗎？我的背包很重。

B Sure. Did you hear anything? Look! An eagle is hovering in the sky.
當然。你有聽到聲音嗎？看！有一隻老鷹在天空中盤旋。

A Let me see. It's not an eagle. I think it's a vulture.
讓我瞧瞧。那不是老鷹。我想那是一隻禿鷹。

B Yes. Will it hurt us?
對耶，牠會傷害我們嗎？

A I don't think so. Let's walk by the stream. I am sure we can find the waterfall on the map.
我不這麼認為。我們沿著小溪走。我確定我們一定可以找到地圖上的瀑布。

Additional Vocabulary & Phrases | 補充單字 & 片語

● **refresh** v 消除…疲勞、重新提起精神
This energy drink will help you refresh.
這個能量飲料能幫助你重新提起精神。

● **hover** v 盤旋
The eagle was hovering above us.
老鷹在我們上空盤旋。

● **vulture** n 禿鷹
I have never seen a vulture.
我從未見過禿鷹。

● **waterfall** n 瀑布
There's a small waterfall over there.
那邊有一個小瀑布。

Daily Sentences 超高頻率使用句 | 一分鐘學一句不怕不夠用 07-05

- Where can I find the lake?
  我可以在哪裡找到湖？

- You can walk along this path. It goes to a big lake in the mountains.
  你可以沿著這條小路走，這條路會通往一個山裡的大湖。

- What is the name of this tree?
  這棵樹叫什麼名字？

- This is a **Maple tree** ★ 1.
  這是楓樹。

- This road is very steep.
  這條路很陡。

- I think we need a cane.
  我想我們需要一根拐杖。

- There is a cable car to go from one peak to the other. We can take it if we do not want to climb mountains.
  有纜車可從一座山峰通到另一座山峰。如果不想爬山的話，我們可以搭乘。

- Listen! It is a **humming bird** ★ 2. I can barely see its wings.
  你聽！那是隻蜂鳥，我幾乎看不到牠的翅膀。

- It's tiring to climb high mountains.
  爬高山很累人的。

★ 換個單字說說看 | 用單字累積句子的豐富度，讓句子更漂亮！

Maple tree★1 可以替換：

| pine tree 松樹 | birch tree 樺樹 | oak tree 橡樹 |

This is a / an _____.
它是_____樹。

humming bird★2 可以替換：

| eagle 老鷹 | swallow 燕子 | dove 鴿子 |

Listen! It is a_____.
你聽！那是隻_____。

Additional Vocabulary & Phrases | 補充單字 & 片語

- **steep** a 陡峭的
  This is a steep hill.
  這是一個陡峭的山丘。

- **cane** n 拐杖
  She needed a cane.
  她需要一個拐杖。

- **cable** n 電纜、鋼索
  They are fixing the cable.
  他們在修理電纜。

- **climb** v 爬
  Please don't climb up on the table.
  請勿爬到桌子上。

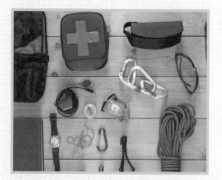

❶ backpack 登山、遠足用的背包

bottle [`bɑtl̩] n̄ ……………………… 大水罐、水壺

provisions [prə`vɪʒənz] n̄ …… 預備的口糧

mountaineering boots ph ……… 登山鞋

cane [ken] n̄ ……………………………… 手杖

compass [`kʌmpəs] n̄ …………… 指南針

first-aid kit ph ……………………… 急救包

❷ mountain 山（脈）

hill [hɪl] n̄ ……………………………………… 丘陵

mountainside [`maʊntən‚saɪd] n̄ …… 山坡、山腰

grassland [`græs‚lænd] n̄ …… 草原，牧草地

forest [`fɔrɪst] n̄ ………………………… 森林

path [pæθ] n̄ …………………………………… 小徑

stream [strim] n̄ …………………………… 小溪

lake [lek] n̄ …………………………………………… 湖

valley [`vælɪ] n̄ ……………………………… 山谷

waterfall [`wɔtɚ‚fɔl] n̄ …………… 瀑布

❸ mountain climbing 登山

map [mæp] n̄ ……………… 地圖

guide [gaɪd] n̄ …………… 嚮導

peak [pik] n̄ ………………… 山頂

cable car ph ……………… 纜車

hiking [haɪkɪŋ] n̄ ……… 爬山、健行

❹ forest 森林

pine [paɪn] n	松樹	**cypress** [ˈsaɪprɪs] n ⋯⋯ 檜樹
cedar [ˈsidɚ] n	杉木	**oak** [ok] n ⋯⋯ 橡樹
birch [bɝtʃ] n	樺樹	**willow** [ˈwɪlo] n ⋯⋯ 柳樹

❺ bird 鳥，禽

woodpecker [ˈwʊdˌpɛkɚ] n ⋯ 啄木鳥
hummingbird [ˈhʌmɪŋˌbɝd] n ⋯ 蜂鳥
swallow [ˈswɑlo] n ⋯⋯⋯⋯ 燕子
vulture [ˈvʌltʃɚ] n ⋯⋯⋯⋯ 禿鷹
eagle [ˈigl̩] n ⋯⋯⋯⋯⋯⋯ 鷹

❻ wild animals 野生動物

squirrel [ˈskwɝəl] n ⋯⋯⋯⋯ 松鼠
black bear ph ⋯⋯⋯⋯⋯⋯ 黑熊
brown bear ph ⋯⋯⋯⋯⋯⋯ 棕熊
raccoon [ræˈkun] n ⋯⋯⋯⋯ 浣熊
andean mountain cat ph ⋯ 山原貓
chital [ˈtʃitəl] n ⋯⋯⋯⋯⋯⋯ 斑鹿

7 sunset 日落

sunrise [ˋsʌnˌraɪz] n ·········· 日出
haze [hez] n ·········· 薄霧
mist [mɪst] n ·········· 山嵐
fog [fɑg] n ·········· 霧
sea of clouds ph ·········· 雲海

8 monkey 猴子

ape [ep] n ·········· 大猩猩
mandrill [ˋmændrɪl] n ·········· 山魈
gelada [dʒəˋladə] n ··· 衣索匹亞大狒狒
orangutan [oˋræŋuˌtæn] n ······· 黑猩猩
Formosan rock-monkey ph 台灣獼猴

Daily Q&A

〔會話一〕

Q▸ I am lost. I can't find my way home.
我迷路了，我找不到回家的路。

A▸ What you need is a compass. It can show you way home.
你所需要的是一個指南針，它可以指出你回家的路。

〔會話二〕

Q▸ Ouch! I cut myself. It hurts.
噢！我割到自己了，好痛喔！

A▸ Let me check my first-aid kit. I can put a band aid on it.
讓我看看我的急救箱，我可以在傷口上貼一個 OK 繃。

〔會話三〕

Q▸ Do you know how old this tree is?
你知道這棵樹幾歲嗎？

A▸ You can tell by its annual rings. One annual ring means one year.
你可以從它的年輪得知。一個年輪代表一歲。

Proverbs & Idioms 道地諺語與慣用語｜讓句子更錦上添花

faith will move mountains 精誠所至，金石為開

Don't feel discouraged. Try again. Your faith will move the mountains.
不要覺得氣餒，再試一次。你將會精誠所至，金石為開。

If a mountain will not come to Mahomet, Mahomet must go to the mountain.
山不轉自轉

You have a fight with your girlfriend? If your girlfriend doesn't call you, you need to call her first. If a mountain will not come to Mahomet, Mahomet must go to the mountain.
你和女朋友吵架啦？如果你女朋友不打電話給你，你就要先打給她。你要山不轉自轉。

make a mountain out of molehill 小題大作

It's not a big deal. Don't make a mountain out of molehill.
那沒什麼，別小題大作。

a mountain to climb 很難的事

Classifying the mountain-high garbage is a mountain to climb.
把像一座山那麼高的垃圾分類是很難的事。

Money does not grow on the tree. 賺錢不容易

"Mom, can I have a computer?" "We can't afford that, you know. Money does not grow on the tree."
「媽，我可以買電腦嗎？」「你知道的，我們負擔不起。賺錢不容易。」

the top of the tree 爬到頂端成功

Nobody would have guessed that Catherine could get to the top of the tree before her talented brother.
沒有人想到凱瑟琳可以在她聰明的弟弟之前成功爬到頂端。

move mountains 有愚公移山的意志達成艱難的任務

He loves her very much. He would move mountains for her.
他深愛著她。為了她，什麼難事他都願意做。

Go to a Farm 農場

07-07

A Wow! This farm is huge and you can do many activities here.
哇，這個農場真的很大，你可以在這裡做很多活動。

B That is true. Some people go camping; some people picking some fresh fruit; some people go boating and some people go grass skiing.
是真的啊。有些人露營，有些人摘新鮮的水果，有些人划船，還有些人滑草。

A I never knew there were so many fun things to do on a farm.
我從來不知道農場上有這麼多好玩的事。

B Well, Let's go to the lake over there. Some people are fishing over there. I haven't had a chance to fish in a lake. I really want to try.
我們去那邊的湖吧，有些人在那邊釣魚。我從來沒有機會在湖裡釣魚，我真的很想試試。

A I think we need to buy some bait and borrow some fishing poles first.
我想我們需要先買一些餌，然後借一些釣竿。

B Yes, we can get what we need at the stands right by the lake. Who do you think will catch a big fish first?
對啊，我們可以在湖邊的那些小攤子上買到那些東西。你覺得誰會先釣到魚？

A Of course, I will.
當然是我啊。

Additional Vocabulary & Phrases | 補充單字 & 片語

- **activity** [n] 活動
  What's your favorite activity?
  你最喜歡的活動是什麼？

- **catch** [v] 捉
  What did the cat catch?
  貓捉到了什麼？

Daily Sentences | 超高頻率使用句 | 一分鐘學一句不怕不夠用
07-08

- Where can I pick some **apples**[1]?
  我可以在哪裡摘蘋果呢？

- All the cows and sheep are kept in the pasture, so we can watch them just right by the fence.
  所有的牛跟羊都被關在籬笆裡，所以我們可以在籬笆旁邊觀賞牠們。

- Is there anything I need to be aware of when I go horseback riding?
  有哪些是我騎馬時需要注意的事嗎？

- You should sit up straight and push your two thighs hard into the horse abdomen when riding a horse.
  騎馬的時候，你應該要坐直，把你的大腿夾緊馬腹。

- Can we go boating in the lake?
  我們可以在湖上划船嗎？

- There are many animal shows in the center of the farm. You can get the show schedule at the booth next to the farm and arrive there 10 minutes before the show starts.
  在農場中間有許多動物的表演，你可以在農場旁取得表演時刻表，然後在每一場表演的前十分鐘到達就可以了。

- We plan to go to the farm for vacation.
  我們計畫到農場渡假。

- We will have some recreation on the farm to enjoy our leisure time.
  我們會在農場做一些娛樂活動來享受我們的休閒時光。

★ **換個單字說說看** | 用單字累積句子的豐富度，讓句子更漂亮！

apples[1] 可以替換：

strawberries 草莓	blueberries 藍莓	blackberries 黑莓	Where can I pick _____? 我們可以在哪裡摘_____呢？

Additional Vocabulary & Phrases | 補充單字 & 片語

- **aware** [a] 注意到、察覺到
  I wasn't aware that she's crying.
  我沒有察覺到她在哭。

- **booth** [n] 小雅座
  We are going to meet at the booth in the restaurant.
  我們會在餐廳的小雅座見面。

- **recreation** [n] 消遣、娛樂
  I like to do some recreation on the weekends.
  我喜歡在周末做些娛樂活動。

- **leisure** [a] 閒暇的
  What do you like to do in your leisure time?
  你在閒暇的時候喜歡做些什麼？

1 countryside 農村

ecology [ɪ`kalədʒɪ] n	·········	生態
scenic spot ph	·········	景點
farmer [`farmɚ] n	·········	農夫
farm [farm] n	·········	農場
field [fild] n	·········	田野
farmhouse [ˌfarmˌhaʊs] n	·········	農舍

2 domestic animals 家畜

sheep [ʃip] n	·····	綿羊	**cattle** [`kætl̩] n	·····	牛
lamb [læm] n	·····	小羊	**horse** [hɔrs] n	·····	馬
cow [kaʊ] n	·····	母牛			

3 turkey 火雞

chicken [`tʃɪkɪn] n	·········	雞
goose [gus] n	·········	鵝
duck [dʌk] n	·········	鴨
pigeon [`pɪdʒɪn] n	·········	鴿子
rooster [`rustɚ] n	·········	公雞
hen [hɛn] n	·········	母雞

4 crops 農作物

wheat [hwit] n	小麥	**buckwheat** [ˋbʌkˌhwit] n 蕎麥
barley [ˋbɑrlɪ] n	大麥	**grain** [gren] n 穀物
maize [mez] n	玉米	**sorghum** [ˋsɔrgəm] n 高粱
rice [raɪs] n	水稻	**millet** [ˋmɪlɪt] n 穀子

5 vegetable 蔬菜

tomato [təˋmeto] n	番茄
potato [pəˋteto] n	馬鈴薯
cabbage [ˋkæbɪdʒ] n	甘藍菜
carrot [ˋkærət] n	紅蘿蔔
yam [jæm] n	番薯
pea [pi] n	碗豆
pumpkin [ˋpʌmpkɪn] n	南瓜

6 fruit 水果

strawberry [ˋstrɔbɛrɪ] n	草莓
cherry [ˋtʃɛrɪ] n	櫻桃
grape [grep] n	葡萄
raspberry [ˋræzˌbɛrɪ] n	覆盆子
apple [ˋæpl̩] n	蘋果

7 **flower 花卉**

sunflower [ˋsʌn͵flauɚ] n ⋯⋯⋯ 太陽花

rose [roz] n ⋯⋯⋯⋯⋯⋯⋯⋯⋯ 薔薇

magnolia [mægˋnolɪə] n ⋯⋯ 木蘭花

coneflower [ˋkon͵flauɚ] n ⋯⋯ 雛菊

tulip [ˋtjuləp] n ⋯⋯⋯⋯⋯⋯⋯ 鬱金香

lily [ˋlɪlɪ] n ⋯⋯⋯⋯⋯⋯⋯⋯⋯ 百合花

butterfly [ˋbʌtɚ͵flaɪ] n ⋯⋯⋯ 蝴蝶

8 **advance 發展**

leisure [ˋliʒɚ] n ⋯⋯⋯⋯⋯ 悠閒

vacation [veˋkeʃən] n ⋯⋯⋯ 假期

recreation [͵rɛkrɪˋeʃən] n ⋯⋯ 娛樂

observe [əbˋzɝv] v ⋯⋯⋯⋯ 觀察

develop [dɪˋvɛləp] v ⋯⋯⋯ 培養

experience [ɪkˋspɪrɪəns] v ⋯⋯ 體驗

camp [kæmp] n ⋯⋯⋯⋯⋯⋯ 露營

grass skiing ph ⋯⋯⋯⋯⋯ 滑草

horseback riding ph ⋯⋯⋯ 騎馬

archery [ˋɑrtʃərɪ] n ⋯⋯⋯⋯ 射箭

fruit picking ph ⋯⋯⋯⋯⋯ 水果採收

go fishing ph ⋯⋯⋯⋯⋯⋯ 釣魚

go boating ph ⋯⋯⋯⋯⋯⋯ 划船

Daily Q&A

〔會話一〕

Q▸ Can we buy some grass to feed the animals on the farm?
我可以買一些草餵農場裡的動物嗎？

A▸ Sure.
當然

〔會話二〕

Q▸ What animals can I see on the farm?
我在農場上可以看到哪些動物？

A▸ You can see lambs, cows and horses.
你可以看到綿羊、牛和馬。

〔會話三〕

Q▸ What activities can I do on the farm?
我可以在農場上做哪些活動？

A▸ You can go fishing, grass skiing, camping, boating and horseback riding.
你可以釣魚、滑草、露營、划船和騎馬。

Proverbs & Idioms **道地諺語與慣用語**｜讓句子更錦上添花

farm someone out　把某人派去為他人工作

I have farmed my secretary out for a week, so I have to arrange all my appointments now.

我把我的祕書外派一週，所以我現在必須自己安排所有的行程。

farm something out　把某事發包給他人

We farm the packaging work out.

我們把包裝發包給別人。

a funny farm　精神病醫院（有冒犯的意思）

If things become worse, they will send me to a funny farm because they think my idea is really too crazy.

如果事情變得愈來愈糟了，他們將會把我送到精神病院，因為他們覺得我的點子實在是太瘋狂了。

bet the farm　把所有的財產賣出來做其他的投資

It is not a wise idea to bet the farm on one investment.

把所有的財產集中在一項投資上，實在不是個聰明的點子。

factory farming　大量快速的農產製造

Due to the modern technology, a lot of food is produced by factory farming.

因為現代科技，很多食物在工廠裡被大量製造。

don't put all your eggs in one basket　不要集中風險（要分散風險）

It's not good to put all your eggs in one basket. You need to cut risks, or you may lose everything.

把所有的雞蛋放置在同一個籃子中並不好。你需要減低風險否則你可能失去所有的東西。

make hay while the sun shines　要把握良機

When there is a great chance, just go for it. We should make hay while the sun shines. Stop spending time wondering.

當有很棒的機會來臨時，就去追求。我們要把握良機。不要花時間想結果。

pigs can fly　不可能的事

It's impossible for our boss to give us any more paid holidays. If he does, pigs can fly.

我們老闆是不可能給我們更多的有薪假期。他如果會，豬就會飛。

Go to the beach 海邊

MP3
07-10

A I can't wait to play in the water. My feet are burning when I stand on the sand.
我等不及去玩水了。我站在沙上的時候，腳快要燒起來了。

B I want to find a good place to enjoy the sunshine and get a perfect tan.
我想找一個好地方，享受陽光並曬個好膚色。

A Did you bring the floats? I need one. I am not a good swimmer. I feel safer when I have them in the water.
你有帶游泳圈嗎？我需要，我不太會游泳。我帶著它會比較安心。

B Don't worry. They are in the bag. Do you want to ride the jet ski?
不用擔心，它們在袋子裡。你想騎水上摩托車嗎？

A Sounds fun. Where can we rent it? Is it costly?
聽起來很有趣，我們可以在哪裡租到？很貴嗎？

B Not at all.
一點也不貴

Additional Vocabulary & Phrases | 補充單字 & 片語

- **burn** v 發熱、燃燒
  The house is burning.
  那棟房子燒了起來了。

- **tan** n 棕褐色、曬成的棕褐的膚色。
  I want to get some nice tan.
  我想要把我的皮膚曬成漂亮一點的棕褐色。

- **rent** v 出租、租用
  She rent a house in Taipei.
  她在台北租了一間房子。

- **costly** a 貴重的、昂貴的
  It is costly to spend a night at that luxury hotel.
  在那間奢華的飯店住一個晚上是非常昂貴的。

Daily Sentences 超高頻率使用句｜一分鐘學一句不怕不夠用 MP3 07-11

- What do we need when we go to the beach?
  我們去沙灘需要準備什麼嗎？

- I will need sunglasses, sunscreen, an ice box, water, hats, swimsuits, a towel and floats.
  我需要太陽眼鏡、防曬油、小冰箱、水、帽子、游泳衣、毛巾和游泳圈。

- It is safer not to swim in a deep water area.
  在深水區游泳是不安全的。

- Where can we rent a **canoe** ★1？
  我們可以在哪裡租到獨木舟？

- Which one do you prefer, snorkeling or scuba diving?
  浮潛和潛水，你比較喜歡哪一個？

- The sun is scorching hot. Let's get some cold drinks.
  太陽很炙熱，我們去買些冷飲吧。

- Put on your swim suit before swimming.
  游泳前，穿上你的泳裝。

- I will bring a big hat and apply a lot of sunscreen before setting off to the beach.
  我會在出發去海灘前，戴一頂大帽子和塗很多防曬油。

- What a lovely day. The sun is shinning and the sky is so blue. It's a perfect day to go to the beach and get a beautiful tan.
  今天天氣真好。陽光普照，而且天空是如此的藍，是個適合去海灘曬太陽的好日子。

- A sun tan symbolizes health and wealth in western countries.
  在西方國家中，曬太陽後的膚色象徵著健康和財富。

★ **換個單字說說看**｜用單字累積句子的豐富度，讓句子更漂亮！

canoe ★1 可以替換：

boat 小船	**speedboat** 快艇	**sailboat** 帆船	Where can we rent a _____？ 我們可以在哪裡租 _____ ？

Additional Vocabulary & Phrases ｜補充單字 & 片語

- **safe** a 安全的
  You are safe here.
  你在這裡是安全的。

- **scorch** v 把……燒焦、使枯萎
  The rose was scorched by the dreaded sun.
  炎炎烈日曬枯了玫瑰花。

1 beachwear 海灘裝

bathing suit ph	泳裝
sunglasses [`sʌn,glæsɪz] n	墨鏡
bikini [bɪ`kinɪ] n	比基尼泳裝
hat [hæt] n	帽子
flip-flops ph	夾腳拖
diving suit ph	潛水衣

2 beachscape 海灘風光

sand [sænd] n	沙灘
sand castle ph	沙堡
sea [si] n	海洋
bay [be] n	灣
coast [kost] n	沿海地區
billow [`bɪlo] n	巨浪；浪濤
wave [wev] n	波浪

3 shearwater 海鷗

palm tree ph	棕櫚樹
seagull [sigʌl] n	海鳥
beach chair ph	沙灘椅

beach umbrella ph	海灘陽傘
relaxed [rɪ`lækst] a	放鬆的

❹ sailboat 帆船

tanker [`tæŋkɚ] n	⋯⋯⋯	油輪
boat [bot] n	⋯⋯⋯	小船
speedboat [`spid,bot] n	⋯⋯	快艇
canoe [kə`nu] n	⋯⋯⋯	獨木舟
yachting [`jɑtɪŋ] n	⋯⋯	乘遊艇

❺ lifeguard 救生員

security [sɪ`kjurətɪ] n	防禦（措施）；防護
drown [draʊn] v	⋯⋯⋯⋯⋯ 死
life jacket ph	⋯⋯⋯ 救生衣
lifeboat [`laɪf,bot] n	⋯⋯ 救生船
kickboard [kɪkbord] n	⋯⋯ 浮板
lifebuoy [`laɪfbɔɪ] n	⋯救生圈；救生帶

❻ seashell 貝殼

starfish [`stɑr,fɪʃ] n	⋯⋯⋯ 海星
sea dollar ph	⋯⋯⋯ 沙錢
mussel [`mʌsl̩] n	⋯⋯⋯ 蚌
hermit crab ph	⋯⋯⋯ 寄居蟹
auger [`ɔgɚ] n	⋯⋯⋯ 螺旋貝

7 scuba diving 水肺潛水

diver [ˋdaɪvɚ] n	⋯	潛水員
sea turtle ph	⋯	海龜
clown fish ph	⋯	小丑魚
sea anemone ph	⋯	海葵
coral reef ph	⋯	珊瑚礁
snorkeling [ˋsnɔrkl̩] n		

使用水下呼吸管潛游

8 surfing 衝浪

surfboard [ˋsɝf͵bord] n ⋯ 衝浪板　　**beach volleyball** ph ⋯ 沙灘排球

beach ball ph ⋯ 沙灘球　　**sunbathe** [ˋsʌnbeθ] n ⋯ 日光浴

beach buggy ph ⋯ 沙灘車　　**jet ski** ph ⋯ 水上摩托車

Daily Q&A

〔會話一〕

Q▸ How can you get a beautiful tan but not sunburn?
要怎麼做，你才能讓皮膚曬得漂亮又不會曬傷？

A▸ Just apply some sunscreen for tanning purpose.
只要塗抹一些適合曬出漂亮膚色的防曬油就可以了。

〔會話二〕

Q▸ People go surfing when the wave is big enough.
人們都在海浪夠大的時候去衝浪。

A▸ Why?
為什麼？

〔會話三〕

Q▸ Do you want to play beach volley ball?
你想要玩沙灘排球嗎？

A▸ Why not?
好啊。

Proverbs & Idioms 道地諺語與慣用語｜讓句子更錦上添花

not be the only pebble on the beach > 成為次重要的人

Jeremy always expects to be the leader of everything. It is time for him to learn not to be the only pebble on the beach.

傑瑞米總是希望擔任每件事的領導者，是他學著當次重要的人的時候了。

between the devil and the deep blue sea > 兩難的選擇

I couldn't make up my mind. I was between the devil and the deep blue sea.

我沒辦法下定決心，我正面臨一個兩難的選擇。

at sea > 困惑

I can't understand at all. I am completely at sea.

我一點都沒辦法瞭解，我完全困惑了。

sea change > 重大的改變

There are too many on-going major plans this year. It is really not time for a sea change.

今年有太多正在進行的重大計畫，實在不是個做重大改變的時機。

get one's sea legs > 適應新生活

After moving to a new city, Jenny got her sea legs by starting her own business.

在搬去新城市之後，珍妮藉著開始她的事業來適應新生活。

boil the ocean > 使海洋沸滾（不可能的事）

You're wasting my time. You might as well be boiling the ocean.

你在浪費我的時間。你可能在做不可能的事。

the coast is clear > 沒有危險

We had to wait until the coast was clear to get out of the building after the earthquake.

地震過後，我們必須等到沒有危險時在走出這棟大樓。

Go to a zoo 動物園

Daily Conversation 日常對話 | 快速融入超擬真的日常對話

MP3
07-13

A Wow! This zoo is really huge.
哇！動物園真的好大。

B Yes, you can find hundreds of various animals here. It is the biggest zoo in Taiwan.
是啊，你可以在這裡看到數以百計不同種類的動物，這是台灣最大的動物園。

A Look at the map. It has different areas, like the marine life, mammals, the polar animals and the insects.
看一下這張地圖。動物園有好幾區，例如海洋生物區、哺乳動物區、北極動物區和昆蟲區。

B Where can we find the giraffes? I think we are here to see the giraffes.
我們可以在哪裡找到長頸鹿呢？我想我們是要來看長頸鹿的。

A We have to go to the mammal area. We are at the gate right now. We need to go straight from here and turn left and go along to the end and make another left turn.
我們必須到哺乳動物區。我們現在在大門這邊，我們需要從這裡直走、左轉走到底，再左轉。

B It will take at least 20 minutes to get there. Are there any shuttle buses?
聽起來好像要花上至少二十分鐘才能到那裡。動物園裡有接駁車嗎？

A Yes, there is one.
是的，有一台。

Additional Vocabulary & Phrases | 補充單字 & 片語

- **huge** a 特大的
  This hamburger is huge.
  這個漢堡真的很大。

- **mammal** a 哺乳類動物
  Giraffes are mammals.
  長頸鹿是哺乳動物。

Daily Sentences 超高頻率使用句｜一分鐘學一句不怕不夠用
07-14

- Can I use the camera in the zoo?
  我在動物園裡可以使用照相機嗎？

- The flash will scare the animals.
  閃光燈會嚇到動物們。

- When you go on safari, remember not to get out of the car because you may be attacked by the wild tigers or lions.
  當你搭著吉普車觀賞野生動物時，記得不要下車，因為你可能會被老虎或獅子攻擊。

- What do the **pandas** *¹ eat?
  貓熊吃什麼呢？

- We can take the shuttle bus provided by the zoo to go around places in the zoo.
  我們可以搭由動物園提供的接駁車，在動物園中遊覽。

- You are not allowed to stick your hands through the bars. It is very dangerous. Some animals do attack people.
  你不能將手伸入籠子裡，這非常危險，有些動物真的會攻擊人類。

- Do not knock on the glass when you see fish in the tank.
  當你在水族箱看到魚的時候，不要敲打玻璃。

- I would like to see the cute **pandas** *².
  我想去看可愛的貓熊。

★ **換個單字說說看**｜用單字累積句子的豐富度，讓句子更漂亮！

pandas*¹ 可以替換：		
tiger 老虎	**elephant** 大象	**zebra** 斑馬

What do the ＿＿＿＿＿＿＿＿ eat?
＿＿＿＿＿＿＿吃什麼呢？

pandas*² 可以替換：		
bunny 小兔子	**pony** 小馬	**lamb** 小羊

I would like to see the cute ＿＿＿＿＿＿＿＿.
我想去看可愛的＿＿＿＿＿＿＿。

Additional Vocabulary & Phrases｜補充單字 & 片語

- **flash** n 閃光燈
  Can you turn off your flash?
  可以請你關掉閃光燈嗎？

- **provide** v 提供
  They provided some free water.
  他們提供了一些免費的水。

- **allow** v 允許、准許
  I am not allowed to go out at night.
  我不被准許晚上出門。

- **knock** v 敲、擊
  Please knock before you come in.
  進來請先敲門。

語言學校都會教的超實用日常單字
MP3
07-15

1 Asian Animals 亞洲動物

panda [ˋpændə] n ⋯⋯⋯⋯⋯⋯ 熊貓
Malayan Tapir ph ⋯⋯⋯⋯⋯ 馬來貘
Formosan black bear ph ⋯ 台灣黑熊
Bengal Tiger ph ⋯⋯⋯⋯⋯ 孟加拉虎
Asian Elephant ph ⋯⋯⋯⋯ 亞洲象

2 Australian animals 澳洲動物

kangaroo [ˌkæŋgəˋru] n ⋯⋯⋯ 袋鼠
koala [koˋɑlə] n ⋯⋯⋯⋯⋯⋯ 無尾熊
Southern Cassowary ph 南方食火雞
kiwi bird ph ⋯⋯⋯⋯⋯⋯⋯ 奇異鳥
eastern gray kangaroo ph ⋯ 灰袋鼠

3 livestock 家畜

pig [pɪg] n ⋯⋯⋯⋯⋯⋯ 豬
dog [dɔg] n ⋯⋯⋯⋯⋯⋯ 狗
cat [kæt] n ⋯⋯⋯⋯⋯⋯ 貓
rabbit [ˋræbɪt] n ⋯⋯⋯ 兔子

horse [hɔrs] n ⋯⋯⋯⋯⋯ 馬
rooster [ˋrustɚ] n ⋯⋯⋯ 公雞
cattle [ˋkætl̩] n ⋯⋯⋯⋯ 牛

④ marine 海洋的

coral [`kɔrəl] n .... 珊瑚

white whale ph .... 白鯨

dolphin [`dɑlfɪn] n .... 海豚

walrus [`wɔlrəs] n .... 海象

sea turtle ph .... 海龜

manatee [ˌmænə`ti] n .... 海牛

sea lion ph .... 海獅

⑤ flying animals 飛行動物

owl [aʊl] n .... 貓頭鷹

bat [bæt] n .... 蝙蝠

mockingbird [`mɑkɪŋˌbɝd] n ... 仿聲鳥

dove [dʌv] n .... 鴿子

hummingbird [`hʌmɪŋˌbɝd] n ... 蜂鳥

⑥ polar animals 極地動物

penguin [`pɛngwɪn] n .... 企鵝

polar bear ph .... 北極熊

seal [sil] n .... 海豹

fat [fæt] n .... 脂肪

Arctic hare ph .... 北極兔

7 amphibian and reptiles
兩棲爬蟲動物

python [`paɪθɑn] n ················· 蟒蛇

snake [snek] n ······················· 蛇

turtle [`tɝtl̩] n ······················· 烏龜

lizard [`lɪzɚd] n ····················· 蜥蜴

chameleon [kə`miljən] n ········· 變色龍

8 African animals 非洲動物

giraffe [dʒəˋræf] n ··············· 長頸鹿

elephant [`ɛləfənt] n ·············· 大象

zebra [`zibrə] n ····················· 斑馬

leopard [`lɛpɚd] n ·················· 豹

lion [`laɪən] n ······················· 獅子

chimpanzee [ˌtʃɪmpænˋzi] n ··· 黑猩猩

tiger [`taɪgɚ] n ······················ 老虎

gazelle [gəˋzɛl] n ·················· 蹬羚

camel [`kæml̩] n ····················· 駱駝

ostrich [`astrɪtʃ] n ·················· 鴕鳥

bushbuck [`buʃˌbʌk] n ······· 非洲羚羊

rhinoceros [raɪˋnɑsərəs] n ········ 犀牛

hippo [`hɪpo] n ······················ 河馬

Daily Q&A

〔會話一〕

Q▶ **Who takes care of these animals in the zoo?**

在動物園裡，誰照顧這些動物？

A▶ **The zookeepers take good care of them.**

動物管理員會照顧牠們。

〔會話二〕

Q▶ **Where can I get the zoo map?**

我可以在哪裡拿到動物園裡的地圖呢？

A▶ **You can find it under the map signs in the zoo.**

你可以在動物園裡的導覽地圖牌下找到。

〔會話三〕

Q▶ **Which area can I find the tigers?**

我在哪一區可以看到老虎？

A▶ **You can go to the mammal area.**

你可以去哺乳動物區。

Proverbs & Idioms 道地諺語與慣用語｜讓句子更錦上添花

a paper tiger 〉 紙老虎

Will India make any changes? Or is it just a paper tiger?

印度會改變嗎？還是只是個紙老虎？

as sly as a fox 〉 像狐狸一般聰明狡猾

Jack is as sly as a fox. He can think of a great idea in just a second.

傑克像狐狸一樣的聰明狡猾，他可以一下子就想到一個好主意。

a bear hug 〉 像熊一般的熱情擁抱

Her boyfriend gave her an affectionate bear hug which almost took her breath away.

她的男朋友給她一個像熊一樣的熱情擁抱，讓她幾乎無法呼吸。

a dark horse 〉 黑馬

I didn't know Sue had written a book. She is a bit of a dark horse, isn't she?

我不知道蘇已經寫過一本書，她實在是一匹黑馬，不是嗎？

have butterflies in one's stomach 〉 胃裡緊張的感覺

She always has butterflies in her stomach before a test.

考試前，她總是緊張到胃痛。

copycat 〉 學人精

Melisa is such a copycat. First, she bought the same bicycle as me, and now she wants to go to the same school as me.

梅莉莎真是個學人精。首先，她買了一台和我一模一樣的腳踏車，然後，現在她想要和我上一樣的學校。

dog days 〉 狗日子（炎熱的日子）

I often go swimming during the dog days in summer.

我在夏天炎熱的日子裡常常去游泳。

- Let's go see the pandas! The news said that two pandas arrived at the zoo last week.

  我們去看貓熊吧！新聞説下星期有兩隻貓熊到動物園。

- How can we get to the zoo？

  我們要怎麼去動物園呢？

- We can take the MRT and get off at the Zoo Station.

  我們可以搭捷運，在動物園站下車。

- If you insist getting to the African animal area on foot, I will keep my mouth shut.

  如果你堅持走路到非洲動物區，我會閉嘴的。

- Let's go to see the penguins after pandas. They are in the polar animal area.

  我們看完貓熊之後，去看企鵝吧，牠們在極地動物區。

- If we are lucky enough, we can see the polar bear. It is right next to the penguins.

  如果我們夠幸運的話，我們可以看到北極熊。牠就在企鵝的正旁邊。

- Have you ever seen crocodiles, black widow spiders, scorpions, elephants and black bears?

  你有看過鱷魚、黑寡婦蜘蛛、蠍子、大象和黑熊嗎？

- What's your favorite animal?

  你最喜歡的動物是什麼？

- I've never seen a polar bear.

  我從沒有看過北極熊。

- That kangaroo is pregnant.

  那隻袋鼠懷孕了。

MEMO

_____

_____

_____

7天就能用英文
行遍全世界！ ◯─◯─◯─◯─**⑤**─◯─◯

Chapter 1
Chapter 2
Chapter 3
Chapter 4
Chapter 5
Chapter 6
Chapter 7
Chapter 8
Chapter 9
Chapter 10

From AM-PM 從早到晚都用得到的必備好用句

- Your credit card is maxed out.
  您的卡片已經刷爆了。

- Have you ever been to a KTV?
  你去過 KTV 嗎？

- What is KTV?
  什麼是 KTV ？

- KTV is a place to sing karaoke.
  KTV 就是可以唱卡拉 OK 的地方。

- KTV is really popular in Taiwan.
  KTV 在台灣很受歡迎。

- Could I have the receipt?
  可以給我收據嗎？

- This price is more than I expected.
  這價格比我想的貴多了。

- It's time to get up.
  該起床了。

- I need to brush my teeth.
  我得要刷牙。

- I was in a rush this morning.
  我今早很趕。

- I need some time to brush my hair and put on make-up.
  我需要時間梳頭和化妝。

MEMO

- I didn't sleep very well last night.
  我昨天晚上沒睡好。

- Have some toast and eggs.
  吃些吐司和蛋吧。

- I prefer drinking apple juice in the morning.
  早上我比較想要喝蘋果汁。

- Breakfast is the most important meal of the day.
  早餐是一天中最重要的一餐。

- What do you usually eat for breakfast?
  你早餐通常吃什麼？

- What do you want for breakfast?
  你早餐想吃什麼？

- Finish your breakfast in 5 minutes.
  五分鐘內吃完早餐。

- I'll give you ten more minutes.
  再給你十分鐘。

- Can I have some ketchup, please?
  能給我些番茄醬嗎？

- I'd like my steak medium-well.
  我的牛排要七分熟。

- The pepperoni pizza looks good.
  義大利肉腸披薩看起來很好吃。

MEMO

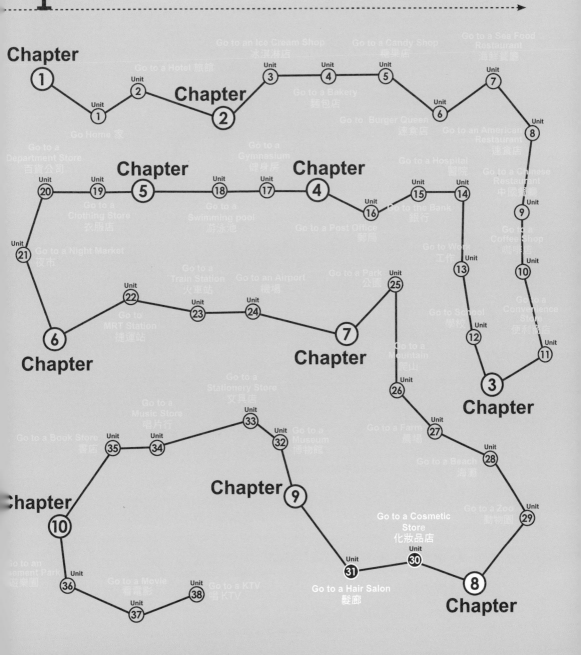

Chapter 8

Make-Over
改頭換面打扮自己

08-01

A Excuse me. I am looking for some useful skin care products to reduce my wrinkles. Do you mind recommending some to me?

不好意思，我在找一些有用的去除皺紋的保養品。妳介意建議我一些不錯的保養品嗎？

B No problem. Let's go to the shelves over there. I can introduce you to some products and you can also try them on the back of your hands to feel texture.

沒問題，我們去那一區。我可以介紹你一些產品，你也可以在手背上試試觸感。

A Sounds like a good idea.

好主意。

B For your crowsfeet, you can try this eye cream. It is also inexpensive. A lot of my customers come back and buy more.

對於你的魚尾紋，你可以試試這一罐眼霜，它也不貴。我的很多顧客都會回來再買一些。

A Can I test it on my skin?

我可以試在我的皮膚上嗎？

B Sure. Let me get a cotton swab. It is better not to use it with your fingers because it is easily contaminated.

當然，我去拿一些棉花棒。你最好不要用你的手指，因為很容易弄髒。

A I see. I will wait here.

我瞭解，我會在這裡等。

Additional Vocabulary & Phrases ｜ 補充單字 & 片語

● **wrinkle** n 皺紋
He has some wrinkles on his face.
他的臉上有一些皺紋。

● **contaminated** a 弄髒的、受汙染的
This glass of water is contaminated by the dust.
這杯水被灰塵弄髒了。

Chapter 1
Chapter 2
Chapter 3
Chapter 4
Chapter 5
Chapter 6
Chapter 7
Chapter 8
Chapter 9
Chapter 10

Daily Sentences 超高頻率使用句 | 一分鐘學一句不怕不夠用
08-02

- You can apply some eye cream around your eyes.

  你可以在眼睛周圍塗一些眼霜。

- To have smoky eyes, you need a thick eyeliner. Use the eyeliner to draw a line around your eyelids and smudge it gently.

  化煙燻妝時，你需要一隻粗的眼線筆。用眼線筆在你的眼瞼處畫一條線，然後慢慢推開。

- To make your eyelashes look longer, you need a good mascara and an eyelash curler.

  想讓眼睫毛看起來長一點，你需要一支好的睫毛膏和一個睫毛夾。

- My skin looks awful. What can I do?

  我的皮膚看起來真的很糟糕。我可以做什麼？

- You can use a concealer to cover the dark circles around your eyes.

  你可以用一些遮暇膏蓋住你眼睛周圍的黑眼圈。

- To have healthy skin, you need to use a makeup remover to completely remove all the makeup on your face.

  想要擁有健康的肌膚，你要用卸妝油徹底的卸掉臉上的妝。

- You need to do a facial treatment regularly. Then, you can try to put on some foundation to make your complexion look better.

  你需要定期做臉，然後你可以試著塗一些粉底，讓你的膚質看起來好一些。

- Can you recommend the latest lipstick ★¹?

  你可以介紹我最新款的口紅嗎？

★ 換個單字說說看 | 用單字累積句子的豐富度，讓句子更漂亮！

lipstick★¹ 可以替換：

| concealer 遮瑕膏 | sunscreen 防曬乳 | B.B cream BB 霜 | Can you recommend the latest _____? 你可以介紹我最新款的_____嗎？ |

Additional Vocabulary & Phrases | 補充單字 & 片語

- **thick** [a] 厚的、粗的
  This board is very thick.
  這塊板子很厚。

- **smudge** [n] 汙點、汙跡
  There's a smudge on the wall.
  牆壁上有一個汙點。

- **gently** [ad] 溫柔地
  My girlfriend holds me gently.
  我的女友溫柔地抱著我。

- **awful** [a] 糟糕的
  His attitude was awful.
  他的態度非常的糟糕

1 **facial** 臉部的

lip [lɪp] n	嘴唇
eyelid [ˋaɪˌlɪd] n	眼皮
cheek [tʃik] n	臉頰
skin [skɪn] n	皮膚
pore [por] n	毛孔

2 **clean** 清潔

facial cleanser ph	洗面乳
make-up remover ph	卸妝油
foaming [fomɪŋ] n	泡沫慕斯
facial scrub ph	臉部磨砂膏
pore cleanser ph	去黑頭

3 **skin care** 護膚

lotion [ˋloʃən] n	護膚乳	**nutrition** [njuˋtrɪʃən] n	滋養
moisturizer [ˋmɔɪstʃəˌraɪzɚ] n		**eye cream** ph	眼霜
	保溼霜／乳／露	**astringent lotion** ph	收斂水
essence [ˋɛsn̩s] n	精華液		

④ mask 面膜

make-up base ph ⋯⋯⋯⋯⋯ 隔離霜

sunscreen [`sʌn͵skrin] n ⋯ 防曬乳液

sun protection factor ph
⋯⋯⋯⋯⋯⋯⋯⋯ 防曬係數（SPF）

concealer n ⋯⋯⋯⋯⋯⋯⋯ 遮瑕膏

lip balm ph ⋯⋯⋯⋯⋯⋯⋯ 護唇膏

⑤ cosmetics 化妝品

foundation [faun`deʃən] n ⋯⋯ 粉底液

powder [`paudɚ] n ⋯⋯⋯⋯ 粉餅；蜜粉

mascara [mæs`kærə] n ⋯⋯⋯⋯ 睫毛膏

eye liner ph ⋯⋯⋯⋯⋯⋯⋯⋯ 眼線筆

eye shadow ph ⋯⋯⋯⋯⋯⋯⋯ 眼影

lipstick [`lɪp͵stɪk] n ⋯⋯⋯⋯⋯ 口紅

lip gloss [`lɪp͵glɔs] ph ⋯⋯⋯⋯ 唇蜜

blush [blʌʃ] n ⋯⋯⋯⋯⋯⋯⋯⋯ 腮紅

⑥ mandelic acid 杏仁酸

hyaluronic acid ph ⋯⋯⋯⋯⋯ 玻尿酸

laser resurfacing ph ⋯⋯⋯⋯ 雷射除疤

intense pulsed light ph ⋯⋯⋯ 脈衝光

chemical peeling ph ⋯⋯⋯⋯ 果酸換膚

botox injection ph ⋯⋯⋯⋯ 打肉毒桿菌

215

7 makeover 美容

exfoliating [ɛks`folɪˌet] 𝗏 ┄┄┄ 去角質
revitalizing [ri`vaɪtˌlaɪzɪŋ] 𝗏 ┄┄┄ 活化
firming [fɝmɪŋ] 𝗏 ┄┄┄ 緊膚
whitening [`hwaɪtnɪŋ] 𝗏 ┄┄┄ 美白
detoxifying [di`tɑksəˌfaɪ] 𝗏 ┄┄┄ 排毒
refresh [rɪ`frɛʃ] 𝗏 ┄┄┄ 更新
acne [`æknɪ] 𝗻 ┄┄┄ 粉刺；青春痘

8 application 工具

eyelash curler ᵖʰ ┄┄┄ 睫毛夾
puff [pʌf] 𝗻 ┄┄┄ 粉撲
brush [brʌʃ] 𝗻 ┄┄┄ 刷子
tweezers [`twizɚz] 𝗻 ┄┄┄ 拔毛鉗
cotton swab ᵖʰ ┄┄┄ 棉花棒

sponge puffs ᵖʰ ┄┄┄ 海綿撲
brow brush ᵖʰ ┄┄┄ 眉刷
lip brush ᵖʰ ┄┄┄ 口紅刷
cotton pads ᵖʰ ┄┄┄ 化妝棉
eye shadow brush ᵖʰ ┄┄┄ 眼影刷

Daily Q&A

〔會話一〕

Q▸ Can you recommend me something useful for my scars?
你可以建議我一些有效去除疤痕的東西嗎？

A▸ You should try this cream. It is good for scars.
你可以試試這個乳霜，它對疤痕很有用。

〔會話二〕

Q▸ I would like to put on some makeup before I go to the interview.
I look pale.
我想要在去面試前點妝，我看起來很慘白。

A▸ You really should. It is also a kind of politeness.
你真的需要，而且化妝也是一種禮貌。

〔會話三〕

Q▸ I did not sleep well last night.
我昨天晚上真的沒睡好。

A▸ I can tell from the dark circles around your eyes.
我可以從你眼睛周圍的黑眼圈看得出來。

Proverbs & Idioms **道地諺語與慣用語**｜讓句子更錦上添花

at first blush 〉 第一眼、當下

At first blush, the room seemed to be perfect. However, we soon found there was no water and no electricity.

第一眼，那間房間看起來好像很完美，但是我們很快就發現，那裡沒水又沒電。

save/spare someone's blushes 〉 避免某人尷尬

The teacher saved the student's blush by scolding him in a private room with no one in it.

老師在一個隱密沒人的房間罵那個學生，以避免他會覺得尷尬。

the cream of the crop 〉 最好的

These artists are the cream of the crop. All of them are very popular with people around the world.

這些藝術家都是最好的，他們全都是世界聞名的。

like the cat that got the cream 〉 洋洋得意（令人討厭）

Tim won the first prize of the lottery. He was sitting there and grinning like the cat that got the cream.

堤姆贏得了樂透頭獎，他坐在那裡笑得洋洋得意，令人討厭。

someone's mask slips 〉 摘下假面具

His mask suddenly slipped, and she saw him as a most terrible and ugliest man that he really was.

他突然摘下假面具，然後她看清楚他真實的面貌是很醜陋又恐怖的。

Beauty is in the eye of the beholder. 〉 情人眼裡出西施

We have different ideas about beautiful girls. You know beauty is in the eye of beholder. Let's stop arguing who is right.

我們對漂亮女生有不同的看法。你知道情人眼裡出西施吧。讓我們不要再爭誰對誰錯了。

Beauty is only skin-deep. 〉 美是件膚淺的事

I hate to upset you. Although Sandra is very beautiful, in her case, beauty is definitely only skin-deep. Her personality is terrible.

我不想讓你失望。雖然珊卓拉非常漂亮，就她而言美麗絕對是一件膚淺的事。她的個性很糟糕。

08-04

A So, how would you like your hair to be like?
那麼，你想要剪什麼樣的髮型？

B I want it to look more stylish. I would like it to be long still. But I want to have some fringe to cover my forehead.
我想要看起來比較有型。我希望我的頭髮還是長的，但是我想要在我的額頭前有一些瀏海。

A I got it. Do you want your hair to be straight, curly or wavy? I think you would look good with wavy hair.
我瞭解了。你想要留直髮、捲髮還是波浪捲？我想你很適合波浪捲。

B I have never tried to make my hair wavy. By the way, I want to color my hair.
我從來沒有試著讓我的頭髮波浪捲過。對了還有，我想要染髮。

A Do you mean you want to dye your hair or just highlight it?
你的意思是說，要染全頭嗎？還是挑染而已呢？

B Just highlight it.
挑染就好。

Additional Vocabulary & Phrases | 補充單字 & 片語

- **stylish** a 有型的
  Tom is very stylish.
  湯姆非常的有型。

- **cover** v 覆蓋、遮蓋
  Can you cover your eyes?
  你能閉上你的眼睛嗎？

- **forehead** n 額頭
  She has a beautiful forehead.
  她的額頭很漂亮。

- **highlight** v 使突出、強調
  Can you highlight this sentence?
  你能把這個句子強調出來嗎？

7天就能用英文
行遍全世界！ ──○──○──○──○──6──○

Chapter 1
Chapter 2
Chapter 3
Chapter 4
Chapter 5
Chapter 6
Chapter 7
Chapter 8
Chapter 9
Chapter 10

Daily Sentences 超高頻率使用句｜一分鐘學一句不怕不夠用 MP3 08-05

- I use some hair spray to make my hair style last longer.
  我噴些定型液好讓我的髮型能維持得更持久。

- If you want to have curly hair, you need to perm it.
  如果你想擁有捲髮，你需要燙。

- I have natural curls. I would like to straighten my hair.
  我有自然捲，我想要把我的頭髮弄直。

- After washing your hair, it's better to apply some hair treatment to maintain the structure of your hair.
  洗髮之後，最好抹上一些護髮霜，來保養頭髮的結構。

- I would like to tie my hair up with a pony tail in the back.
  我想要在腦杓後方綁一個馬尾。

- I would like to leave my hair down to make me look more attractive.
  我要把頭髮放下來，讓我看起來更有吸引力。

- Can you quickly use the hairdryer to dry my hair?
  你可以快速的用吹風機吹乾我的頭髮嗎？

- Can you **braid**★1 my hair?
  可以幫我編一下頭髮嗎？

- Can you recommend a good hairdresser to me?
  你可以推薦我一個好的髮型設計師嗎？

★ **換個單字說說看**｜用單字累積句子的豐富度，讓句子更漂亮！

braid★1 可以替換：

| cut 剪 | wash 洗 | tie 綁 | Can you _____my hair? 可以幫我_____一下頭髮嗎？ |

Additional Vocabulary & Phrases ｜ 補充單字 & 片語

- **maintain** v 保持、維持、保養
  She maintains her piano very well.
  她把她的鋼琴保養得很好。

- **structure** n 結構
  The structure of this article is very strong.
  這篇文章的結構很強。

- **tie** v 綁
  Can you tie my hair?
  你能幫我綁頭髮嗎？

- **recommend** v 推薦
  Can you recommend me a nice hotel?
  你能推薦我一間好的飯店嗎？

1 **hair** 頭髮

long hair ph	長髮	**bangs** [bæŋs] n	瀏海
short hair ph	短髮	**curly hair** ph	捲髮
medium hair ph	中長髮	**straight hair** ph	直髮

2 **hair salon** 髮廊

hair dresser ph 髮型設計師
mirror [ˋmɪrɚ] n 鏡子
salon chair ph 美髮椅
designer assistant ph 設計師助理
design [dɪˋzaɪn] v 設計

3 **shampoo** 洗頭；洗髮精

conditioner [kənˋdɪʃənɚ] n 潤絲精
hair spray ph 髮型定型液
treatment [ˋtritmənt] n 對待；治療
essential hair oil ph 護髮乳

4 tools 工具；器具；用具

scissors [ˈsɪzɚz] n	剪刀	rubber band ph 橡皮筋
hair dryer ph	吹風機	hair curler ph 電棒捲
hair clip ph	髮夾	hair straightener ph 離子夾
razor [ˈrezɚ] n	剃刀	

5 technique 技術

procedure [prəˈsidʒɚ] n 程序
thinning [ˈθɪnɪŋ] v 打薄
wave [wev] n （頭髮等）呈波形；捲曲
layer [ˈleɚ] n 層次
straighten [ˈstretn̩] v 燙直
permanent [ˈpɝmənənt] n 燙髮
haircut [ˈhɛr.kʌt] n 理髮
dye [daɪ] n 染髮

6 comb 梳子

wide tooth comb ph 寬齒梳
rat tail comb ph 扁平梳
barber comb ph 理髮用梳
roller brush ph 圓梳
paddle brush ph 板梳

221

7 hairstyle 髮型

afro [ˋæfro] n	爆炸頭
crew cut ph	平頭
bob [ˋbɑb] n	鮑伯頭
Pixie cut ph	精靈頭
finger wave ph	手指波浪髮

8 braids 髮辮

ponytail [ˋponɪˌtel] n	馬尾	**crown braid** ph	皇冠式髮辮
pigtails [ˋpɪɡˌtels] n	兩個（馬尾）	**fishtail hair** ph	魚骨編
French twist ph	法式髮髻		

Daily Q&A

〔會話一〕

Q▸ How would you like to part your hair?
你想要怎麼旁分你的頭髮？

A▸ I would like to part my hair on the left.
我想要左分。

〔會話二〕

Q▸ Would you like to dye your hair?
你想要染頭髮嗎？

A▸ No, thanks.
不用，謝謝！

〔會話三〕

Q▸ How much is the shampoo?
這瓶洗髮乳多少錢？

A▸ It's 1,000 dollars.
一千元。

Proverbs & Idioms ## 道地諺語與慣用語｜讓句子更錦上添花

not have a hair out of place 〉 一絲不苟

She is so tidy and clean. She does not have a hair out of place.
她是如此的整齊和乾淨，連頭髮都梳得整整齊齊，看起來就是一絲不苟的樣子。

a bad hair day 〉 不幸運的日子

It has been a bad hair day. My cell phone was not working when I talked to my girlfriend. I found my bike was stolen when I came back home.
今天真是個不幸的日子，我的手機在和女朋友講話時壞了；我回家的時候又發現，我的腳踏車被偷了。

hair-raising experience 〉 恐怖的經驗

Driving through the mountains is a hair-raising experience.
開山路真是個恐怖的經驗。

not turn a hair 〉 不受壞消息所影響

I thought she would be furious. However, she did not turn a hair.
我本來以為她一定會很生氣，但她絲毫不受壞消息所影響。

put on a hair shirt 〉 選擇不享受樂趣來苦修

I don't think you need to put on a hair shirt in order to be a teacher. Life is short. You should do something more interesting and make yourself to feel happier.
我不認為老師只能嚴格的管理自己，而不能享樂。人生很短暫，應該做一些有趣而且快樂的事。

make one's hair stand on end 〉 讓人驚嚇

Hearing the news about earthquakes made my hair stand on end.
聽到關於地震的消息讓我驚嚇不已。

let your hair down 〉 放輕鬆 做自己想做的事

The party gives you a chance to let your hair down at the end of the week.
這個派對給你一個機會讓你在周末放鬆心情做自己想做的事

gray hair 〉 白頭髮

My grandfather is 78 years old now. She has a lot of gray hair.
我奶奶現在 78 歲了。她有很多白頭髮。

hang by a hair 〉 薄弱的證據

Your whole argument is hanging by a hair.
你的整個論述證據薄弱。

- Your hair loses its style. You need to go to a hair salon. I can introduce my hair dresser to you.

  你的頭髮沒有型了。你需要去髮廊，我可以介紹我的髮型設計師給你。

- Let's make an appointment first before we go there.

  在我們去那裡之前，先預約一下。

- I am thinking about going to a hair salon. I look stupid with my hair like this.

  我正想去髮廊。我頭髮這樣看起來真的很呆。

- I was the one who made an appointment with Jimmy 30 minutes ago. My friend wants to change her hair style.

  我就是那個三十分鐘前和吉米預約的人。我的朋友想要改變他的髮型。

- Welcome to ABC Hair Salon. Did you make an appointment with any of our hair dressers?

  歡迎來到 ABC 髮廊，你們有先跟我們哪一位髮型設計師預約嗎？

- I will bring you to your place.

  我會帶你到座位上。

- I will sit on the sofa and wait for you here.

  我在這裡，坐在沙發上等你。

- If you dye you hair, you make all your hair in just one color. If you just highlight your hair, you just change part of your hair into a different color.

  如果你要染全染，你把全部的頭髮變成單一的顏色；如果你只是挑染，你只改變局部的頭髮變成不一樣的顏色。

- How long would you like your hair to be?

  你想要你的頭髮多長？

- In about one or two hours, you can see a whole new me.

  大概一到兩個小時，你就會看到全新的我了。

- I would like my hair to be a little over shoulder.

  我想要我的頭髮過肩一點點。

From AM-PM 從早到晚都用得到的必備好用句

- How about getting some spaghetti with meatballs?
  來些義大利麵配肉丸怎麼樣？

- What does the German sausage taste like?
  德國香腸吃起來味道如何？

- Cake is a nice dessert.
  蛋糕是很棒的甜點。

- The pie is too greasy.
  這餡餅太油了。

- The cookie is too sweet.
  這餅乾太甜了。

- A lot of people come to this coffee shop to chat and drink coffee.
  很多人來這家咖啡店喝咖啡聊天。

- Don't waste your food.
  不要浪費食物。

- Vegetables are good for you. Eat more.
  蔬菜對你很好，多吃點。

- Thanks for cooking dinner, mom.
  媽，謝謝您做的晚餐。

- Would you please say grace for us?
  能請你幫我們說謝飯禱文嗎？

- Fast food is quick and cheap.
  速食又快又便宜。

MEMO

- Eating too much fast food will make you fat.
  吃太多速食會變胖。

- I'll order a cheeseburger with fries and Coke, please.
  我要點起司漢堡、薯條和可樂，謝謝。

- This food is really greasy.
  這食物好油喔！

- The presentation of this dish is beautiful.
  這道料理的擺盤設計很漂亮。

- Do you eat sashimi?
  你吃生魚片嗎？

- What kind of meat do you want in your tepanyaki?
  你的鐵板燒要什麼肉？

- Could we have some more broths in the hot pot?
  能請你幫我們在鍋裡加點湯嗎？

- Watch out! The soup is boiling.
  小心！湯滾了！

- Do you want to try the spicy hot pot?
  你想試試看麻辣火鍋嗎？

- Are you looking for a particular brand of shoes?
  你是在找特定品牌的鞋款嗎？

- Those are a nice pair of basketball shoes.
  那是雙相當不錯的籃球鞋款。

MEMO

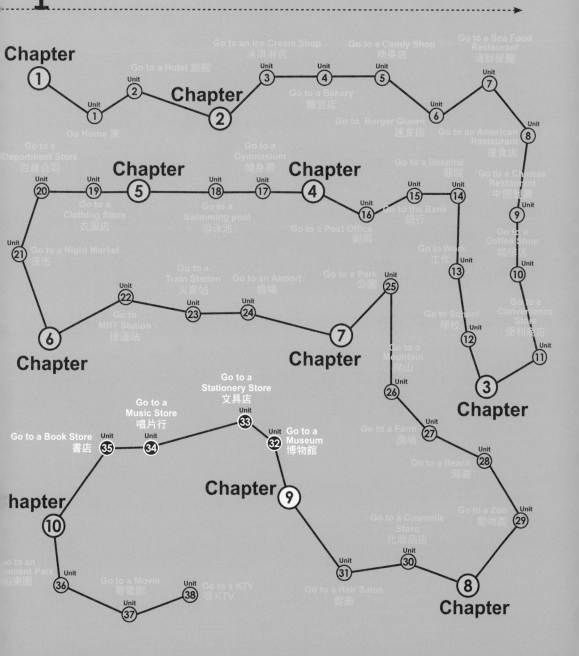

Chapter 9

Art Enthusiast
知性文青

Chapter
①

Unit
①

Go Home 家

Go to a Hotel 旅館

Unit
②

Chapter
②

Go to a Bakery
麵包店

Go to an Ice Cream Shop
冰淇淋店

Unit
③

Unit
④

Go to a Candy Shop
糖果店

Unit
⑤

Go to a Sea Food
Restaurant
海鮮餐廳

Unit
⑦

Unit
⑥

Go to Burger Queen
速食店

Go to an American
Restaurant
速食店

Unit
⑧

Go to a
Department Store
百貨公司

Unit
⑳

Unit
⑲

Chapter
⑤

Go to a Clothing Store
衣服店

Go to a
Gymnasium
健身房

Unit
⑱

Unit
⑰

Go to a
Swimming pool
游泳池

Chapter
④

Go to a Hospital
醫院

Unit
⑯

Go to the Bank
銀行

Unit
⑮

Unit
⑭

Go to a Chinese
Restaurant
中國餐廳

Unit
⑨

Go to a
Coffee Shop
咖啡店

Go to a Post Office
郵局

Go to Work
工作

Unit
㉑

Go to a Night Market
夜市

Go to a
Train Station
火車站

Go to an Airport
機場

Go to a Park
公園

Unit
㉕

Unit
⑬

Go to School
學校

Unit
⑩

Go to a
Convenience
Store
便利商店

Unit
㉒

Unit
㉓

Unit
㉔

Go to a
MRT Station
捷運站

Chapter
⑦

Unit
⑫

Unit
⑪

Chapter
⑥

Go to a
Mountain
爬山

Chapter
③

Unit
㉖

Go to a
Stationery Store
文具店

Unit
㉗

Go to a Farm
農場

Go to a
Music Store
唱片行

Unit
㉝

Unit
㉜

Go to a
Museum
博物館

Unit
㉘

Go to a Beach
海灘

Go to a Book Store
書店

Unit
㉟

Unit
㉞

Chapter
⑨

Go to a Cosmetic
Store
化妝品店

Go to a Zoo
動物園

Unit
㉙

hapter
⑩

Go to an
mement Park
遊樂園

Unit
㊱

Go to a Movie
看電影

Unit
㊲

Unit
㊳

Go to a KTV
唱 KTV

Go to a Hair Salon
髮廊

Unit
㉛

Unit
㉚

Chapter
⑧

A Which floor is the art exhibition we are going to on?
我們要去藝術展的哪一層樓？

B I have no idea. Let me take a closer look at my museum map.
我不知道耶。讓我仔細看一看我的藝術館地圖。

A Sure, take your time. We have a whole day.
好啊，慢慢來。我們有一整天的時間。

B It's on the 2nd floor. We are going to see some beautiful paintings of ancient Greek.
在二樓。我們去那裡看一些和古希臘有關的漂亮的畫吧！

A Look at the museum guide. It says there are also some sculptures and potteries in this area. Let's rent an audio guide.
看看那個藝術館導覽！上面說在這裡有一些雕像和陶器，我們去租個語音導覽吧！

Additional Vocabulary & Phrases | 補充單字 & 片語

● **map** [n] 地圖
I need a map.
我需要一張地圖。

● **whole** [a] 全部
The whole class passed the exam.
全班都通過了考試。

● **ancient** [a] 古代的
It is an ancient story.
這是一個古老的故事。

● **pottery** [n] 陶器
My grandma likes to collect potteries.
我奶奶喜歡收集陶器。

7天就能用英文
行遍全世界！

6

Chapter 1
Chapter 2
Chapter 3
Chapter 4
Chapter 5
Chapter 6
Chapter 7
Chapter 8
Chapter 9
Chapter 10

Daily Sentences 超高頻率使用句│一分鐘學一句不怕不夠用
09-02

- What exhibition is shown on the **ground floor**[1]?
  一樓有什麼展覽？

- This exhibition is about the history of **Spain**[2].
  這是關於西班牙歷史的展覽。

- What is the opening hours of the museum?
  博物館的開放時間是幾點到幾點？

- I would like to make a phone call to enquire about the museum. Do you have the number?
  我想打個電話到博物館問一些訊息。你有電話號碼嗎？

- The museum is open from 9 am to 7 pm every day.
  博物館的開放時間是每天的早上九點到下午七點。

- Every three to four hours, you can wait next to the information desk. A museum guide will tell you some detailed information about the exhibition.
  每三到四小時，你可以在詢問台旁邊等，博物館導覽員會告訴你一些關於展覽的詳細資訊。

- Excuse me, where can I find Monet's paintings in this museum?
  不好意思，我可以在這個博物館裡找到莫內的畫嗎？

- Can I take photos here?
  我可以在這裡照相嗎？

★ **換個單字說說看**│用單字累積句子的豐富度，讓句子更漂亮！

ground floor[1] 可以替換：

basement 地下室	**2nd floor** 二樓	**top floor** 頂樓

What exhibition is shown on the _____?
_____ 有什麼展覽？

Spain[2] 可以替換：

German 德國	**America** 美國	**France** 法國

This exhibition is about the history of _____.
這是關於_____歷史的展覽。

Additional Vocabulary & Phrases │ 補充單字 & 片語

- **history** [n] 歷史
  My favorite subject is history.
  我最喜歡的科目是歷史。

- **opening hour** [ph] 開放時間
  The opening hour of library is 7am-10pm.
  圖書館的開放時間是早上七點到晚上十點。

- **enquire** [v] 詢問、查詢
  I enquired about the graduate programs of Ohio State University.
  我詢問了有關俄亥俄州立大學的碩士學程。

- **detail** [n] 細節
  He told me the detail of the story.
  他告訴我那個故事的細節。

1 topic 主題

science [ˋsaɪəns] [n]	科學
history [ˋhɪstərɪ] [n]	歷史
astronomy [əsˋtrɑnəmɪ] [n]	天文
humanity [hjuˋmænətɪ] [n]	人文
art [ɑrt] [n]	藝術
antique [ænˋtik] [a]	古代的
modern [ˋmɑdən] [a]	現代的

2 exhibition 展覽

display [dɪˋsple] [n]	展示
period [ˋpɪrɪəd] [n]	時代
memory [ˋmɛmərɪ] [n]	紀念
on tour [ph]	巡迴的
hold [hold] [v]	舉辦
preview [ˋpriˏvju] [n]	預告
review [rɪˋvju] [n]	回顧

3 visit 參觀

audio guide [ph]	語音導覽	**ticket** [ˋtɪkɪt] [n]	門票
handbook [ˋhændˏbuk] [n]	手冊	**plan** [plæn] [n]	平面圖
route [rut] [n]	路線	**introduction** [ˏɪntrəˋdʌkʃən] [n]	介紹

④ hall 走廊

area [`ɛrɪə] n ⋯⋯⋯⋯⋯⋯ 區域
audio-visual room ph ⋯⋯⋯ 視聽室

ticket booth ph ⋯⋯⋯⋯ 售票室
souvenir [`suvə.nɪr] n ⋯⋯⋯ 紀念品

⑤ era 時代

renaissance [rə`nesn̩s] n ⋯⋯⋯⋯ 文藝復興時期
gothic [`gɑθɪk] n ⋯⋯⋯⋯⋯⋯⋯⋯⋯ 哥德式
Baroque [bə`rok] n ⋯⋯⋯⋯⋯⋯ 巴洛克藝術
Rococo [rə`koko] n ⋯⋯⋯⋯⋯⋯⋯ 洛可可式
Romanticism [ro`mæntə.sɪzəm] n ⋯⋯ 浪漫主義
Impressionism [ɪm`prɛʃən.ɪzəm] n ⋯⋯ 印象派

⑥ artist 藝術家

Leonardo da Vinci n ⋯⋯⋯⋯ 達文西
Raphael n ⋯⋯⋯⋯⋯⋯⋯⋯⋯ 拉斐爾
Michelangelo n ⋯⋯⋯⋯⋯ 米開朗基羅
Millet n ⋯⋯⋯⋯⋯⋯⋯⋯⋯⋯ 米勒
Vincent van Gogh n ⋯⋯⋯⋯ 梵谷

231

7 collection 收藏品

sculpture [ˋskʌlptʃɚ] n ⸺ 雕塑
pottery [ˋpatɚrɪ] n ⸺ 陶器
copper [ˋkapɚ] n ⸺ 銅製品
jade [dʒed] n ⸺ 玉製品
classic [ˋklæsɪk] a ⸺ 典藏的

8 painting 繪畫

calligraphy [kəˋlɪgrəfɪ] n ⸺ 書法
ink painting ph ⸺ 水墨畫
oil painting ph ⸺ 油畫

egg tempera ph ⸺ 蛋彩畫
mural painting ph ⸺ 壁畫
watercolor [ˋwatɚ͵kʌlɚ] n ⸺ 水彩

Daily Q&A

〔會話一〕

Q▸ How much do I need to pay for the entrance fee in this museum?
這間博物館的門票要付多少錢？

A▸ About 200 dollars.
大約兩百塊。

〔會話二〕

Q▸ Where can we rent an audio guide?
我們在哪裡可以租到語音導覽？

A▸ It's at the desk next to the ticket booth.
在售票亭旁邊的櫃台。

〔會話三〕

Q▸ Do you know how to use the museum map?
你知道怎樣看博物館的地圖嗎？

A▸ It's easy. Just turn your map like this.
很簡單，只要把地圖轉成這樣。

Proverbs & Idioms **道地諺語與慣用語** | 讓句子更錦上添花

take a collection up from (sb.) for (sb. or sth.) ＞ 從某人那邊募款給某人或某事

The teacher took a collection up from every student for the poor student who was not able to pay for his tuition.

老師從每一個同學那邊募款給無法交學費的窮苦學生。

make an exhibition of (oneself) ＞ 盡情表現

She is not only dancing but making an exhibition of herself in the public.

她不只跳舞，而且也盡情在大家面前表現自己。

be no oil painting ＞ 不吸引人

She has a very beautiful face but is no oil painting.

她有漂亮的臉蛋，但是一點都不吸引人。

history repeats itself ＞ 舊事重演

I think the two parties in that country are having fight again because history repeats itself.

我想那個國家的兩個政黨又將產生爭執，因為舊事會一再重演。

happy is the country which has no history ＞ 沒有歷史的國家是快樂的

History of that country is full of greed, anger and dishonest. Happy is the country which has no history.

那個國家的歷史充滿了貪婪、憤怒和不誠實，沒有歷史的國家反而是快樂的。

museum piece ＞ 老（舊）式的東西

Look at the car over there! It is absolutely a museum piece.

看那邊那輛車！它絕對是老東西。

make an exhibition of oneself ＞ 讓自己出洋相

He is drunk. If he keeps drinking, he is going to end up making an exhibition of himself.

他喝醉了。如果讓他繼續喝酒，他最後會讓自已出洋相。

Unit 33 Go to a Stationery Store 文具店

A I have to go to shelf number 3 first to get my markers, color pencils, highlighters and some brushes.
我們必須先去三號架找我的馬克筆、彩色筆、螢光筆和一些水彩刷。

B I also need some thumbtacks, whiteout and paper clips. Which shelf are they on? I can't find the number.
我需要一些圖釘、立可白和迴紋針，它們在哪一個架上？我找不到號碼。

A It's at the back. I think you are near-sighted. You had better get yourself a pair of nice glasses.
在後面，我想你有近視喔。你最好買一副好的眼鏡。

B No, I am not near-sighted. I just did not notice it.
不，我沒有近視，我只是沒有發現。

A OK. Let's go find the things separately and meet here again after 1 hour. Is that fine with you?
好，我們分頭去找東西，一個小時後在這裡碰面。你覺得這樣好嗎？

B That sounds like a perfect idea. We can save plenty of time.
聽起來是個完美的點子，我可以省很多時間。

Additional Vocabulary & Phrases | 補充單字 & 片語

- **near-sighted** ph 近視
  She is near-sighted.
  她有近視。

- **notice** v 注意
  Did you notice that she was crying?
  你有注意到她在哭嗎？

- **separately** ad 分別地、個別地
  You need to wash the dishes separately.
  妳需要分開洗盤子。

- **plenty** n 充足、大量
  I have plenty of chocolate.
  我有很多巧克力。

Daily Sentences 超高頻率使用句｜一分鐘學一句不怕不夠用
MP3 09-05

- I need some notebooks, paper, whiteout, highlighters and pens.
  我需要一些筆記本、紙、立可白、螢光筆和筆。

- Where do you put **binder clips** ★¹?
  你們的長尾夾放哪裡？

- The notebooks are on the shelf next to the markers.
  筆記本在麥克筆旁邊的架子上。

- How many colors does this box of colored pencils have?
  這盒色鉛筆最多有幾個顏色？

- We ran out of pens. Let's go to the stationery store.
  我們的筆用完了，我們去文具店吧。

- Where is the nearest stationery store?
  最近的文具店在哪裡？

- What time does the stationery store close?
  文具店幾點關門？

- How much is a box of **ball point pens** ★²?
  這一盒原子筆多少錢？

- We need to do a group report tomorrow. I need to go to the stationery store to buy something for the posters.
  我們明天要做小組報告，我要去文具店買一些做海報的東西。

★ **換個單字說說看**｜用單字累積句子的豐富度，讓句子更漂亮！

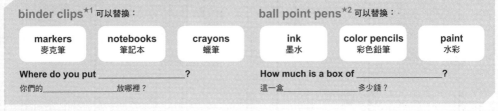

binder clips★¹ 可以替換：			ball point pens★² 可以替換：		
markers 麥克筆	**notebooks** 筆記本	**crayons** 蠟筆	**ink** 墨水	**color pencils** 彩色鉛筆	**paint** 水彩

Where do you put _____?
你們的_____放哪裡？

How much is a box of _____?
這一盒_____多少錢？

Additional Vocabulary & Phrases｜補充單字 & 片語

- **near** a 近的
  Sandy lives near my house.
  仙蒂住在我家附近。

- **poster** n 海報
  This poster is well designed.
  這張海報設計得很好。

1 paper 紙

card [kɑrd] n	卡片
sticky note ph	便利貼
memo pad ph	便條本
business card ph	名片卡
carbon paper ph	複寫紙

2 tape 膠帶

double-sided sticky tape ph	雙面膠帶
glue [glu] n	膠水
glue stick ph	口紅膠
acrylic foam tape ph	泡棉膠
scotch tape ph	透明膠

3 file 文件夾；公文箱

envelope [ˋɛnvəˏlop] n	信封
letter paper ph	信箋
folder [ˋfoldɚ] n	文書夾
telephone directory ph	電話簿
binder [ˋbaɪndɚ] n	文件夾

④ ball point pen 原子筆

pencil [ˋpɛnsl̩] n ················· 鉛筆

mechanical pencil ph ······ 自動鉛筆

fountain pen ph ················· 鋼筆

gel ink pen ph ················· 中性筆

white out ph ················· 修正液

eraser [ɪˋresɚ] n ················· 橡皮擦

mechanical pencil lead ph 自動鉛筆筆芯

⑤ crayon 粉蠟筆

highlighter [ˋhaɪˌlaɪtɚ] n ········· 螢光筆

marker [markɚ] n ················· 麥克筆

brush [brʌʃ] n ················· 毛筆；畫筆

watercolor [ˋwɑtɚˌkʌlɚ] n ········· 水彩

complement [ˋkɑmpləmənt] n 補充物

ink [ɪŋk] n ················· 墨水；油墨

⑥ drafting 製圖

ruler [ˋrulɚ] n ················· 尺

compass [ˋkʌmpəs] n ················· 圓規

protractor [proˋtræktɚ] n ······ 量角器

setsquare [ˋsɛtˌskwɛr] n ········· 三角板

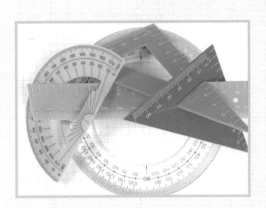

237

❼ hardware 五金器具

scissors [ˈsɪzɚz] n	剪刀
blade [bled] n	刀片
craft knife ph	美工刀

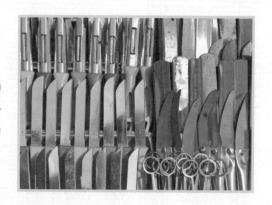

❽ binder clips 長尾夾

paper clips ph	迴紋針
thumbtack [ˈθʌmˌtæk] n	圖釘
pin [pɪn] n	大頭針；別針
staples [ˈstepl̩z] n	釘書針

❾ business machine 事務機器

stapler [ˈsteplɚ] n	訂書機
shredder [ˈʃrɛdɚ] n	碎紙機
computer [kəmˈpjutɚ] n	電腦
paper puncher ph	打孔機
paper trimmer ph	裁紙機
pencil sharpener ph	削鉛筆機

Daily Q&A

〔會話一〕

Q▸ Do you have any paper shredder?
你有碎紙機嗎？

A▸ I am sorry. Our store does not sell any paper shredders.
對不起，我們的店沒有賣碎紙機。

〔會話二〕

Q▸ How can I find everything on my shopping list in this store?
我如何能在這家店找到我購物清單上的所有東西？

A▸ You can look at the signs on top of the shelves.
你可以看架上頂端的指示牌。

〔會話三〕

Q▸ Do you have any discount?
你們有打折嗎？

A▸ Yes, if you are our VIP member, you can get 20% discount.
有的，如果你是我們的 VIP 會員，你可以享有八折的優惠。

Proverbs & Idioms 道地諺語與慣用語｜讓句子更錦上添花

be in the bull pen 〉 準備好回報他人

I am ready to be in the bull pen. Just call me whenever you need my help.

我準備好要報答你，只要你有需要的時候，就打電話給我。

pen is mightier than the sword 〉 文字論述比武力戰爭有力

Believing that pen is mightier than the sword, the students decided to put what they were against in the newspapers instead of going on the street.

你要相信文字論述比武力戰爭更有力，那些學生決定把他們反對的事情登在報紙上，而不是走上街頭。

a poison-pen letter 〉 黑函

After the man was accused of laundering the money, his family soon received many poison-pen letters.

那個男人在被提告洗錢之後，他的家人立刻收到很多黑函。

put pen to paper 〉 付諸行動

Tim keeps thinking about writing to his dream lover, but he never puts pen to paper because he is afraid of being rejected.

提姆一直想著寫信給他的夢中情人，但是他從沒付諸行動過，因為他很害怕被拒絕。

a pen pusher 〉 作家

He is a pen pusher who always dreams about traveling through the whole USA.

他是一個夢想旅遊全美的作家。

glued to the spot 〉 被嚇到定住不動

Raymond stood there glued to the spot as the shadow of a thief came nearer and nearer.

當小偷的影子越來越逼近時，雷蒙被嚇到定住不動。

glued to something 〉 （受到吸引）目光注視一處

During the football season, everyone's glued to the TV.

在足球季每個人的目光都黏在電視上。

Go to a Music Store 唱片行

09-07

A This music store is really huge. You can find all kinds of CDs and tapes. If you want to learn how to play the musical instruments, you can also find a good one here.

這間唱片行真的很大,你可以找到各式各樣的 CD 和錄音帶。如果你想要學樂器的話,你也可以在這裡找到一個好樂器。

B Wow, I can see thousands of CDs and tapes on this side and on the other side I can see many different kinds of musical instruments displayed over there.

哇,我看到數以千計的 CD 和唱片陳列在這裡,而在另一邊,我看到不同種類的樂器。

A I love music. I always come here to buy the CDs I like because I can always find what I want.

我愛音樂,我總是來這裡買我喜歡的 CD,因為我一定可以找到我要的。

B How can you find the CD you want to buy? I mean this store is really huge.

你怎麼能夠找到你想要買的 CD ?我的意思是,這間唱片行真的很大。

A Actually, it is not difficult at all. If you have the title, you can go to the counter and ask the counter helper to check whether they have it in the stock.

事實上,這一點也不難。如果你有唱片名,你可以去櫃台,然後請櫃台的人幫你查查有沒有庫存。

Additional Vocabulary & Phrases | 補充單字 & 片語

- **thousand** a 一千的
  Why do you always have thousands of questions?
  為什麼你總是有好幾千種問題?

- **display** v 陳列
  The cookies are displayed in the window.
  餅乾陳列在櫥窗裡。

- **difficult** a 困難的
  It's difficult to learn a new language.
  學習一種新的語言是困難的。

- **stock** n 存貨
  We still have many stocks.
  我們還有很多存貨。

Daily Sentences 超高頻率使用句│一分鐘學一句不怕不夠用
09-08

- How many people are there in this band?
  這個樂團有幾個人？

- I am looking for a good piano. Can you recommend one to me?
  我在找一台好的鋼琴，你可以推薦我嗎？

- Do you have the score of this music?
  你有這首音樂的樂譜嗎？

- There are 5 people in this rock band, two vocalists, two drummers and a guitarist.
  這個搖滾樂團有五個人。兩個主唱，兩個鼓手和一個吉他手。

- Does this album come in tapes?
  這張專輯有出卡帶嗎？

- Are these CDs on special sale?
  這些 CD 有特別的折扣嗎？

- Does your music store have a website?
  你們的唱片行有網站嗎？

- Excuse me, I am looking for this CD. Do you have it in stock?
  不好意思，我在找這個 CD，你們有貨嗎？

- I like **classical music**★1.
  我喜歡古典樂。

- I went to Super Junior's concert last night. It was fantastic.
  我昨晚去 Super Junior 的音樂會，真的很棒。

★ 換個單字說說看│用單字累積句子的豐富度，讓句子更漂亮！

classical music★1 可以替換：

| country music 鄉村音樂 | rock music 搖滾音樂 | pop music 流行音樂 | I like _____.
我喜歡_____。 |

Additional Vocabulary & Phrases │補充單字 & 片語

- **look for** ph 尋找
  I am looking for some yummy cheese.
  我在找一些好吃的起司。

- **website** n 網站
  You can go on our website and order the products.
  你可以到我們的網站預定商品。

① concert 音樂會

stage [stedʒ] n ⸺⸺⸺ 舞台
show [ʃo] n ⸺⸺⸺⸺ 表演
audience [`ɔdɪəns] n ⸺⸺ 聽眾
spot light ph ⸺⸺⸺ 聚光燈

② band 樂團

vocalist [`vokəlɪst] n ⸺⸺ 主唱
keyboard player ph ⸺⸺ 鍵盤手
guitar player ph ⸺⸺ 吉他手
drummer [`drʌmɚ] n ⸺⸺ 鼓手
bass player ph ⸺⸺ 貝斯手

③ chorus 合唱團

alto [`ælto] n ⸺⸺⸺ 中音部
soprano [sə`præno] n ⸺⸺ 高音部
tenor [`tɛnɚ] n ⸺⸺⸺ 次中音

bass [`bes] n ⸺⸺⸺ 低音部
choir [kwaɪr] n ⸺⸺⸺ 合唱

4 **singer** 歌手

lyricist [ˋlɪrɪsɪst] n ⸺ 寫詞人

composer [kəmˋpozɚ] n ⸺ 作曲者

lyrics [ˋlɪrɪks] n ⸺ 歌詞

score [skor] n ⸺ 樂譜

recommend [͵rɛkəˋmɛnd] v 推薦；介紹

popular [ˋpɑpjəlɚ] a ⸺ 大眾化的

billboard [ˋbɪl͵bord] n ⸺ 排行榜

album [ˋælbəm] n ⸺ 專輯

5 **orchestra** 管弦樂器

instrument [ˋɪnstrəmənt] n ⸺ 樂器

piano [pɪˋæno] n ⸺ 鋼琴

flute [flut] n ⸺ 長笛

trumpet [ˋtrʌmpɪt] n ⸺ 小號；喇叭

violin [͵vaɪəˋlɪn] n ⸺ 小提琴

cello [ˋtʃɛlo] n ⸺ 大提琴

6 **guitar** 吉他

drum [drʌm] n ⸺ 鼓

bass [ˋbes] n ⸺ 貝斯

keyboard [ˋki͵bord] n ⸺ 鍵盤樂器

electronic guitar ph ⸺ 電吉他

7 audio 音響裝置

compact disc [ph] ············· CD、唱片
tape [tep] [n] ·························· 卡帶
earphone [ˋɪr͵fon] [n] ··········· 耳機
microphone [ˋmaɪkrə͵fon] [n] ······· 擴音器；麥克風
MP3 player [ph] ············· MP3 播放器
CD player [ph] ··············· CD 播放器

8 musical types 音樂類型

pop [pɑp] [n] ·················· 流行音樂
jazz [dʒæz] [n] ················ 爵士樂
rap music [ph] ·············· 饒舌音樂
classical music [ph] ·········· 古典樂
electronic music [ph] ········ 電子音樂
rock-and-roll [ph] ············ 搖滾樂

blues [bluz] [n] ·············· 藍調音樂
Britpop [n] ················ 英式搖滾樂
folk music [ph] ················ 民謠
hip hop [ph] ············ 節奏強烈的音樂
opera [ˋopərə] [n] ············· 歌劇
punk rock [ph] ··········· 龐客搖滾樂

Daily Q&A

〔會話一〕

Q▸ Is Super Junior's new album available now?
現在買得到 Super Junior 的新專輯嗎？

A▸ Yes, you can find their CDs at the music store.
可以啊，你可以在唱片行找到他們的 CD。

〔會話二〕

Q▸ I love this band a lot. They always make good rock and roll music.
我真的很喜歡這個樂團，他們總是可以創作出很好的搖滾樂。

A▸ Who is the vocal? Who is the drummer?
主唱是誰？鼓手是誰？

〔會話三〕

Q▸ What kind of music do you like?
你喜歡哪種音樂？

A▸ I like classical music.
我喜歡古典樂。

Proverbs & Idioms ｜ **道地諺語與慣用語** ｜ 讓句子更錦上添花

face the music 〉 面對現實

Not being able to be accepted by the school is a fact. You should face the music.

沒被學校錄取是個事實，你要面對現實。

make chin music 〉 說話談論

Jim loves talking. He will make hours of chin music to let everyone listen to him.

吉姆很愛說話，他會讓別人聽他講幾小時的話。

music to someone's ears 〉 令人悅耳的話

A: You look so beautiful tonight.
A: 妳今天看起來真漂亮。
B: Ah, that is music to my ears.
B: 哈，這真是令人悅耳的話。

preach to the choir 〉 在已認同你的人面前闡述自己的言論

I finally realized that all I was doing was preaching to the choir. The men who really needed to hear this did not come.

我最後瞭解到，我所做的都是在已經認同我的人面前說服他們，真的需要被說服的人卻都沒來聽。

jazz something up 〉 使有型、使有趣

Mom, you need to jazz up your wardrobe. All your clothes are old fashioned.

媽咪，妳要讓妳的衣櫥更有型，妳的衣服都很老氣耶。

strike a false note 〉 做錯的或是不合宜的事

David found out that he struck a false note when he arrived at the theme party with wrong dress code.

當大衛穿錯衣服參加主題派對時，他發現他做了件不合宜的事。

ring a bell 〉 熟悉的事

Melisa? The name rings a bell but I don't remember her.

梅麗莎？這名字好熟悉但是我想不起來她是誰。

Go to a Bookstore 書店

09-10

A Excuse me, Ma'am. I am looking for books about business. Where is the business section?
不好意思，女士。我們在找商業相關的書，商業書籍區在哪裡？

B Go straight and turn left. It's next to the computer section. If you know the title of the book, I can search the book for you on the Internet.
直走左轉，它在電腦區的旁邊。如果你知道書名，我可以在網路上替你查詢。

A OK. I think I will look around first.
好，我會先到處看看。

B Just tell me when you need my help.
有需要時就叫我。

A No problem. Thank you very much.
沒問題，謝謝你。

B You're welcome. It's my pleasure.
不客氣，這是我的榮幸。

Additional Vocabulary & Phrases | 補充單字 & 片語

- **section** n 部分、地區
  What's your favorite activity?
  你最喜歡的活動是什麼？

- **title** n 標題、書名
  What's the title of the book?
  那本書的書名是什麼？

- **search** v 搜查、搜尋
  What are you searching for?
  你在找什麼？

- **pleasure** n 愉快、高興、滿足
  It is such a pleasure to spend time with you.
  花時間和你相處真的很愉快。

Daily Sentences 超高頻率使用句｜一分鐘學一句不怕不夠用
09-11

- I would like to find books about literature. Where are they?
  我想找文學相關的書籍，它們在哪裡？

- Language learning books are next to the literature section down the aisle.
  語言工具書在走道底的文學書籍區的旁邊。

- Can you check whether you have this book in your shop or not?
  你可以幫我找找你們店裡有這本書嗎？

- What's the book title and the writer's name?
  這本書的書名和作者是誰？

- Do you know any good bookstore in this neighborhood?
  你知道這附近有好的書店嗎？

- There is a big bookstore in Taipei 101. You can find a lot of interesting books there.
  台北 101 裡有一間大書店，你可以在那裡找到很多有趣的書。

- How much money do you spend on books every year?
  你每一年花多少錢買書？

- What kinds of books interest you?
  你對哪種書有興趣？

- I would like to get a **map** *¹ at a bookstore.
  我要在書店買一張地圖。

★ 換個單字說說看｜用單字累積句子的豐富度，讓句子更漂亮！

map*¹ 可以替換：

| novel 小說 | poem 詩集 | dictionary 字典 | I would like to get a _____ at a bookstore. 我要在書店買_____。 |

Additional Vocabulary & Phrases｜補充單字 & 片語

- **aisle** n 走道
  Dictionaries are located at aisle number 2.
  字典位在第二走道裡。

- **check** v 檢查、核對
  Can you check this list for me?
  你能幫我核對這張清單嗎？

- **neighborhood** n 鄰近地區
  Sandy lives around our neighborhood.
  仙蒂住在我們家附近。

- **interesting** a 有趣的
  This book is very interesting.
  這本書很有趣。

❶ magazine 雜誌

periodical [ˌpɪrɪˋɑdɪkḷ] n	········	期刊
sketchbook [ˋskɛtʃˌbʊk] n	········	繪本
comic [ˋkɑmɪk] n	········	漫畫
newspaper [ˋnjuzˌpepɚ] n	········	報紙

❷ genre 文學類型

poem [ˋpoɪm] n	········	詩
novel [ˋnɑvḷ] n	········	小說
drama [ˋdrɑmə] n	········	戲劇
short story ph	········	短篇小說
myth [mɪθ] n	········	神話
graphic novel ph	········	連環小說

❸ language 語言

simplified Chinese ph	···· 簡體字	**English** [ˋɪŋglɪʃ] n	····	英語
foreign language ph	···· 外文	**Chinese** [ˋtʃaɪˋniz] n	····	中文
Japanese [ˌdʒæpəˋniz] n	···· 日語	**dictionary** [ˋdɪkʃənˌɛrɪ] n	····	字典

④ writer 作家

novelist [`navḷıst] n ⋯⋯⋯⋯⋯⋯⋯ 小說家

poet [`poıt] n ⋯⋯⋯⋯⋯⋯⋯ 詩人

masterpiece [`mæstɚ͵pis] n ⋯⋯⋯ 名著

translator [træns`letɚ] n ⋯⋯⋯⋯ 譯者

manuscript [`mænjə͵skrıpt] n ⋯ 手稿

⑤ bookstore 書局

check-out counter ph ⋯⋯⋯⋯⋯ 工作台

bestseller n ⋯⋯⋯⋯⋯⋯⋯ 暢銷作家

borrow [`baro] v ⋯⋯⋯⋯⋯⋯⋯⋯ 借

return [rı`tɚn] v ⋯⋯⋯⋯⋯⋯⋯ 歸還

storage [`storıdʒ] n ⋯⋯⋯⋯⋯⋯ 倉庫

check [tʃɛk] v ⋯⋯⋯⋯⋯⋯⋯⋯ 盤點

⑥ publisher 出版社

editor [`ɛdıtɚ] n ⋯⋯⋯⋯⋯⋯⋯ 編輯

marketing [`markıtıŋ] n ⋯⋯⋯⋯ 行銷

publishing [`pʌblıʃıŋ] n ⋯⋯⋯⋯ 出版

copyright [`kapı͵raıt] n ⋯⋯⋯⋯ 版權

royalty [`rɔıəltı] n ⋯⋯⋯⋯⋯⋯ 版稅

7 book binding 裝訂

hardcover ph 精裝書
paperback [`pepɚ͵bæk] n 平裝書
bookmark [`buk͵mark] n 書籤
perfect binding ph 膠裝書
second-hand book ph 二手書

8 category 種類

business [`bɪznɪs] n 商業
philosophy [fə`lasəfɪ] n 哲學
social [`soʃəl] n 社會
psychology [saɪ`kɑlədʒɪ] n 心理
design [dɪ`zaɪn] v 設計
cooking [`kʊkɪŋ] n 烹飪

architecture [`arkə͵tɛktʃɚ] n 建築
education [͵ɛdʒʊ`keʃən] n 教育
literature [`lɪtərətʃɚ] n 文學
computer [kəm`pjutɚ] n 電腦
photography [fə`tagrəfɪ] n 攝影
politics [`palətɪks] n 政治

Daily Q&A

〔會話一〕

Q▶ Do you have this book in English version?
你有這本書的英文版嗎？

A▶ Let me check. Yes, it is in front of the check-out counter.
讓我查一查。有，它在結帳櫃台前。

〔會話二〕

Q▶ Can you recommend me a good philosophy book?
你可以推薦我一本好的哲學書嗎？

A▶ Sure. *Sophie's World* **is a good book.**
當然，《蘇菲的世界》是本好書。

〔會話三〕

Q▶ Excuse me. On which floor is the bookstore?
不好意思，書店在哪一樓？

A▶ It's on the 10th floor.
在十樓。

Proverbs & Idioms **道地諺語與慣用語** | 讓句子更錦上添花

cook the book 〉 記假帳

The accountant had been cooking the book. Our company had been losing money because of that.

那個會計一直都在做假帳，我們的公司之前因為這樣損失了不少錢。

be an open book 〉 率直的人

Tina is an open book, so you will know right away if she does not like something or someone.

緹娜是個很率直的人，如果她不喜歡某件事或某人，你可以馬上就知道。

cuddle up with a book 〉 曲著身體認真的閱讀一本書

In my free time, I like to cuddle up with a good book.

在我有空的時候，我喜歡曲著身體認真的看一本書。

crack a book 〉 打開書

Kevin failed his test because he seldom cracked his book.

凱文考不及格，因為他很少看書。

have a nose in a book 〉 埋首苦讀

Sam always has his nose in a book whenever I see him. He never does any exercise.

每次我看到山姆的時候，他都埋首苦讀。他很少運動。

every trick in the book 〉 用盡所有方法成功

He used every trick in the book to reach his goal. He does not care about whether he is honest. What he really cares is to win in every game.

他用盡所有的方法成功的達到他的目標，他從不在乎他是否誠實，他只在乎贏得每一場遊戲。

don't / never judge a book by its cover 〉 不要以貌取人

Jenny looks a bit sloppy, but don't judge a book by its cover. She is the smartest student at her school.

珍妮看起來有些邋遢，但是不要以貌取人。她是全校最聰明的學生。

take a page out from someone's book 〉 模仿；仿效

Many modern inventors took a page from Edison's book and began inventing useful little things.

現在很多發明家都仿效愛迪生並且研發出很多實用的東西。

- I need to buy some books. Do you want to go to the bookstore with me?
  我需要買一些書，你要跟我一起去書店嗎？

- I need to do a report about business. I want to find some books that I can apply some of the ideas in them.
  我要做一篇商業的報告，我想找一些我可以取用裡頭點子的書。

- I think I can read some comics and novels there while you are searching for your book.
  我想我可以在你找書的時候，看些漫畫和小說。

- I am free today. I can go with you to the bookstore. What kinds of books do you want to buy?
  我今天有空，我可以跟你一起去書店。你想要買哪一種書？

- The clerk is very helpful and friendly. She wears a sweet smile all the time.
  那位店員很願意幫忙，而且很友善。她總是帶著甜甜的微笑。

- I will read my comic books and novels there. When you are ready to go home, just come and find me.
  我會先在那裡看我的漫畫和小說，你要回家的時候就來找我。

- What's your favorite book?
  你最喜歡哪本書？

- Who's your favorite author?
  你最喜歡的作家是誰？

- Have you heard of *Fifty shades of Grey*?
  你有聽過《格雷的五十道陰影》嗎？

- Ellen DeGeneres is one of the most famous bestseller.
  艾倫狄珍妮是最有名的暢銷作家之一。

- Mitch Albom is one of my favorite author.
  米奇艾爾邦是我最喜歡的作家之一。

MEMO

_____

_____

_____

From AM-PM 從早到晚都用得到的必備好用句

- They're too expensive.
  它們太貴了。

- High heels give me blisters.
  高跟鞋讓我的腳起水泡。

- $30 is too much. How about $20?
  30 美元太貴了，20 塊如何？

- You should always try to bargain for a better price.
  你每次都該試著殺價好拿便宜一點的價錢。

- How much are these?
  這些多少錢？

- What's the price after the discount?
  打折後是多少？

- You can count sheep if you cannot fall asleep.
  如果你睡不著你可以數羊。

- I've been lying in bed for an hour.
  我已經躺在床上一小時了。

- It's three in the morning and I still can't fall asleep.
  已經早上三點了，我還不能入睡。

- I haven't been able to fall asleep for days.
  我已經好多天睡不著了。

- Would you like to have a cup of coffee?
  你想要來一杯咖啡嗎？

MEMO

- I would prefer a cup of tea.
  我比較想喝一杯茶。

- I would like to have a piece of cake.
  我想吃一塊蛋糕。

- I'd like a large latte.
  我要一杯大杯拿鐵。

- Can I have a small mocha, please?
  一杯小杯摩卡，謝謝。

- Could you give me a packet of sugar with my coffee?
  你能幫我的咖啡加一包糖嗎？

- I'd like a cup of black coffee.
  我想要一杯黑咖啡。

- Let's play basketball in the park.
  我們去公園打籃球吧！

- I enjoy watching baseball on TV.
  我喜歡看電視棒球轉播。

- How long does it take for you to go home?
  你回家要多久？

- I'm in a rush to get back home today.
  我今天趕著要回家。

- It's time for dinner!
  晚餐時間到囉！

MEMO

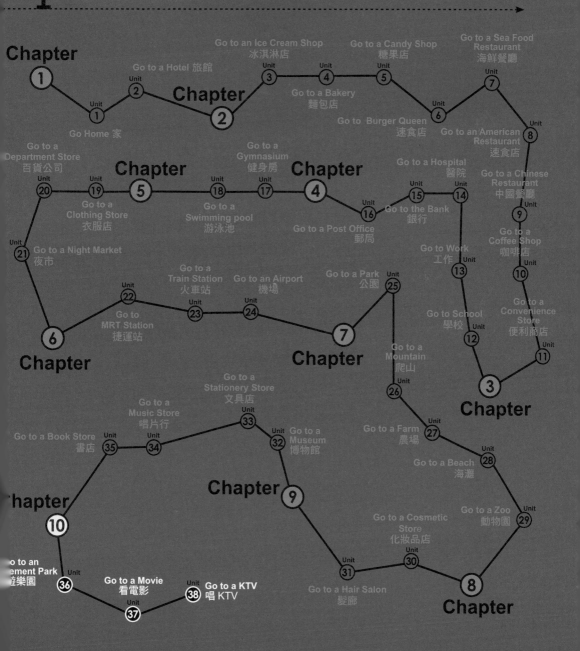

Chapter 10

Entertainment
放鬆娛樂一下

Chapter
① Unit ① Go Home 家
Unit ② Go to a Hotel 旅館
Chapter ②
Unit ③ Go to an Ice Cream Shop 冰淇淋店
Unit ④ Go to a Bakery 麵包店
Unit ⑤ Go to a Candy Shop 糖果店
Unit ⑥ Go to Burger Queen 速食店
Unit ⑦ Go to a Sea Food Restaurant 海鮮餐廳
Unit ⑧ Go to an American Restaurant 速食店

Go to a Department Store 百貨公司
Unit ⑳ Unit ⑲
Chapter ⑤
Go to a Clothing Store 衣服店
Unit ⑱ Go to a Swimming pool 游泳池
Go to a Gymnasium 健身房
Unit ⑰
Chapter ④
Unit ⑯ Go to a Post Office 郵局
Go to the Bank 銀行
Unit ⑮ Unit ⑭
Go to a Hospital 醫院
Go to a Chinese Restaurant 中國餐廳
Unit ⑨
Go to a Coffee Shop 咖啡店

Unit ㉑ Go to a Night Market 夜市
Go to Work 工作
Unit ⑬
Unit ⑩
Go to a Convenience Store 便利商店
Unit ⑪

Unit ㉒ Go to MRT Station 捷運站
Go to a Train Station 火車站
Unit ㉓
Go to an Airport 機場
Unit ㉔
Go to a Park 公園
Unit ㉕
Go to School 學校
Unit ⑫
Chapter ③

Chapter ⑥
⑥
⑦
Chapter ⑦
Go to a Mountain 爬山
Unit ㉖
Go to a Farm 農場
Unit ㉗
Go to a Beach 海灘
Unit ㉘

Go to a Stationery Store 文具店
Unit ㉝
Go to a Music Store 唱片行
Unit ㉞
Go to a Book Store 書店
Unit ㉟
Go to a Museum 博物館
Unit ㉜
Chapter ⑨
Go to a Zoo 動物園
Unit ㉙

Chapter ⑩
Go to an Amusement Park 遊樂園
Unit ㊱
Go to a Movie 看電影
Unit ㊲
Go to a KTV 唱 KTV
Unit ㊳
Go to a Cosmetic Store 化妝品店
Unit ㉛
Go to a Hair Salon 髮廊
Unit ㉚
Chapter ⑧

Go to an Amusement Park 遊樂園

A I love the roller coaster. It is my favorite ride in every amusement park. I love the sensation of the wind blowing on my face. It is really exciting.
我最愛雲霄飛車了，那是我在每一個遊樂園裡頭的最愛。我喜歡風吹過臉頰時的興奮感，真的很刺激。

B I love the pirate boat. It rocks back and forth. It is pretty scary because the only thing you can hold onto is just a bar in front of you.
我最愛海盜船，它往前又往後搖，實在還滿可怕的，因為你唯一可以抓住的東西只有你前面的那根杆子。

A Do you know if there are any new exciting rides in this amusement park?
你知道這間遊樂園裡，有新的、刺激的遊樂設施嗎？

B Yup, there are a few. My friend recommended a new ride called The Oil Well. She said the well could turn people upside down up in the sky. Nine out of ten people who have taken the ride can't help but scream loudly.
是的，有一些。我的朋友介紹我一個新的遊樂設施，叫做「老油井」，她說那個老油井可以把人們倒吊在空中，玩過的人，十個有九個都會忍不住尖叫。

A Wow. That sounds really attractive to me. How can I miss taking such an exciting ride?
哇！聽起來好吸引人喔，我怎麼能錯過這麼刺激的遊樂設施呢？

B Let's line up over there to take the roller coaster frist.
我們先排隊去玩那個雲霄飛車吧！

Additional Vocabulary & Phrases | 補充單字 & 片語

- **sensation** n 感覺、知覺
  Cotton candy gives a sensation of tender.
  棉花糖給人一種柔軟感覺

- **wind** n 風
  The wind is so strong today.
  今天刮的風很強。

- **pirate** n 海盜
  The pirate robbed the passengers.
  那群海盜搶劫那些旅客。

- **scream** v 尖叫
  Please don't scream at the bookstore.
  在書店請不要大聲尖叫。

Daily Sentences 超高頻率使用句｜一分鐘學一句不怕不夠用
10-02

- Where can we buy tickets for the amusement park?
  我們在哪裡可以買到遊樂園的票呢？

- Where is the **Merry-Go-Round**[1]?
  旋轉木馬在哪裡？

- Are there any food vendors?
  這裡有賣吃的攤販嗎？

- You can buy it at the booth in front of the gate.
  你可以在大門前的售票亭買到。

- I would like to buy some souvenirs. Can you show me how to get to the souvenir shop from here?
  我想買一些紀念品，你可以告訴我怎麼從這裡到紀念品商店嗎？

- What is your favorite ride in an amusement park?
  遊樂園裡頭，你最喜歡的遊樂設施是什麼？

- Can you recommend some interesting rides in an amusement park to us?
  你可以建議我一些遊樂園裡有趣的遊樂設施嗎？

- I do not like the haunted house because it is fake and is not scary at all.
  我不喜歡鬼屋，因為它好假，而且一點都不可怕。

- I am thirsty. I see a food vendor over there. Let's go buy something to drink after riding the roller coaster.
  我好渴喔。我看到那裡有一些賣食物的攤販，我們玩完雲霄飛車後，去買些東西來喝吧！

★ **換個單字說說看**｜用單字累積句子的豐富度，讓句子更漂亮！

Merry-Go-Round[1] 可以替換：

| roller coaster 雲霄飛車 | pirate boat 海盜船 | haunted house 鬼屋 | Where is the _____? _____ 在哪裡？ |

Additional Vocabulary & Phrases｜補充單字 & 片語

- **vendor** n 小販、叫賣者
  Are there any candy vendors in the amusement park?
  遊樂園裡面有賣糖果的小販嗎？

- **souvenir** n 紀念品
  I want to buy some souvenir for my girlfriend.
  我想要幫我女友買些紀念品。

- **haunted** a 鬧鬼的
  This house is said to be haunted.
  傳說這棟房子鬧鬼。

- **fake** a 假的、冒充
  This is just a fake doll.
  這只是一個假娃娃。

1 ticket window 售票口

ticket [ˋtɪkɪt] n		入場券
adult [əˋdʌlt] n		成人
child [tʃaɪld] n		小孩
disabled [dɪsˋebḷd] a		殘障的
group [grup] n		團體
teenager [ˋtinˏedʒɚ] n		青少年
free [fri] a		免費的

2 cotton candy 棉花糖

lollipop [ˋlalɪˏpap] n		棒棒糖
popsicle [ˋpapsəkəl] n		冰棒
ice cream sandwich ph		
		冰淇淋三明治
hot dog ph		熱狗
ice cream cone ph		甜筒冰淇淋

3 amusement 娛樂

funny [ˋfʌnɪ] a		有趣的
exciting [ɪkˋsaɪtɪŋ] a		刺激；使興奮
happy [ˋhæpɪ] a		快樂的
enjoyable [ɪnˋdʒɔɪəbḷ] a		享受的
joyful [ˋdʒɔɪfəl] a		充滿喜悅的
horror [ˋhɔrɚ] a		恐怖的
scary [ˋskɛrɪ] a		驚嚇的

4 theme 主題

water park ph	················	水上樂園
land park ph	················	陸上樂園

fantasy land ph	··········	奇幻世界
magic kingdom ph	·········	魔法王國
animal kingdom ph	········	動物王國

5 castle 城堡

princess [`prɪnsɪs] n	········	公主
prince [prɪns] n	········	王子
king [kɪŋ] n	········	國王
queen [`kwin] n	········	皇后
crown [kraʊn] n	········	皇冠
fireworks [`faɪr͵wɝks] n	········	煙火

6 safari 非洲狩獵

jeep [dʒip] n	········	吉普車
desert [`dɛzɚt] n	········	沙漠
jungle [`dʒʌŋgl̩] n	········	叢林
giraffe [dʒəˋræf] n	········	長頸鹿
lion [`laɪən] n	········	獅子

Chapter 1
Chapter 2
Chapter 3
Chapter 4
Chapter 5
Chapter 6
Chapter 7
Chapter 8
Chapter 9
Chapter 10

❼ pay attention 注意

maintenance [ˋmentənəns] n
.... 維修；保養

restrict [rɪˋstrɪkt] v .... 限制

forbid [fɚˋbɪd] v .... 禁止

pause [pɔz] n .... 暫停

emergency [ɪˋmɝdʒənsɪ] n 緊急情況

cooperation [koˌɑpəˋreʃən] n ..... 合作

heart attack ph .... 心臟病

❽ facility 設施

merry-go-round [ˋmɛrɪgoˌraund] n
.... 旋轉木馬

roller coaster ph .... 雲霄飛車

bumper car ph .... 碰碰車

ferris wheel ph .... 摩天輪

go-kart ph .... 賽車

pirate ship ph .... 海盜船

haunted house ph .... 鬼屋

shuttle train ph .... 遊園火車

great fall ph .... 大怒神

octopus [ˋɑktəpəs] n .... 章魚轉

raft [ræft] n .... 橡皮艇

Daily Q&A

〔會話一〕

Q▶ Where is the entrance of the ride?
這個遊樂設施的入口在哪裡？

A▶ It's near the small wooden booth over there.
在靠近那裡的一座小的木製售票亭。

〔會話二〕

Q▶ Where is the exit of the ride?
那個遊樂設施的出口在哪裡？

A▶ Follow the sign, and you can find the way to go out.
跟著標示走，你可以找到出去的路。

〔會話三〕

Q▶ The lines are long.
那排隊伍真長。

A▶ Yup, we will have to wait more than 30 minutes.
是的，我們至少要等超過三十分鐘。

Proverbs & Idioms 道地諺語與慣用語｜讓句子更錦上添花

a bumpy ride 〉 不好的時機

The construction industry is in for a bumpy ride next year.
明年是營造業時機不好的一年。

ride a wave of (something) 〉 受到某種好的事物的愛戴

The candidate rides a wave of good feelings among voters that makes him unlikely to lose the election.
候選人受到選民的愛戴，讓他不可能輸掉這場選戰。

free ride 〉 搭便車

I got a free ride from Jack last week.
我上一週搭傑克的便車。

thumb a ride 〉 做出搭便車的手勢

My car broke down on the highway, and I have to thumb a ride to get back to Taipei.
我的車在高速公路上壞了，所以我做出搭便車的手勢，搭便車到台北。

if two ride on a horse, one must ride behind 〉
一山難容二虎，需要有一方妥協

We can only decide to do one thing when we need to work together. If two ride a horse, one must ride behind.
當我們一起工作時，我們只能決定一件事情。一山難容二虎，需要有一方妥協。

a level playing field 〉 公平的狀況

People call for new rules in order to allow them to compete on a level playing field with other football teams.
人們要求新的規則讓他們和其他的足球隊公平競賽。

foul play 〉 不正當的手段

A virus wiped out all our computer-held records. We suspect foul play on the part of an ex-employee.
病毒清除我們公司整個電腦檔案。我們懷疑這是之前員工所做的破壞手段。

MP3
10-04

A There are many new movies coming out this week. Let me look at the movie schedule and see when the earliest show is.

這一週有很多新的電影上映。讓我看一下電影時刻表，然後看一下離現在最接近的場次是什麼時候。

B I have checked it online. I think it is the one at 6:30 pm.

我在網路上查過了，我想是六點半那一場。

A It's 6:40 pm. We are late for the movie. I think it is better for us to see the next show.

現在已經六點四十，我們已經遲到了。我想我們最好看下一場。

B We can still see that one since trailers at the beginning of the movies usually take about 20 minutes. In this case, we are still on time.

我們還是可以看這一場，因為每場電影前的預告片通常都會有二十分鐘長。依照這個慣例，我們還是能準時看到這場電影。

A You are right. How come I did not think of this?

你是對的，我怎麼沒有想到呢？

B Well, two heads are always better than one. Let's go into the movie theater now.

嗯，三個臭皮匠勝過一個諸葛亮。我們趕快進去電影院吧！

Additional Vocabulary & Phrases ｜補充單字 & 片語

● **come out** ph （電影）上映
Fifty Shades of Grey is coming out next week.
《格雷的五十道陰影》下周會上映。

● **beginning** n 開始；起點
I fell in love with her in the beginning.
我一開始就愛上她了。

Daily Sentences 超高頻率使用句 | 一分鐘學一句不怕不夠用 🎧 MP3 10-05

● Can we reserve the movie tickets online?
我們可以在網路預訂電影票嗎？

● I like **horror movies** ★1.
我喜歡恐怖片。

● The movies are rated in 5 groups. They are G (general audience), PG (parental guidance suggested), PG-13 (under 13 parents strongly cautioned), R (restricted-under 17 requires parents or adult accompanying) and, NC-17 (no one 17 or under 17 suggested).
電影被分為五級，它們是：普級、輔導級、十三歲以下的輔導級、十七歲以下需由成人陪同的限制級，以及十七歲以上的限制級。

● What kind of movies do you like?
你喜歡哪種電影？

● You can go to the website for the movie theater and reserve the seats and the tickets online.
你可以去這個電影院的網址，然後在網路上預約你的座位和票就可以了。

● What movie genres do you know?
你知道的電影種類有哪些？

● Which room is *Harry Potter 3* playing in?
《哈利波特3》在哪一廳播放？

● Do you have any promotional tickets?
你有公關票嗎？

● Who is in the movie?
電影裡有哪些明星？

★ 換個單字說說看 | 用單字累積句子的豐富度，讓句子更漂亮！

horror movies★1 可替換：

| **romance**
浪漫愛情片 | **comedy**
喜劇 | **action movie**
動作片 | I like _____.
我喜歡_____。 |

Additional Vocabulary & Phrases | 補充單字 & 片語

● **guidance** n 指導；引導
I need your guidance.
我需要你的指導。

● **caution** n 小心；謹慎
Mom always drives with caution.
媽媽開車總是很小心。

● **accompany** v 陪同；伴隨
She always accompanies me whenever I need her.
每當我需要她的時候她都陪著我。

● **promotional** a 增進的；促銷的
They have a promotional sale.
他們有一個促銷特賣。

1 film genre 電影種類

comedy [ˋkɑmədɪ] n	喜劇
tragedy [ˋtrædʒədɪ] n	悲劇
romantic movie ph	愛情片
action movie ph	動作片
horror movie ph	恐怖片
sitcom [ˋsɪtˏkɑm] n	情境喜劇
soap opera ph	肥皂劇

2 food bar 食物吧

popcorn [ˋpɑpˏkɔrn] n	爆米花
pop [pɑp] n	氣泡飲料
churros n	吉拿棒
sundae [ˋsʌnde] n	聖代
hot chocolate ph	熱可可
cinnamon bun ph	肉桂捲

3 seat 座位

audience [ˋɔdɪəns] n	觀眾	**projector** [prəˋdʒɛktɚ] n	投影機
curtain [ˋkɝtn̩] n	簾幕	**cinema** [ˋsɪnəmə] n	電影院
screen [skrin] n	銀幕	**theater** [ˋθɪətɚ] n	電影院

264

④ notice 公告；通知

trailer [ˋtrelɚ] n ⋯⋯⋯⋯⋯ 預告片

advertise [ˋædvɚˌtaɪz] v ⋯ 為…宣傳

announce [əˋnaʊns] v ⋯⋯ 宣佈

intellectual property rights ph
⋯⋯⋯⋯⋯⋯⋯⋯⋯⋯⋯⋯⋯ 智慧財產權

copy [ˋkɑpɪ] v ⋯⋯⋯⋯⋯⋯ 拷貝

sponsor [ˋspɑnsɚ] n ⋯⋯ 贊助廠商

⑤ festival 戲劇節；音樂節

film [fɪlm] n ⋯⋯⋯⋯⋯⋯⋯ 電影

program [ˋprogræm] n ⋯⋯ 節目

competition [ˌkɑmpəˋtɪʃən] n
⋯⋯⋯⋯⋯⋯⋯⋯⋯⋯⋯⋯ 角逐；競賽

topic [ˋtɑpɪk] n ⋯⋯⋯⋯⋯ 主題

⑥ award 獎

Oscar [ˋɔskɚ] n ⋯⋯⋯⋯⋯ 奧斯卡

red carpet ph ⋯⋯⋯⋯⋯⋯ 紅毯

celebrity [sɪˋlɛbrətɪ] n ⋯⋯ 明星

trophy [ˋtrofɪ] n ⋯⋯⋯⋯⋯ 獎盃

critic [ˋkrɪtɪk] n ⋯⋯⋯⋯⋯ 評論

7 award category 獎項分類

best picture ph ⋯⋯⋯⋯⋯⋯ 最佳影片

best director ph ⋯⋯⋯⋯⋯ 最佳導演

best actress ph ⋯⋯⋯⋯ 最佳女主角

best actor ph ⋯⋯⋯⋯⋯ 最佳男主角

best supporting actress / actor ph
⋯⋯⋯⋯⋯⋯⋯⋯⋯⋯ 最佳女 / 男配角

best screenplay ph ⋯⋯⋯ 最佳原著劇本

best adapted screenplay ph
⋯⋯⋯⋯⋯⋯⋯⋯⋯ 最佳改編劇本

best film editing ph ⋯⋯⋯⋯ 最佳剪輯

best visual effects ph ⋯ 最佳視覺效果

best sound mixing ph ⋯⋯⋯ 最佳音效

best foreign feature ph ⋯ 最佳外語片

8 staff 工作人員

director [dəˋrɛktɚ] n ⋯⋯⋯⋯⋯⋯ 導演

assistant [əˋsɪstənt] n ⋯⋯⋯⋯⋯ 助理

camera operator ph ⋯⋯⋯⋯⋯ 攝影師

make-up artist ph ⋯⋯⋯⋯⋯ 化妝師

modeling artist ph ⋯⋯⋯⋯⋯ 造型師

hair stylist ph ⋯⋯⋯⋯⋯⋯ 髮型設計師

Daily Q&A

〔會話一〕

Q▶ What movies are on screen right now?

現在哪部電影正在上映中？

A▶ They are listed and introduced in the theater brochure.

電影院製作的小冊子裡都有列出介紹。

〔會話二〕

Q▶ Has the movie *Harry Potter 5*, come out yet?

《哈利波特 5》上映了嗎？

A▶ Not yet. It will come out on September 28th.

還沒有，它九月二十八日才上映。

〔會話三〕

Q▶ Are we allowed to bring our food to the theater?

我們可以帶食物到電影院裡嗎？

A▶ Nope.

不可以。

Proverbs & Idioms 道地諺語與慣用語｜讓句子更錦上添花

snuff movie 〉 關於謀殺血腥的電影

I really don't like snuff movies. The murders in the movies are always bloody, cruel and very violent.
我真的不喜歡有關謀殺、血腥的電影。在電影裡，謀殺的人總是非常血腥殘酷，而且非常的暴力。

silver screen 〉 電影院

All the stars of the silver screen are here tonight to celebrate the New Year.
電影裡的所有明星，今晚都聚在這裡慶祝新年。

award someone something 〉 頒獎某人某物

The company awarded the employees prizes for full attendance in one month.
這個公司頒發全勤獎給一個月都沒請假的員工。

movie genre 〉 電影種類

The movie genres include horror, sci-fi, romantic, comedy, tragedy and so on.
電影的種類包含有恐怖、科幻、浪漫、喜劇、悲劇等等。

movie review 〉 電影影評

The movie review of this movie says "It is a movie you can't miss once in your life time."
這部電影的影評說：「這是一部你一生不能錯過的電影。」

film over 〉 蒙上一層薄膜

The windows had filmed over because of all the humidity.
因為濕氣窗戶早已經蒙上一層薄膜。

double feature 〉 雙片放映的電影

Rocky Horror Film is a double feature movie. It consists of two stories.
《洛基恐怖秀》是一部雙片放映的電影。它是由兩個故事組成。

spook somebody out 〉 驚嚇某人

That horror movie really spooked me out.
那部恐怖片真的讓我很驚嚇。

killer 很厲害或很棒的事

The concert was a killer.
那演唱會棒極了。

Go to a KTV 唱 KTV

Daily Conversation 日常對話｜快速融入超擬真的日常對話

A Wow! The song books are like dictionaries. Let me check whether they have Jolin's new song.
哇！這些歌本就像字典一樣，讓我查查它們是不是有蔡依林的那首新歌。

B Look at the front page. The newly released songs are usually listed on the first page.
看一下第一頁，新發行的歌通常都會被列在第一頁。

A Yes! It's there. Let me key in the number of this song. My voice is low. How can I adjust the pitch?
對耶，在那裡！讓我把歌曲號編輸入進去。我的聲音很低，我要怎麼調整音調呢？

B You can use the remote control. Can you see the buttons for low and high keys?
你可以用遙控器。你有看到調音調高低的按鈕嗎？

A Yes. If I want to turn up the key, do I press the high key and vice versa?
是的。如果我要調高音調，我就按「高音調」的按鈕嗎？低音調也是嗎？

B Absolutely!
對！

Additional Vocabulary & Phrases ｜ 補充單字 & 片語

- **front** n 前面、正面
  Please write your name on the front.
  請在前面寫下你的名字。

- **release** v 釋放、解放
  He released the dog.
  他把狗給放了。

- **adjust** v 調整、適應
  I cannot adjust the life in India.
  我無法適應在印度的生活。

- **absolutely** ad 絕對地、完全地
  It's absolutely none of your business.
  這件事情與你一點關係也沒有。

Daily Sentences 超高頻率使用句｜一分鐘學一句不怕不夠用
10-08

- How can I search for the songs into the song book?

  我要如何在歌本裡找到這些歌呢？

- You can search for them by using the number of the words in the name of the song.

  你可以用歌名的字數來找。

- Can we reserve a room for 15 people?

  我們可以預約一個十五人的包廂嗎？

- We have one more friend is coming. Can we leave a message in the guestbook?

  我們還有一個朋友會來。我們可以在訪客留言本上留言嗎？

- Do you accept **credit cards**[1]?

  你們有收信用卡嗎？

- Are we required to pay a minimum charge?

  我們有基本消費嗎？

- If you need anything in the room at a KTV, you can press the button to ask for service.

  如果你在 KTV 的包廂裡需要什麼東西的話，只要按服務鈴就可以了。

- Is there a restroom in the room or do we have to use the one in the hallway?

  包廂裡有廁所嗎？還是我們得用走道上的那一個？

- What songs do you want to sing then? Tell me the number and I can key it in for you.

  你想唱的歌是哪些呢？告訴我號碼，我可以幫你輸入。

★ **換個單字說說看**｜用單字累積句子的豐富度，讓句子更漂亮！

credit cards[1] 可以替換：

| **debit card**
現金卡 | **check**
支票 | **cash**
現金 | Do you accept _____?
你們有收_____嗎？ |

Additional Vocabulary & Phrases｜補充單字 & 片語

- **reserve** [v] 預約、預定
  I have reserved a table at the restaurant.
  我在餐廳預訂了一桌。

- **guestbook** [n] 來賓簽名本、訪客留言本
  We need to prepare a guestbook for her wedding.
  我們需要在她的婚禮上準備一本來賓簽名本。

- **require** [v] 需要
  The professor requires us to write an essay.
  教授要求我們要寫一篇小論文。

- **hallway** [n] 走廊
  They kissed at the hallway.
  他們在走廊上相吻。

Chapter **10**

語言學校都會教的超實用日常單字
MP3
10-09

① service 服務

reservation [ˌrɛzɚ`veʃən] n		預訂
option [`apʃən] n		選擇
consume [kən`sjum] v		消費
clean [klin] v		清潔
reserved room ph		包廂
assign [ə`saɪn] v		指定

② sing 唱歌

request a song ph		點歌
cancel [`kænsl̩] v		取消
insert [ɪn`sɝt] v		插入
function [`fʌŋkʃən] n		功能
karaoke [ˌkarɑ`oke] n		卡拉 OK
songbook [`sɔŋˏbʊk] n		歌集
voice activation ph		聲控

③ facility 設備

microphone [`maɪkrəˏfon] n	麥克風	**cocktail** [`kakˏtel] n		雞尾酒
disco ball ph	迪斯可球	**groove** [gruv] v		盡情享受
flirt [flɝt] v	搭訕	**music video** ph		音樂錄影帶

4 purpose 目的

pastime [ˈpæsˌtaɪm] n ······ 消遣；娛樂

party [ˈpɑrtɪ] n ······ 聚會；派對

contest [ˈkɑntɛst] n ······ 比賽

practice [ˈpræktɪs] n v ······ 練習

5 song 歌曲

singer [ˈsɪŋɚ] n ······ 歌手

composer [kəmˈpozɚ] n 歌曲作曲家

lyricist [ˈlɪrɪsɪst] n ······ 作詞；作曲

critic [ˈkrɪtɪk] n ······ 評論家

6 tone 音調

pitch [pɪtʃ] n ······ 音高

tune [tjun] n ······ 旋律；準確的音調

high [haɪ] a ······ 高音調的

low [lo] a ······ 低音的

voice [vɔɪs] n ······ 聲音

7 types of music 音樂種類

K-pop n	....	韓國流行音樂
J-pop n	....	日本流行音樂
blues [bluz] n	....	藍調
rap [ræp] n	....	饒舌
jazz [dʒæz] n	....	爵士
electronic [ɪlɛk`trɑnɪk] n	....	電子

8 music awards 音樂獎項

Grammy Awards ph ·····葛萊美音樂獎

World Music Awards ph 世界音樂獎

American Music Awards ph
·························· 全美音樂獎

MTV Europe Music Awards ph
························· 歐洲音樂大獎

Golden Melody Awards ph ···金曲獎

Daily Q&A

〔會話一〕	〔會話二〕	〔會話三〕
Q▸ What's your past time activity?	**Q▸ Let's have a singing contest!**	**Q▸ How often do you go to KTV?**
你的休閒活動是什麼？	我們來唱歌比賽吧！	你多久去一次 KTV？
A▸ I like to sing at the KTV.	**A▸ Why not!**	**A▸ I go there twice a month.**
我喜歡在 KTV 唱歌。	好啊！	我一個月去兩次。

7天就能用英文
行過全世界！ ○─○─○─○─○─**7**

Chapter 1
Chapter 2
Chapter 3
Chapter 4
Chapter 5
Chapter 6
Chapter 7
Chapter 8
Chapter 9

Proverbs & Idioms 道地諺語與慣用語 | 讓句子更錦上添花

sell something for a song > 以便宜的價格出售

The man had to sell his house for a song because he needed money in a hurry.

那個男人以便宜的價格出售自己的房子，因為他急需用錢。

swan song > 過世與退休前最後一個表演作品

The actress is going to retire soon. The show last night was her swan song.

那個女演員即將退休，昨天晚上是她的告別作。

set the tone > 訂定活動進行的氛圍

He was very angry at her lateness for the party yesterday evening, and that also set the tone for the whole evening.

他對她昨天晚上在派對上遲到很生氣，那破壞了整個晚上的氣氛。

lower the tone > 降低標準與格調

Please do not tell rude jokes. It is certain to lower the tone of the whole evening.

不要講低級的笑話，那一定會降低整個夜晚的格調。

out of tune > 走調；不協調

Your idea is out of tune with my idea of what we are supposed to be doing.

你的點子和我們最初想做的完全不一樣。

lay low and sing small > 低調行事

Jack is looking for you, and he sure was angry. You'd better lay low and sing small.

傑克到處在找你，當然他很生氣。你最好低調行事一點。

sing for someone's supper > 幫某人做事以換取食物做報酬

Howard's upstairs fixing my computer. I'm making him sing for his supper.

豪爾在樓上幫我修東西；我等下會請他吃東西。

sing the blues > 抱怨

Many graduates are singing the blues because economy is bad and it is hard to find a good job.

很多畢業生抱怨因為經濟不好找不到好工作。

- We are planning to have a class reunion next week. Any suggestions?
  下星期，我們要舉辦班聚。有任何建議嗎？

- Jolin's new song just came out last week. I want to practice singing it before our reunion and show it in our reunion.
  蔡依林的新歌上週才剛出來，我想在我們班聚前先練唱然後在班聚的時候秀給大家看。

- We can go to Hollyday KTV. They are having special offers for students.
  我們可以去 Hollday KTV。他們有給學生特別的優惠。

- I am Jim Chen. We reserved a room for two.
  我是陳吉姆。我有預約一個兩人的包廂。

- Welcome to Hollyday KTV! Did you make your reservation?
  歡迎來到 Hollyday KTV，你們有預約嗎？

- Wow! This KTV is so big and beautiful.
  哇！這間 KTV 真的好大又好漂亮喔！

- Let me check my list. Your box is room 534. It's on the 5th floor.
  讓我看看我的名單。是的，你們的包廂是 534 房，在五樓。

- This KTV has a reputation for its song books. They include all kinds of songs. You never need to worry about not being able to find the songs you want.
  這間 KTV 的歌本是出了名的。它們包含了各式各樣的歌曲，你永遠不用擔心找不到你要唱的歌。

- Did the song just come out one week ago?
  這首歌是一星期前才發行的嗎？

- You can order some drinks when we are in the box.
  我們到包廂的時候可以點些飲料。

- The music of your song is on TV now. You should get ready to show your voice.
  沒關係，你的歌已經出現在電視上了。你可以準備一展歌喉了。

MEMO

_____

_____

_____

_____

From AM-PM 從早到晚都用得到的必備好用句

- It's time to eat!
  吃飯了！

- I would like to have beef noodles for dinner.
  我晚餐想吃牛肉麵。

- You have to eat everything.
  你必須全部吃光。

- Beef is very nutritious.
  牛肉很有營養。

- You have to eat more.
  你必須多吃一點。

- These French fries are stale.
  這些薯條都不新鮮。

- This pizza is greasy.
  這披薩很油膩。

- How many pieces of fried chicken do you want?
  您想要幾塊炸雞？

- I can only eat three pieces of pizza.
  我只想吃三塊披薩。

- What kind of soft drink do you want?
  你想喝什麼飲料？

- Are you sure you grilled the meat long enough?
  你確定你的肉烤得夠久嗎？

MEMO

_____

_____

_____

_____

- This meat is really tender.
  這肉非常嫩。

- The smoke from the grill keeps blowing on my face.
  烤肉架的煙一直吹到我臉上。

- Let's order some vegetables along with the meat.
  我們點些蔬菜來搭配肉。

- What kind of meat is this?
  這是什麼肉？

- Could you clean the grill for us?
  你能幫我們清一下烤肉架嗎？

- I need to buy some mascara.
  我要買睫毛膏。

- I like this pink lipstick.
  我喜歡這支粉色口紅。

- I don't wear make up.
  我不化妝的。

- I don't think you need to wear make up.
  我不認為你需要靠化妝。

- Where is the cosmetics section?
  化妝品區在哪邊？

- Could you show me how to apply this make up?
  你能示範給我看這化妝品要如何塗抹嗎？

MEMO

_____

_____

_____

_____

- The quality of this product isn't good!
  這東西品質沒有那麼好。

- I would like to pay by credit card.
  我要用信用卡付款。

- It's time to turn off the TV.
  該是關電視的時候了。

- There's no more hot water for a bath.
  沒有熱水洗澡了。

- I think I'll go to bed now.
  我想我得去睡覺了。

- I'm going to sleep early tonight.
  我今晚要早點睡。

- What do you think of these boots?
  您覺得這些靴子如何呢？

- I have too many pairs of shoes at home.
  我家裡有太多雙鞋子了。

- Why don't you try them on?
  你何不試穿一下呢？

- What's your budget for the present?
  你買禮物的預算是多少？

- Could you take the price tag off for me?
  能請你幫我把價格標籤拿掉嗎？

Chapter 1
Chapter 2
Chapter 3
Chapter 4
Chapter 5
Chapter 6
Chapter 7
Chapter 8
Chapter 9
Chapter 10

MEMO

- Don't put too much food in the hot pot.
  不要放太多食材到火鍋裡。

- Do you want to eat Japanese or Korean BBQ?
  你想吃日式還是韓式烤肉？

- I know a good all-you-can-eat BBQ restaurant near my house.
  我知道我家附近有一間不錯的吃到飽燒烤店。

- Oh no! I forgot to do my homework!
  噢，不！我忘記做功課了！

- Can I borrow a pencil?
  我能借枝鉛筆嗎？

- Don't sit there and daydream.
  別坐在那做白日夢啦。

- What chapter are we on?
  現在在上第幾章？

- What class do we have next?
  我們下一堂是什麼課？

- Do you feel like eating some Chinese food?
  你想吃中式料理嗎？

- I love Indian food.
  我喜歡印度料理。

- Do you have any lunch specials?
  你們有任何午餐特餐嗎？

MEMO

- We're ready to order.
  我們準備好點餐了。

- It's time for coffee break.
  休息時間到了。

- There's a coffee shop around the corner. Let's go!
  轉角那邊有一家咖啡館。我們走吧！

- How was work?
  今天工作還好嗎？

- I have no idea what to cook for dinner.
  我不知道晚餐要煮什麼？

- What's for dinner?
  今天晚上吃什麼？

- We're having fried rice for dinner.
  我們晚上吃炒飯。

- Dinner will be ready in ten minutes.
  再十分鐘晚餐就好了。

- I'll have a medium-sized Coke.
  我要中杯可樂。

- The kid's meal comes with a toy.
  兒童餐有附玩具。

- Can I have a pack of ketchup for my fries?
  可以給我一包番茄醬好配薯條嗎？

MEMO

_____

_____

_____

- Would you like to upgrade your drink and fries?
  您想把飲料和薯條升級嗎？

- Dipping your meat and vegetables in this sauce will make it taste better.
  把你的肉和菜沾一點這些醬會更好吃。

- Be careful not to burn yourself.
  小心不要燙到。

- I don't like the taste of chicken.
  我不喜歡雞肉的味道。

- Make sure you grill the meat thoroughly.
  確定你有將肉烤熟。

- This meat doesn't look very fresh.
  這肉看起來不太新鮮。

- We're having a BBQ on our rooftop tonight.
  我們今天晚上要在屋頂烤肉。

- Could we get some meat with less fat?
  我們可以點一些比較沒脂肪的肉嗎？

- Be careful not to burn the meat.
  小心不要把肉烤焦了。

- Thanks for taking me out for dinner.
  謝謝你帶我出來吃晚餐。

- Please help me clean the table.
  請幫我清桌子。

MEMO

- I'm stuffed!
  我好飽！

- This is not what I ordered.
  這不是我點的食物。

- Could you please pass me the salt and pepper?
  麻煩你把鹽和胡椒遞給我好嗎？

- The food here tastes excellent.
  這裡的食物真是好吃。

- Would you like some cream and sugar in your coffee?
  您的咖啡要加奶油和糖嗎？

- Wash your hands before you eat.
  吃飯前先洗手。

- I made you favorite dish.
  我做了你最愛吃的菜。

- Could you set the table, please?
  你能幫忙放碗筷嗎？

- There's more rice in the cooker if you're still hungry.
  如果你還沒吃飽，飯鍋裡還有飯。

- Could you please hurry up in the bathroom?
  你廁所能不能用快一點啊？

- I can't find my shoes.
  我找不到我的鞋。

MEMO

- It doesn't take me very long to get ready in the morning.
  我早上準備不用太多時間。

- Taking a shower helps me wake up.
  沖個澡可以讓我清醒一點。

- Could you brew some coffee for me?
  你能幫我煮些咖啡嗎？

- I don't feel like eating anything this morning.
  今天早上我不太想吃東西。

- Do we have any butter for the toast?
  我們還有奶油好抹吐司嗎？

- I usually skip breakfast in the morning.
  我早上通常不吃早餐。

- I'm usually not hungry in the morning.
  我早上通常不餓。

- Take off your pajamas.
  把睡衣脫掉。

- Put on your coat.
  穿上你的外套。

- Put on your pants.
  穿上你的褲子。

- I hate sitting in traffic.
  我討厭被困在車陣中。

MEMO

你敢跟外國人對話嗎？

只要4週！

即刻變身英文
聽、說、讀、寫高手！

學校老師永遠教不會的
英文
聽力・口說
技巧

〔全亞洲同步**修訂版**〕

全亞洲人都在用這本！

本書在台灣、港澳、中國、新加坡、馬來西亞等各國熱銷狀況10萬冊・暢銷！台灣、福州及泉州（福建古音中）年度仍同掀一起出入全亞洲讀者掌聲的行列。

成為超完美英文口語大師
Jacob Lavender

亞洲暢銷多年屹立不搖的補教名師
Josephine Lin /著

 Week ① ② ③ ④

1週學會一個技巧；4週成為英文聽說達人！

「關鍵字」、「輕重音」、「語調」、「連音」，先讓入五單，能用套能學習式。

英語證書再多都沒用，重點在「敢不敢和外國人對話」！
亞洲讀者學生大量現考試撫定，反而別把基本的英文發問。談能力。
滾除出你補習五認上費句每五文。你有什麼資格在社會上競爭！

中、美名師首次聯手出擊！
只有補教名師Josephine Lin才能聽解亞洲英語漢者學生到英文聽說的學習關鍵。
而Jacob Lavender用美國人的音要式解，說技巧，教學帶生如何深只國字真語地道進英文聽，認能力。

能開口，就能聽懂！能聽懂，就能說出口！
1,424句會話＋1,424個片語＋3,050個單字，文法與重點剖析，
不僅是與校外讀入真語，也能掌握聽力、口說考試技巧，交友、是遊、考試、讀書、一次搞定。

求職面試、全民英檢、托福、雅思、新多益聽說測驗完全適用！

《學校老師永遠教不會的
英文聽力・口說技巧（全亞洲同步修訂版）》
定價／**349**元

學校老師永遠教不會的
英文
翻譯・寫作
技巧

蔡詠琳 /著　　**Chris Fluellen** /審訂

Google翻譯不了的英文，就交給人腦吧！

人腦＋電腦＝超完美 **英文翻譯＋英文寫作**
人工智慧再發達，翻譯還是缺乏靈魂感覺，電腦就只再會，遇是有做不到的步驟！人腦＋電腦才是最完美組合。

 Step ① ② ③

只要遵循三個步驟，就能成為英文翻譯、寫作達人！

電腦翻譯一聲現問題＝人腦翻譯。只要遵循三個步驟，就能讓電腦成為最好的幫手。
再加上第一天、五沙達用，每個人都能成為英文翻譯、寫作達人！

利用電腦翻譯不可恥，重點在有沒有「判斷翻譯正確性」的能力！
英文翻譯軟體或許繁多參步，如何有對不懂不能判斷及認識翻譯的好壞！
沒有審閱的能力，就會犯下惱似美洲的「亂馬翻譯正成「Seven America」也確冗惡的笑話！

電腦再強，還是有做不到的事情！
說言是活的，每次翻譯此更新再快，也無法理解不有的特殊用語及文法處理。
只有增強自己的文能力，才能與數電腦的不足，電腦不會，你你一定要會！

能英翻中，就能中翻英；能寫，就能說！
企書分成「英文翻中文」，「中文翻英文」兩大章節，並針對生佳情境，文法眼部分做說解。
再附配美篇老師朗誦的MP3，讓你隨時聽誦的不足。

（適用對象）所有曾經借助翻譯軟體翻譯過文字的使用者們！

《學校老師永遠教不會的
英文翻譯・寫作技巧》
定價／**299**元

1週學會一個技巧；4週成為英文聽說達人
只要遵循三個步驟，就能成為英文翻譯、寫作達人

I'm 我識出版集團
I'm Publishing Group

我識客服：（02）2345-7222　http://www.17buy.com.tw
我識傳真：（02）2345-5758　iam.group@17buy.com.tw

〔全國各大書店熱烈搶購中！大量訂購，另有折扣
劃撥帳號◆ 19793190 戶名◆我識出版社